"Maybe you should get a god."

"We have one."

"Oh, really?" Janet raised an eyebrow. "Is he hot? Or is he even a he? Did you go the goddess route?"

"No, he's a he."

"Cool. So is he hot?"

"He's a raccoon."

"Like with the striped tail and the cute little paws?"

Teri nodded.

"Very retro."

Praise for *DIVINE MISFORTUNE*:

"A. Lee Martinez is the American Terry Pratchett. While Martinez deals in more contemporary settings, he is every bit as witty and funny as Pratchett, and one hopes his career is just as long and successful."

—graspingforthewind.com

"*Divine Misfortune* is a light and wonderful read from start to finish."

—sfsignal.com

"*Divine Misfortune* reads like a mash-up of Neil Gaiman, Monty Python, and a sugar-bombed nine-year old."

—*Locus*

By A. Lee Martinez

A. LEE MARTINEZ

DIVINE
MISFORTUNE

www.orbitbooks.net

Copyright © 2010 by A. Lee Martinez
Excerpt from *Chasing the Moon* copyright © 2011 by A. Lee Martinez
All rights reserved. Except as permitted under the U.S. Copyright Act of 1976, no part of this publication may be reproduced, distributed, or transmitted in any form or by any means, or stored in a database or retrieval system, without the prior written permission of the publisher.

Orbit
Hachette Book Group
237 Park Avenue
New York, NY 10017
Visit our website at www.orbitbooks.net

Orbit is an imprint of Hachette Book Group. The Orbit name and logo are trademarks of Little, Brown Book Group Limited.

The publisher is not responsible for websites (or their content) that are not owned by the publisher.

Printed in the United States of America

Originally published in hardcover, March 2010
First mass market edition, April 2011

10 9 8 7 6 5 4 3 2

ATTENTION CORPORATIONS AND ORGANIZATIONS:
Most HACHETTE BOOK GROUP books are available at quantity discounts with bulk purchase for educational, business, or sales promotional use. For information, please call or write:

Special Markets Department, Hachette Book Group
237 Park Avenue, New York, NY 10017
Telephone: 1-800-222-6747 Fax: 1-800-477-5925

To Mom and the DFWWW, for all the usual reasons.

To Sally, just because I know she'll be really, really excited to be mentioned in a dedication, and anyone who can put up with me for this long deserves some kind of acknowledgment.

To World of Warcraft. *For the Horde!*

To me, because it's been a while since I've dedicated a book to myself, and damn it, I've earned it with this one.

And to Squirrel Girl, greatest superhero ever. And, yes, she did defeat Thanos single-handedly. It's in continuity. Deal with it.

DIVINE

MISFORTUNE

1

"Hello. My name is Anubis. I like long walks on the
beach, carrying departed souls into the underworld, and
the cinema of Mr. Woody Allen."

Wincing, Teri pushed the PAUSE button. "Oh, ick."

"What? What's wrong with this one?" After an hour
of watching Internet videos, Phil's patience was wearing thin. It seemed no god would be good enough for his
wife.

"Look at him," she said. "He's got a dog head."

"Jackal," corrected Phil. "It's a jackal head."

She frowned. "Eww. That's even worse."

"How is that worse?"

She shrugged. "I don't know. It just is. I mean, dogs are
nice, at least. But jackals... who has anything nice to say
about them?"

"He isn't a jackal, honey," he said, with an edge on
the term of endearment. "He just has a jackal head." He

loved his wife dearly, but she was making this difficult. If it had been up to him, he'd just pick one. Any old low-maintenance god would've worked.

"But what about that *cinema of Mr. Woody Allen* line?"

"You like Woody Allen," countered Phil.

"Yes, I like him. But who says *cinema*?"

"Now you're just nitpicking."

"But it's important. The words someone chooses say a lot about them. And people who say *cinema* are pretentious."

He rolled his eyes. "He's a god. He's allowed to be pretentious."

"Not my god. No, thank you."

Phil scrolled through Anubis's profile. "He's a pretty good find. I think we should sign up with him while we can."

Teri looked at him coldly. She didn't use the look a lot, but it meant there was no changing her mind. He didn't feel like fighting about it anyway. There were plenty of other gods. Somewhere in the hundreds of listed profiles, there had to be one she couldn't find anything wrong with.

She was right. It wasn't a decision to be taken lightly. The string of events that had led him to peruse the digital pages of Pantheon.com, the Internet's second-largest deity matching service, hadn't made him forget that.

First had been the promotion. Another one passing him over. The fourth opening in as many months. Instead, that kiss-ass Bob had taken Phil's step up the corporate ladder. Phil had been practicing his brownnosing and was damn good at it. Better than Bob. So good in fact that Phil had actually swallowed his outrage and walked up to Bob's new corner office to congratulate his new boss.

He'd found Bob, chanting in Sumerian, hunched over a small altar.

"Hey, Phil." Bob, his face covered in black and red paint, smiled.

"Hello, sir," replied Phil, trying his damnedest not to sound annoyed. "Didn't mean to interrupt. I'll come back later."

"Oh, please. Don't worry about it." He made a casual sweeping gesture at the altar. "Five minutes won't kill the old boy."

Phil leaned in against the doorway, perched on the edge of Bob's corner office with its plush carpeting and obnoxiously large desk clearly made from some rare and expensive wood that Phil couldn't recognize but still resented. He tried not to notice the lovely view of the park just below.

"Something I can do for you?" asked Bob.

"Just wanted to say congratulations. You deserve it."

"Thanks. Honestly, I'm surprised you didn't get it. I thought for sure that fatted calf I offered ol' Baal here wasn't going to be enough. What did you offer?"

"Nothing."

"Ah, that explains it. You know, it never hurts to stain the sacrificial altar now and then. Keeps the boys upstairs happy."

"I don't have one." Phil crossed his arms tight enough to cut off the circulation. "An old boy, I mean."

"Really?" A curious expression crossed Bob's face, as if Phil had just admitted to being a cross-dressing jewel thief clown in his spare time. "You really should get one. They're an absolute necessity. I don't see how anyone gets along without some upstairs help."

That alone wasn't enough to push Phil into the decision.

On the car ride home, distracted by his worries, he'd been in a minor fender bender. The damage wasn't serious, just a dented bumper and an ugly scrape to his paint job. But the other driver's car didn't have a scratch.

The other driver pulled out a special knife and ran it across his palm, drawing some blood to offer to his god as he incanted, "Blessed be Marduk, who keeps my insurance premiums down."

Phil arrived home. As he pulled into the driveway, the first thing he noticed (the first thing he *always* noticed) was his lawn. It taunted him, a symbol of his promising life, once green and flourishing, now greenish and wilted. He watered and fertilized it. Had even brought in a specialist. But it was dying, and there was no way to stop it. He took comfort in the fact that nobody else in the neighborhood could get their grass to grow either. There was something in the soil, a lingering curse laid by Coyote on this spot of land for the injustices the Native Americans had suffered at the hands of the Europeans. The natives got smallpox, and the suburbs got yellowed grass. A light punishment for stealing a continent, Phil had to admit, but still annoying.

Except his next-door neighbor Ellen had a lush green lawn today.

Phil didn't have to guess what had happened. The four-foot-high faux granite goddess statue told him everything he needed to know.

Ellen's car pulled into her own driveway, and she noticed Phil eyeing the lawn.

"Pretty cool, huh?"

He stifled a scream. "I thought you already had a god. That weird one. The one with the horns and the nine arms."

"Oh, sure. That's still working out for me, but he's a jealous old goat," she said. "But he doesn't do lawns. So I just hired an outside service. They stick up the statue, offer the tribute, and my god doesn't get jealous and smite me dead. It's a win-win." Ellen knelt down and ran her hand across her lawn in an almost obscene manner. "That Demeter sure knows how to handle crabgrass, doesn't she?"

And that was that. The next day Phil went online and signed up on Pantheon.com.

Teri was against the idea at first.

"You knew I didn't want any gods before we were married," she said. "We had a long talk about this."

"I know, but—"

"My grandfather was killed by a desert god, y'know," she said. "Just for cutting his hair."

"I know, but—"

"In the end, they always get you, Phil. They always screw you over. Read your history."

He took her in his arms. She offered some resistance, then hugged him back.

"Honey," she said, "I know you're frustrated with how things have been going lately, but I don't think you're thinking this through."

"I am," he said. "I've thought about it a lot, and it makes sense to me."

She pulled away from him. "We're not doing so bad, are we?"

Phil looked at his house. It wasn't big, but it was big enough. They had the finest furniture IKEA could supply, a television larger than would have been sane ten years ago, and enough bric-a-brac and art hanging from the walls to keep Teri happy but not appear too cluttered. Although he could've done without the sailboat motif. Something he'd always found odd, considering he'd never heard Teri even talk about sailing once since he'd met her.

They were paying the bills, and they weren't that far in debt. Not more than anyone else. And he had a wife who loved him. He knew it should've been enough. More than enough for any man.

It wasn't. Not when any idiot willing to throw a lamb onto a pyre was able to get ahead while they struggled to make it. Everything would be great if they could just get a little divine intervention.

She turned her back to him. "I just think it's a bad idea, Phil. That's all."

"Okay, tell you what. Let's think about it for a couple more days. Will you at least promise me that you'll think about it?"

"If that's what you want."

A week passed. Phil went online and watched clips of various gods. He even considered signing up with one in secret. Teri didn't have to know. He could always keep the altar or shrine or whatever somewhere else. Maybe at a friend's house. Or in the toolshed. He told himself that it would be a good thing, that it would improve their life, and that if Teri wasn't signed up, too, then it would work out great for her since she'd get all the benefits without any of the obligations.

He couldn't do it. Not behind her back. If they were going to do it, they needed to do it together or not at all. Teri would never budge on this issue, and maybe she was right. He already had a lot of responsibilities. He didn't need any more. Especially responsibilities that involved temperamental deities who had a tendency to smite first and never even bother asking questions later. The longer he thought about it, the more he knew it had been a bad idea and that Teri had done him a big favor by talking him out of it. That was why he loved her. She had the common sense he didn't.

The next day, she called him at work.

"Let's do it."

"Do what?" he asked.

"The god thing. Let's do it."

It took Phil a few moments to remember the debate, so far back had he pushed it in his mind. "But I thought you said you didn't—"

"I didn't. Not then. But I've changed my mind."

"Oh yeah? Why is that?"

"I saw a cat come back from the dead today."

"Okay." Phil sat back. "I like cats, too, honey, but I don't think that qualifies as a sign."

"Just listen. I ran over the cat."

"Oh, I'm sorry."

"Let me finish," she said. "I got out and checked on it, but it was dead. Then this little girl who was watching came over and touched it, and it was alive again. Just like that."

He scowled. "Children shouldn't be allowed to play with divine favor."

"The point is that she was able to save a life. And I thought, if a little girl can save a cat, what could I do with that kind of power? And I thought maybe you were right. It's not the gods. It's what we choose to do with their gifts."

"So now you want to do it? The god thing?"

"Yes," she said. "Maybe. I don't know. It's not something to take lightly, and maybe I'll change my mind later. But it can't hurt to look, I suppose."

Phil hesitated.

"It was your idea in the first place," she said.

"True." He shrugged. "I guess it can't hurt to look."

And now, six hours later, here they were back on Pantheon, trying to find the god for them.

They ran through dozens more. Teri found a reason to disqualify most of them, and the few she did approve of didn't suit Phil. Choosing a god wasn't as simple as he'd first thought. All the really useful gods were in high demand, and they knew it. And the more powerful a deity, the more demanded of his followers. You had to pass a credit check to merely look at Zeus's profile, and Tyr demanded you cut off one of your hands as a show of devotion if you wanted full benefits. And that was if you were even accepted in the first place. Some gods wanted blood. Others wanted money. Most wanted blood and money. But there were other costs. Vows of silence, poverty, chastity, ruthlessness, and so on. There was always a price, even for the most minor and inconsequential of divine favors, and Phil and Teri found they weren't usually willing to pay it.

He sat back and rubbed his eyes. He was about to suggest that they just abandon their quest when Teri chimed in.

"This one looks interesting. Luka, god of prosperity and good fortune."

"He has a raccoon head," remarked Phil. "I thought you didn't want one with an animal head."

"No, I didn't want one with a jackal head. I can live with a raccoon head."

"What's the difference?"

"Raccoons are cute."

"Raccoons are vermin," he countered. "And they can carry disease."

She glared at him, and he realized he didn't know why he was arguing. Aside from the odd head, Luka stood tall, lean, and proud. He wore long rainbow-colored robes and had a Chinese-style hat on. Phil didn't know the name for it, but it was one of those hats that the emperor's advisers always wore in the kung fu movies. Luka's hands were tucked into his loose sleeves, and he was smiling. Many of the lesser gods they'd seen today had been smiling, too. But there had been a quiet desperation hidden underneath, a neediness that Phil had found off-putting. Luka's smile seemed genuine.

She clicked the PLAY button for his video.

"Is it on?" Luka looked over the camera. "It is? It's on? Cool." He smoothed his robes and adjusted his hat. "Hi, I'm Luka, god of prosperity and good fortune. I…uh…what am I supposed to say?"

Someone offscreen mumbled a reply.

"I really hate these things." Luka frowned. "Let's be honest here. You don't care about what I like or don't. You just want to know what I can give you and what I want in return. I've seen better days. Kind of ironic, considering I'm a god of luck." He chuckled. "All I really need is a fresh start, and maybe that's all you need, too. I don't need your blood. None of that animal sacrifice nonsense. You won't have to mutilate yourself or promise to wear your shoes backward or leave the lid off your trash can. And I'll admit that I won't change your life in any big way. Not my thing. I'm more of a serendipity specialist, but the world can turn on a moment, and that's where I come in. You won't become king of the universe or beloved by everyone or a super sex god. But if you allow me into your heart and hearth, all I ask for in return is a percentage of the good I help you attain. Say...ten percent? I could maybe go as low as eight. But that's my bottom line."

He bowed and stared at the camera for a few seconds.

"Is it still on? Should I say some—"

The video ended.

"I like him," said Teri.

So did Phil. Most gods were too...godly. So full of themselves. Even the lesser ones had an aura of entitlement, as if you were lucky to have them. But this one seemed different. Luka was regal but relaxed. He seemed refreshingly down-to-earth.

They read the whole profile just to be sure what they were getting into. No blood offerings, weird rituals, or big demands. Just a standard "welcoming into the home" arrangement. They'd expected that. They'd already picked out the corner where they would stick their new idol.

"I think he's perfect," said Teri.

Phil was happy to discover a choice he and his wife agreed on. He was also overjoyed that it was finally done. He didn't feel like scrolling through any more profiles. The site said that Luka was ready, and they met his minimum qualifications. Approval was just a click away.

They pricked their fingers with a needle and prepared to click on the ACCEPT button together.

She studied the blood on her fingertip. "This better not screw up my mouse."

They clicked the button together. Teri retrieved some paper towels to wipe off the red stain. They spent a few more minutes filling out consent forms and double- and triple-clicking confirmation buttons. With the establishment of the Court of Divine Affairs, worship had become much more paperwork-intensive.

"Do we have to go pick up the idol ourselves?" she asked. "Or do they drop it off as part of the service?"

The doorbell rang.

They answered it together.

A small mound of rainbow-colored luggage occupied their porch. On top of it sat a raccoon in an unbuttoned Hawaiian shirt and denim shorts. He wore sunglasses, even though it was night.

"You must be Phil and Teri, right?"

They nodded.

The raccoon hopped up, put his hands on his hips, and struck a dramatic pose. "Behold your new god. Luka, lord of prosperity and good fortune."

He lowered his sunglasses to the end of his nose and smiled.

"Where should I put my stuff?"

"Nice digs," said Luka as he pushed his way past Phil and Teri. "Not exactly the palace of the High Magistrate of Atlantis, but beggars can't be choosers, right?"

"You're Luka?" asked Teri.

"The one and only. And, please, call me Lucky." He tucked his sunglasses into his pocket and imitated a gun with his finger, once at each of them. "Anything to drink? I just descended from the heavens and could really use some juice."

"We have soda," said Teri. "Sorry, no juice."

"I'll take a Coke, thanks."

She went into the kitchen. Awkward silence filled the room. Phil didn't look directly at Lucky. Then he felt weird about it, so he made eye contact with his new god. Lucky winked.

Teri returned. "All we had was Dr. Pepper."

"That'll do." He chugged the entire beverage in one long drink. "So do I throw this away or do you recycle?"

Teri took the can and went back to the kitchen. She didn't return right away, leaving Phil and Lucky to stare at each other some more.

"Something wrong, Phil?" asked Lucky.

"No, no," Phil replied quickly. "I mean, no, not really. It's just…"

"It's just you thought I'd be taller."

Phil nodded.

"Like this." Lucky transformed into the more traditional figure seen in the video. Human in proportion, though the head remained the same. "This is for show. Helps to get people's attention. But it's not how I always look. Do you think Hermes always wears the winged sandals? Or that Osiris keeps that falcon head on all the time?"

"It's not his real head?"

"Naw. He just wears it to hide his bald spot. You didn't hear that from me. We're gods. Our bodies are like your clothes. They're largely a matter of personal preference." He transformed back into his smaller, more casual form. "I'm just more comfortable this way. If it's all the same to you. Not going to be a problem, is it?"

Phil shook his head.

"Cool. So where's your bathroom?"

Phil pointed down the hall.

"Thanks. Be right back. What are we having for dinner tonight? I have a hankering for tacos."

He shut the door behind him.

Teri dared to venture from the kitchen. "Did he leave?"

"He's in the bathroom," said Phil.

"Gods use the bathroom?" asked Teri.

"Maybe he wants to wash his hands. I think raccoons like to do that."

"But he's not really a raccoon, is he?"

Phil lowered his voice, afraid Lucky might hear them. "I don't think so, but maybe he has some of their tendencies while in that form."

The toilet flushed. They heard the water in the sink run, and Phil elbowed Teri to point out that he was right about the hand-washing.

Lucky came out, drying his hands on his shirt.

"I've been thinking about it, and tonight feels more like a burger night. But I'm open."

He took a seat on the couch and used the remote to turn on the television. "Aw, shoot. This isn't high-def, is it?"

"No," said Phil. "We're sorry, uh, Master."

"How many channels do you get?"

Phil and Teri each waited for the other to answer the question.

"I'm not really sure," Phil finally said.

"You've got premium, right?" asked Lucky.

Phil hesitated. "It's just basic."

"Aw, crud," said Lucky.

"Our apologies . . . Master."

"Will you cut out that master stuff? It's Lucky. Just Lucky. It's not your fault. It's that damn matchmaking service. You'd think with all the forms you have to fill out they'd have a space for cable package somewhere, right? It's not ideal, but I can live with it. Maybe your next paycheck you might consider getting an upgrade. I'm not trying to impose or anything, but a nice, upstanding American couple like yourselves can really do better than basic cable. Still, as long as we've got Oxygen and Discovery, I guess I'm good."

He flipped through the channels too rapidly to even see what was on.

"How are those burgers coming along, kids?"

"I don't think we have everything we need here," said Phil.

"Well, they have these great new things called grocery stores. Very handy. Or, if you prefer, you can swing through a drive-through. I'll take a Big Mac and a cherry pie. But before you go, we should probably get my stuff inside first. Where's my room?"

"Room?" repeated Teri.

"Don't tell me. No room. Disappointing, but heck, I don't mind crashing on the couch."

"Excuse me," said Teri, "but you want to move in?"

"You bet."

"Here?"

Lucky nodded.

"In our house?"

Lucky muted the television. "Let's get down to brass tacks, shall we? I'm not one of those gods who sits up high on his mountain and looks down upon his followers like interchangeable minions. I'm more hands-on. Quality not quantity, that's my motto. And I have a good feeling about you two. I'm not just in this for myself. Sure, when you guys do better, the divine karmic feedback loop means that I do better. But that's just a fringe benefit. I want you to be happy, and the only way I can feel comfortable doing that is to be down here, in the trenches, with you fine folks."

Phil and Teri smiled weakly.

"I know, I know," said Lucky. "Too good to be true, isn't it?"

"Would you excuse us for a moment?" asked Teri.

"Sure. I'll just grab something to nosh on until dinner, if that's all right with you?"

"Please, help yourself."

They kept their feeble smiles until Lucky went to the kitchen.

"He can't stay here," Teri harshly whispered.

"I don't think we have a choice," said Phil. "We agreed to allow him into our home."

"But I thought that meant an altar or an idol or something like that. Isn't that normally how it works? Your parents had a god, right? You should know."

"There was an idol. Once a month, they sacrificed a dove to it, I think."

She glared.

"What? They didn't involve me in it. It was only a minor pact with a minor god. Just something to keep the house from needing repairs."

"I don't want him in my house," she said. "You have to tell him."

"Me? Why?"

"Because it was your idea to do this."

Phil said, "But when I changed my mind, you're the one who said we should do it. Remember the cat? The freakin' miracle cat?"

"I wouldn't have had a miracle cat if you hadn't put the idea in my head in the first place."

"We both accepted the deal," said Phil. "We can't just tell him to leave. It could be dangerous. One month, my dad decided it wouldn't hurt anything to put off a sacrifice by a day. By next week, the house was infested with termites, the plumbing backed up, the fireplace started belching sulfur into the living room, and all the carpet became moist and moldy."

"But he's a luck god, right? What's the worst that could happen?"

"Did I mention the dead rats that filled the attic crawl space?"

Teri bit her lip. "You're right. I just wasn't expecting this."

"He's not very big," said Phil, "and he seems nice."

Lucky came back in, chewing on a cold chicken leg. He'd stripped off most of the flesh and was gnawing on the bone. "Is there a problem, gang?"

Phil and Teri waited for the other to say something first.

"Can we cut the crap?" asked Lucky. "Let's be honest, shall we? I'm sensing some reluctance on your part. You were looking for a heavenly benefactor, not a roommate. And now you're having second thoughts."

They nodded.

Lucky transformed in a flash into a hulking raccoon monster, as big as a bull, with slavering jaws, fearsome tusks, and burning red eyes.

"Blasphemers!" He stomped his feet with a crack of thunder. "Thou hast rejected thy god and roused mine righteous fury." He roared, blasting them with his hot breath and divine saliva. "Prepare thyselves for the Hell of Great, Nibbly Agonies and an eternity of great and...uh... nibbly..." Lucky's burning eyes furrowed.

"Agonies," finished Phil timidly.

He changed back into his raccoon form and winked.

"You got moxie, kids."

"You aren't going to smite us?" asked Phil.

"No, I was just having some fun. You should've seen your faces. Half-fear, half-confusion. It was like one part of you was afraid for your life and the other couldn't believe you were about to be eaten by a giant raccoon." He chuckled. "Priceless."

He grabbed the chicken bone, picked off the carpet fuzz, and sucked on it.

"Don't worry. I don't plan on any smiting, though it is well within my rights. But I'm not that kind of god. Never was a casual smiter. Sure, I've smote a few mortals in my day. I'm not proud of it, but it was back in the old days. Everyone was doing it, and I just wanted to be cool. But I'm past that sort of heavy-handed disciplinary action. It's good for a laugh occasionally, but I don't want to be your god because you're afraid of me. I want us to be buddies, compadres. Heck, we're practically family.

"But I'm not going to force myself on you. I don't need to. You'll see the benefits of having me around soon enough. You don't want to put me up for the night, that's cool. Though I did notice you have a very nice guest room. But I'll leave. No smiting. No wrath. Providing you make me a sandwich at least."

Teri made a bologna-and-ham offering for their new god.

Lucky stood beside his luggage on the porch. "Extra mustard. Just like I like it." He saluted. "I'll be seeing you, kids. Hopefully sooner than later, but that's your call. Thanks for the sandwich. Verily, I am pleased. I suggest you check under your couch cushions."

A luminous ball of light enveloped the god and his luggage.

"Wait," said Phil, "uh, please, sir."

The light faded, and Lucky raised a brow.

"Is there a way you'd prefer for us to contact you?" asked Phil. "Like a special prayer or chant or something?"

"Oh, right. Almost forgot." Lucky reached into his pocket and handed them a business card. "You can reach me at this number when you're ready to commit. But don't call before noon." He put on his sunglasses with a smile. "I like to sleep in."

The sphere of light engulfed him. He shot skyward and sailed off into the horizon.

Phil and Teri flipped the cushions, revealing thousands of coins. Enough to cover the entire surface. Mostly pennies, a few dozen buttons, and a handful of coins of foreign currency. There was also a doubloon, an earring Teri had lost over a year ago, and an old key they couldn't place.

Phil shook the change jar. "Not a bad exchange for a sandwich."

"Maybe we should've asked him to stay," said Teri.

"You're the one who didn't want him here."

"I know, but now I feel kind of bad about it."

They put the cushions back and sat. "I'm sure it isn't that big of a deal." He put his arm around Teri. "I thought for sure he was going to smite us."

She laughed. "He seemed like a good guy. For a god. Why would he want to live with us?"

"He said he was down on his luck," said Phil. "And I've heard that the rent on Mount Olympus is pretty steep."

She elbowed him gently in the ribs. "Where did you hear that?"

"CNN had a special report a few months ago. Did you know that Odin bought a house in San Diego?"

"Seems a little sunny for a Norse god."

"Probably got tired of all that snow." Phil glanced

around the room. "Have you seen the remote?" he asked. "I could've sworn I left it on the end table."

"I'm sure it'll turn up, honey."

It didn't. Neither gave it much thought at the time, but it was the beginning.

The next morning, Teri slipped in the shower. It wasn't a serious fall, though she did bruise her tailbone and skin her calf on the faucet. Phil's car had a flat tire, and when he tried to change it, he ended up stripping the lug nuts. Teri gave him a ride to work. She spilled coffee on her lap. It didn't burn, but it did ruin her favorite skirt.

"I'll pick you up around six," she said as she gave him a kiss. "Love ya, babe."

"Love you, too." He stepped onto the curb, and she pulled away, tearing off the end of his sleeve, which was stuck in her door.

Grumbling, Phil trudged into the building. Hank, the security guard, remarked on Phil's appearance. Some kind of joke that Phil didn't catch, but he nodded and smiled anyway. As he was signing in, the pen broke. More accurately, it exploded, splattering his fingers and shirt with blue ink.

"Son of a..."

Hank handed Phil some paper towels. "Looks like you're having one of those days, huh?"

Phil dabbed at the mess with the towels, accomplishing nothing. "What?"

"Hey, we all have them. One of those days when everything goes wrong."

Phil lowered the towel.

"Something wrong?" asked Hank.

"No, everything's fine. Excuse me. I have to make a phone call."

His cell battery was dead.

Phil stopped at the row of elevators. People pushed past him, but he hesitated. So far the bad luck had been minor, but he saw no reason to tempt the wrath of his new god by getting into an elevator.

He took the stairs. One step at a time, very slowly, with a death grip on the railing. He made it to his cubicle without tearing any more clothes or breaking any bones.

Elliot peered over the cubicle's edge. "Geez, buddy, you look like hell."

"Long story." Phil searched his wallet, but couldn't find Lucky's card.

"How'd that god search go?" asked Elliot. "Did you and Teri find one you agreed on?"

Phil nodded.

"So you did it?" Elliot came around and sat on Phil's desk. "You actually did it."

"Yes."

"I didn't think you'd actually follow through with it, buddy. I mean, I thought you might, but I was sure you weren't going to be able to get Teri to commit."

"She saw a miracle cat," said Phil.

Elliot chuckled. He took a bite of his doughnut. Jelly squirted out and struck Phil in the eye.

"Dude, I am so sorry."

"Don't worry about it."

"How's it working out?" asked Elliot.

Phil wiped the jelly from his face. "Not so great. I think I've been smote."

"Already? That has to be a record." Elliot tried to act casual, but exited the cubicle, continuing the conversation from a distance. "Should I be on the lookout for lightning bolts?"

"I don't think it's as serious as that," said Phil. "My god isn't that type."

"Just the same, buddy, you should probably appease him before it's too late. This kind of thing can get out of hand quickly. Did Teri catch any divine wrath?"

"I think so."

"Bet she's not happy about that."

"I'll let you know."

Elliot went back to his cubicle, and Phil dialed Teri's cell number. She didn't answer. Her battery was probably dead, too. He decided not to panic. There was no need for it yet. All the smiting had been annoying, a string of bad luck from an angry prosperity god. Nothing life-threatening to this point.

His imagination worked against him. He could see the wheel coming off her car, sending her skidding into the path of a speeding semi. Or her tripping at the top of a flight of stairs and falling. Or getting electrocuted by a fax machine. Or a million other grim possibilities. It was all luck in the end. If probability had it in for you, there wasn't much you could do to stop it.

He pushed aside his concerns and let work occupy his thoughts. He kept glancing at the clock. A minute after she should've made it to work, he called. She wasn't there yet.

He waited fifteen minutes, then called again. Teri still wasn't in.

Phil started getting nervous.

"Problem, buddy?" asked Elliot, his head poking above the cubicle partition.

"It's nothing."

"Are you sure? You aren't typing. Normally, the clickity-click of your keyboard is like a machine gun."

Phil's hands rested in his lap. "It's fine."

But it wasn't fine. He should've listened to Teri when she said no to getting a god. And he shouldn't have listened to her when she'd said she'd changed her mind. Now she was the victim of an angry raccoon god, and it was all his fault. If he hadn't brought it up in the first place then everything would have been fine.

The phone rang. He answered it so fast, he didn't even realize it was to his ear until he heard Teri's voice.

"Phil, has something gone wrong? Are you okay?"

He slumped in his chair and blew out a calming breath. "I'm good." He pondered the jelly and ink stains on his shirt as he formulated his next sentence. If Teri hadn't figured out what was happening by now, there was no reason to upset her. He could appease Lucky on his own time, and she might never know.

"I just called to say I love you," he said.

"Uh-huh. Love you, too."

The line was silent as Teri formulated her own reply.

"So we've been smote, right?"

"I'm fairly certain we have been," he agreed.

"Damn. And to think I was feeling sorry for that little bastard."

Phil winced. "Honey, I don't think it's a good idea to profane our new god right now."

"Sorry. I knew this was a bad idea. Why didn't you talk me out of it?"

"Why did you talk me into it?" he replied.

"We have to fix it. Maybe we could renounce him."

Phil said, "I don't know. That costs a lot of money. Lawyers in the Divine Court aren't cheap. Plus it takes time. Sometimes months."

He imagined having another day like this, one right after another. Even if it didn't eventually kill him, he wasn't looking forward to it. Teri had the same thought.

"So we appease him, right?" she asked. "That shouldn't be too hard. He said we could just call him when we were ready to commit."

"I left the number at the house."

"Why did you do that?"

"I didn't do it on purpose," he said through clenched teeth. "It was just some bad luck."

"I suppose you're going to blame Lucky for that, too."

"This is no big deal," he said. "We can handle this. It's just one bad day. Tonight, you'll pick me up—"

"Yes, about that. Someone else will have to take you home tonight. I ran over a hubcap, and it broke my axle."

"Damn it, do you know how much that's going to cost us?"

"More than a jar of pennies," she replied. "I don't want to talk about it. I just want this fixed. Now."

He heard a thud on the line.

"Ow, son of a bitch! My paperweight just dropped on my foot. Jeez, that hurts. Phil..."

"I'll take care of it. Don't worry."

"Make it quick, okay?" she said. "I have an important meeting at two and I know if I end up setting the board-room on fire it'll probably earn me a write-up."

He hung up and tried to save his work. Sickly green filled his monitor and smoke rose from his computer. Phil quickly unplugged it.

Elliot popped up. "Do I smell something burning?"

Phil waved away the smoke. "I need to borrow your car."

Elliot narrowed his eyes suspiciously. "Why don't you have yours?"

"Flat tire."

"This isn't wrath-related, is it?"

Phil considered lying, but he wasn't very good at it. "Maybe."

"Forget it."

"Remember that time I caught you and Ginger in the broom closet during the vernal equinox party?" said Phil. "And your wife was about to discover you, too, if I hadn't stalled her, if I remember right."

"That's no fair. I was drunk. It was just a little making out anyway. Nothing serious."

"I'm sure Amy would've been fine with seeing you and Ginger dry-humping next to the mops."

Elliot threw his keys at Phil.

"We're even now. But please be careful with that car. I just bought it, and my insurance doesn't cover acts of gods."

4

Bonnie would later think about how random it all was, and how an entire life could change because of a stolen motorcycle. They never found the thief. She sometimes liked to believe that it was destiny, that an emissary of fate had snatched her prized Harley as part of a larger plot. Perhaps right now the cycle was being used to tow the sun across the heavens, too. She could live with that.

She knew better. If there was one thing her dealings with the divine would teach her, it was that there was no larger plan. Mortals might not like that. Gods might do their best to deny it. But Whim was the true ruler of the universe. Bonnie had bought her Harley on a whim. Someone had stolen it on another whim. It was a whim of public transportation that there was a bus stop just a block from her apartment, and a whim of nature that the morning was so beautiful she left early to sit on the bench and enjoy the crisp weather.

A lone woman occupied the bench. She was disheveled, with dirty brown hair. She wore a dress that must have been beautiful a decade ago, but now was tattered and dirty. She sat slumped. Her face was hidden and she wore gloves, so Bonnie couldn't guess her age. Bonnie wondered if the woman was homeless or a burned-out hippie or something else. Bonnie had expected more people since it was the morning commute, but maybe the woman had scared them away.

Bonnie almost walked away but decided she was being judgmental. She wasn't going to let a snap judgment ruin her day.

"Hello," she said as warmly as she could.

The woman turned her head. Her hair fell across her eyes and obscured everything but her chin. It was smooth and pale. Too pale. As if her skin had never been exposed to sunlight. Or any light at all. Like an albino. She didn't smile.

"Hello." There was a slight rasp in her flat voice.

"Beautiful day, isn't it?"

"Is it?" The woman raised her head. Her hair clung to her face, refusing to show any more of it. "I hadn't noticed."

Bonnie decided the woman was weird, but harmless. If she did scare away the other commuters, it just gave Bonnie more room on the bench. She sat down. A chill passed through her.

"You shouldn't have done that," said the woman, shaking her head.

"I'm sorry?"

"You shouldn't have sat there."

The woman sighed deeply and a frozen wind swept across the bench. The birdsongs turned shrill. Darkness blotted out the sun, and a gray shadow fell across the bus stop and only the bus stop. The rest of the world was just as bright and warm as before, but the miniature eclipse enveloped the stop in raw, all-consuming hopelessness. There was no other word for it.

The darkness passed. It didn't fade so much as bleed into the ground and slide into place as the woman's shadow. The cold lessened but didn't disappear. Bonnie jumped off the bench and rubbed her hands together.

"It's too late for that," said the tattered woman.

Bonnie's cell rang. The ring tone told her it was her boyfriend.

"I'm sorry," said the woman.

Bonnie flipped open the phone. "Hi, Walter. You would not believe what just happened to—"

He broke up with her. He wasn't rude, but he didn't feign politeness either. Just told her it was over, and hung up. She didn't have time to absorb the news, much less formulate a response. She tried calling him back, five times, but he didn't answer.

"I'm sorry," said the woman, "but I did tell you not to sit there."

"No, you didn't."

"I didn't? Are you certain about that? Because I'm pretty sure I did."

"No, I'm pretty sure you didn't."

Bonnie dialed her boyfriend again with the same result. She left another message.

"Well, maybe if you had said something to me before you sat," said the tattered woman, "I could've warned you. It's only polite to acknowledge others."

"I said hello."

"Did you? That's something, I suppose."

Bonnie dialed her phone again but snapped it shut before the call went through. "I talked to you about the day, too. About the weather!"

"I suppose." She grunted. "Though you didn't sound like you really meant it."

"I didn't mean it."

"So you admit it?"

"Of course I admit it," said Bonnie. "It's the weather. It doesn't mean anything. It's just polite conversation."

"I guess that counts for mortal politeness in this new age."

Bonnie paced in a tight circle, staring at her phone, willing it to ring.

"He's not going to call," said the tattered woman. "It'll just be easier to let him go."

"But we're in love."

"You were in love, and I guess you still are. More than ever now. But he'll never speak to you again."

A palpable misery emanated from her, a wave of icy numbness. The bench grayed. Its color ran down the street and into a storm drain. Bonnie felt every ounce of the rising melancholy. She wanted to die then. Just collapse and wither away until she was nothing but dust. Then she hoped the sun would explode and vaporize the entire planet, erasing every remnant of this moment from the memory of time.

Bonnie had to get away. She ran back to her apartment, shut the door behind her, and wiped away her tears. The weight of despair lessened, but it didn't fade. Not completely.

Someone rattled around in her kitchenette. She knew who it was without having to look.

The tattered goddess floated into view. She carried two glasses of tomato juice and offered one to Bonnie. "Here. Drink this. It won't solve your problem, but it's chock-full of vitamins."

Bonnie slapped the glass out of the goddess's hand. Juice spilled across her carpet, couch, and wall. "You did this! You did something to Walter!"

"Actually, I did something to you," said the goddess. "Your boyfriend was just some collateral damage." The goddess sipped her juice, leaving a red mustache on her pale flesh. "And I did say I was sorry."

She brushed her limp hair away, allowing Bonnie a brief glimpse of the goddess's face. Her large, sad eyes were as colorless as the rest of her.

"Take it back. Please, I'll do anything."

Her relationship with Walter had been good, but nothing spectacular. She loved him, but it wasn't head-over-heels. Just some good times and reliable, comforting familiarity. So why did she miss him so much now? She ached for his touch, his smile, his clumsy but competent sex. Even things that she'd found annoying somehow seemed endearing at this moment.

She stifled a sob. Her lip quivered, but she swallowed the pain.

"That's good," said the goddess. "Bury it deep. You'll last longer that way." She sighed and a nearby frame holding Walter's photo cracked.

"Will you stop doing that?" asked Bonnie. "Stop sighing!"

"Sorry. I can't help it. Or you."

Bonnie slapped the second glass out of the goddess's hand. The juice covered Bonnie's shoes, but none of it splashed the goddess. "Get the hell out of my apartment!"

"I can't do that. You invited me into your life, and here I shall remain until..."

The goddess sighed, and Walter's photo burst into flame. Bonnie stomped it out, but not fast enough to prevent a scorch mark in the carpet. The loss of her apartment deposit didn't add any joy to her day.

"What do I have to do to get rid of you?" asked Bonnie.

"There's nothing you can do." The goddess floated to the couch and had a seat.

"But you just said you're in my life until..."

The goddess turned on the television. "Oh, good. You have cable. The last one didn't."

"Don't change the subject. You said I was stuck with you until..." Bonnie paused to give the goddess a chance to insert the end of the sentence, but she didn't oblige.

"*When Harry Met Sally* is on," said the goddess. "I hate that movie. So tragic when they die in that car accident."

"That doesn't happen in the movie," said Bonnie.

"It does when I watch it."

Bonnie stepped in front of the television and glared at the goddess.

"Your pain will end, Bonnie. Eventually. In the mercy that ends all mortal pain."

"Death? You're saying I'm stuck with you until I die?"

The goddess shrugged. "I'm sorry. If it's any consolation, it's worse for me. You're only the victim of heartbreak, but I'm the goddess of it."

"Why are you doing this to me?"

"As I keep telling you, I have no choice. Do you think I want to ruin your life? Or anyone's? I wasn't always like this. Once, I was...different. But that was a long time ago. Now, I am what I am, and pain and suffering are all I bring to those who allow me into their lives."

"But I just said hello."

"You also sat on the bench."

"That's absurd. You're telling me that just because I sat on a bench with a goddess of heartbreak that my whole life is ruined?"

The goddess almost sighed, but caught herself this once. "I know it's unfair. You were just being friendly. You shouldn't have to carry this burden, but look at it this way. By carrying the pain, you are keeping someone else from having to carry it. Your sacrifice will allow others to know love and joy. It won't be in vain."

"Well, whoop-de-fuckin'-doo."

Bonnie stormed into the kitchen and drank tomato juice right out of the carton. It spilled down her blouse. She didn't care.

"Nothing would make me happier than to leave you alone," said the goddess from the living room. "Well, actually, something would make me happier, but let's not dwell on impossibilities."

Bonnie leaned against the refrigerator. The emptiness inside her would stay, she realized. A yawning, devouring cold that would eventually consume her. She yanked a dirty steak knife out of the sink and held it in tight white knuckles.

She had to end it.

The goddess stood in the kitchen doorway. "I'm sorry, Bonnie. I really am."

"Stop saying that!"

Bonnie charged. She pushed the goddess to the floor

and stabbed her in the heart. Bonnie plunged the blade in over and over and over. Every stab stoked the flames of rage, fueled by a need to feel anything besides nothing. Five minutes later, her fury faded but the emptiness remained.

The goddess, her sad face etched with boredom, looked up at Bonnie.

"Are you through?"

There wasn't a drop of blood on the knife, nor a mark left on the goddess's flesh. Bonnie dropped the weapon and dragged herself to the sofa. The goddess sat beside her.

The sound of a car crash drew her attention to the movie playing on the TV and the depiction of twisted steel and broken glass. And blood. So much blood.

The goddess opened her mouth.

"Don't," interrupted Bonnie. "Just don't say it."

Phil hit every bug on the drive from the office. By the time he made it home, the windshield was a mess of smeared insects. There was no wiper fluid, but he managed to avoid driving Elliot's car off a cliff, though by the end he was peering through a few inches of semi-clear glass. He pulled into his driveway and cringed at the sound of breaking glass. Even with supernatural bad luck, he didn't see how it was possible to run over three separate bottles and a rusty nail, flattening all four tires.

He walked very carefully across his lawn. Somehow, he managed to step in dog crap anyway. Twice. He left his shoes on the porch.

The card wasn't where Phil had left it. He searched all over the house for it, stubbing his toes on every piece of furniture before slipping on a new pair of shoes. He checked under the couch cushions, in every drawer. He looked in the refrigerator, behind the entertainment center, and in the trash.

He couldn't find it. He gave up after an hour.

Phil sat on the couch and stared at the phone. What kind of god didn't have a prayer? It was a little old-fashioned but a lot harder to lose than a business card. Phil pulled out his wallet and checked it. He'd already checked it a dozen times, but he didn't have any other ideas.

The card fell into his lap. He questioned if it had been there the whole time and it'd just been his bad luck to not see it until now. Or had it materialized in his wallet after his god had deemed that Phil had suffered enough?

The phone rang for about twenty seconds before someone answered.

"Yello."

He didn't recognize the voice.

"May I speak to Lucky, please?" Phil asked.

There was a pause.

"He's asleep right now," replied the voice. "Can I take a message?"

"Asleep?"

"He likes to sleep in. Am I speaking to Phil?"

"Uh...yes."

"Hey, Phil. I'm Tom."

"Hi...Tom."

Awkward silence as Phil tried to figure out what to say next.

"Could you maybe wake Lucky?" he asked. "This is a bit of an emergency."

"Love to help you," said Tom, "but no can do. I'll leave a message on the refrigerator. He'll get it when he wakes up. In the meantime, you'll just have to stick it out. It'll only be another couple of hours of misfortune. Take my advice and sit still, don't do anything, and you'll be fine."

"But..."

"Talk to you later, Phil. Praise Luka."

"Praise Luka," echoed Phil reflexively.

He followed Tom's advice and planted himself on the couch. He went to the kitchen once to get some soda. He turned on the TV, but without the remote control, he was stuck watching soaps. When he went to use the bathroom, the toilet clogged. Even though he only peed. When he tried to fix it, the plunger got stuck.

The phone rang at half past eleven. It was Teri, not Lucky, calling to check on Phil's progress. She sounded exhausted, rattling off a short list of the misfortunes that had befallen her. He was only half-listening. He gave her the same advice Tom had given him and told her he was expecting a call, and that he'd let her know when things were corrected.

Noon rolled around. The phone didn't ring. He gave it ten minutes, then decided it couldn't hurt to call again.

"Yello." It was Tom.

"Hi, this is Phil. I called earlier—"

"Yeah. I remember. Hold on a second..."

Phil made out Tom's muffled shout.

"Hey, Lucky! It's Phil!"

Lucky's reply was too muffled to decipher.

"He says he'll be right over after he finishes his cornflakes and takes a shower. Forty minutes, tops."

Phil almost complained but decided it would be smarter to play it safe. He stared at the TV and zoned out. The doorbell rang an hour later. Phil jumped off the sofa. In his eagerness to answer it, he slammed his hip hard into an end table. The lamp fell over and shattered. Grumbling, he limped the rest of the way.

Lucky stood on the porch. He didn't have any luggage.

"Hey, buddy. What's up?"

Phil knelt. Not easy to do with his bruised hip. He prostrated himself, trying to get his head lower than Lucky's. That wasn't easy either.

"Oh, Great and Merciful Luka, Lord of Prosperity and Good Fortune. We have wronged you and humbly beg your forgiveness—"

"Knock it off, kid."

Phil dared to raise his head. Lucky smiled at him.

"Get up. I appreciate the old-school supplication, but it's not necessary."

"Does that mean you've unsmote us?"

"I never smote you in the first place."

"But since you left we've had nothing but—"

"I could go for a pizza. Want to grab a pizza?"

"I am a little hungry," said Phil. "But my car has four flat tires."

"No problem. I'll fly us there."

Lucky snapped his fingers. A shining globe wrapped around them, and Phil was lifted off the ground to zip over the city. Lucky surveyed the landscape, quickly spotting a cheesy themed pizzeria designed to appeal to children. Since it was a weekday and school was in session, the place was empty. The globe of light pushed through the front doors and deposited Lucky and Phil at the front counter.

"So what do you like on your pie? I'm partial to anchovies myself."

Lucky surveyed the menu posted behind the clerk, who was festooned in a bright yellow-and-blue uniform with a name tag proclaiming him Gary.

"Sir," said Gary, "I'm afraid animals aren't allowed in here."

"Hold on a second." Lucky searched through his pockets and produced a standard-issue deity identification card. Gary gave it a cursory inspection.

"Your order, sir?" he asked.

"We'll take a large pie, extra anchovies."

"We no longer carry anchovies, sir."

"Check in the back. I have a feeling you'll find an old tin behind the canned pepperoni."

"We use only the freshest ingredients, sir," said Gary.

Lucky chuckled. "Just do me a favor and check. I'll also take a large cola and a side salad. Get whatever else you want, Phil. I'll be over by skeeball."

After he walked away, Gary asked, "Is that your god? Or is it just some god you know?"

"Mine."

"And he hangs out with you? That's pretty cool. My family gods just send us a newsletter four times a year. Oh, and I got a drop cloth of invisibility on my eighteenth birthday."

"That must've been nice."

"I lost it by the end of the week." Gary shrugged. "Damn thing was invisible."

Phil paid for the pizza. He forgot to get a receipt, but he wasn't in the habit of considering deity-related tax write-offs yet.

He joined Lucky in the arcade. The raccoon pointed to a couple playing the machine on the far end.

"Watch this."

The man rolled the wooden ball up the ramp. It hopped perfectly into the highest-scoring and most difficult hole.

The machine spit out a stream of tickets. The woman took a turn and repeated the success. They continued, scoring perfect with every throw. They gathered up all their tickets and ran to the redemption counter.

"Are they your followers, too?" asked Phil.

"Nope. Never met them before."

"But you help them out while me you smite?"

"The only one who smote you...is you." Lucky said, "Oooh, they have a classic Asteroids console machine! I love those. Do you have any quarters?"

"They don't take quarters anymore," said Phil.

"Really? Things change so fast with you mortals, don't they?"

Phil bought some tokens. Lucky pulled up a stool to the Asteroids machine. He played while explaining.

"Do you know any basic theology, Phil?"

"A little. High school stuff. I don't remember very much."

"Do you at least remember the first law of divine embodiment? It states that gods manifest their natures in the world around them. The effect and intensity varies by god. It's not always the same, and it's not always reliable. But it still applies as a general rule. As a god of prosperity and good fortune, I make good things happen. Just by being me. It's like a tree spitting out oxygen. It doesn't choose to do it. It just does it."

He paused to concentrate on blasting an onslaught of meteors.

"Anyway, you and your lovely wife whose name escapes me at this moment in time..."

"Teri."

"Thanks. When you and Teri signed on to follow me,

you invited good fortune into your home. And when you let me leave, I took that fortune with me. I didn't want to. It just left with me because that's how it works."

"You couldn't make it stay behind?"

"Nope. See, that's a common misconception you mortals have about us gods. Just because we're divine that doesn't mean we're all-powerful. We have limits. We don't like to advertise that, but it's true." He sniffed the air. "Is that anchovies I smell? I think our pizza is up."

Lucky's nose was right. They found a table in front of the animatronic animal band. The drummer was a robotic raccoon, and Lucky frowned.

"The drummer never scores. At least he's doing better than the octopus with the tambourines." He raised his glass to the cephalopod. "I feel for you, pal."

The pizza was a lukewarm bread disk slathered with tomato paste and cheese. Lucky helped himself to the first slice.

"You're not going to have any?" he asked.

"I don't like anchovies."

"More for me then."

Lucky picked the little fish off a slice and devoured them. Then he put the cleaned slice on a plate and slid it before Phil. Phil took a bite. It wasn't very good, still retaining a bit of salty anchovy flavor. But he was hungry, and he didn't want to insult Lucky.

"Why didn't you warn us what would happen?" Phil asked.

"I find a demonstration makes the point so much better than mere explanation." Lucky flashed a smile. "Plus, I'm a god. I'm allowed to be petty. You can't tell me you weren't honestly expecting a little wrath. You're fortunate you didn't try to pull that a few hundred years ago. Back then, I probably would've dropped a meteor on your house. Lucky for you I've mellowed over the centuries."

His eyes twinkled, and Phil found himself forgiving Lucky.

"Why didn't you ask me to stay?" Lucky asked. "You came to me, after all. I wouldn't have even been there if you hadn't signed up."

"No reason."

"Riiiight." Lucky said, "If you don't want to tell me, that's cool. But I already figured it was Teri's call, right?"

"No." Phil took a long drink of his soda. "It was me."

"That's sweet, kid. Don't know many people who would risk divine wrath to protect their spouse. But don't bother lying. I saw it in her eyes. She's reluctant."

Phil tried denying it, but Lucky wasn't buying it.

"Her grandfather was killed by wrath."

"Say no more. I understand. Being reluctant is fine. It shows she's smart. I never trust mortals who are too eager to follow. Means they don't take the responsibilities seriously."

"She's okay then?"

"Depends. Do I have her permission to crash at your place?"

"Yes."

"Terrific, but just to make things official, I'll need to hear it from her. Have your cell handy?"

"The battery's dead."

"Check again."

Phil wasn't surprised to see the phone fully charged. He dialed and asked for Teri. Lucky took the phone before she picked up. That made Phil nervous. She wanted the bad luck fixed, but he wasn't certain she would agree to this. Her behavior over the course of this entire thing had been unpredictable. First against it, then for it. Then against it. If he explained the situation to her, how it worked, he was positive she'd allow Lucky into their home. That's why he wanted to talk to her first.

"Teri," said Lucky. "How's it going?"

He turned his back and walked out of eavesdropping range. Phil nibbled on a slice of pizza and waited. The conversation took longer than a simple yes would've required. Lucky did most of the talking.

He returned. "Great news. She's in."

Lucky convinced Phil to blow off work and take the rest of the afternoon off. It wasn't like Phil, but the god offered a wink and a smile accompanied by his trademark finger snap/gun-imitation point, and Phil found himself agreeing. They finished their meal, then played video games.

As gods went, Lucky seemed fairly laid-back. A teenager jumped ahead of him at a Whack-A-Mole game. Lucky didn't say anything, but Phil noticed that the machines started eating the teen's tokens afterward. Phil wondered if it was an intentional affliction or just a side effect of the prosperity god's displeasure. Either way, it wasn't as bad as it could've been, a small misery for a small transgression.

As they were leaving, Lucky said, "I almost forgot. Mind if I use your phone to call Tom and let him know I'm moving out?"

"Will he be upset?" asked Phil. "Won't you take his fortune with you if you leave?"

"That's what I like about you, kid. You think about

others. Most everyone else wouldn't even consider that. You're good people."

Phil smiled. It was nice to get a compliment, and since it was coming from his god, it had to count for a few extra points of karma.

"Don't worry about Tom," said Lucky. "He'll set up an altar. I'll be moving out, but I won't be leaving. Not in the metaphorical sense."

"Why do you want to move out anyway?"

"Tom's a good guy," replied Lucky, "but he lives in Varney, Wisconsin. Ever heard of Varney?"

"No."

"Exactly. Nobody has. It's not a good place for a god to regain his popularity. Plus there's nothing to do there. And the cheese . . . it's not as good as you'd expect."

Lucky walked away as he placed his call.

Phil wandered outside and waited for Lucky to finish. The day was beautiful. He had a good feeling about the future. His god wasn't prestigious or all-powerful, but Lucky seemed like a good god to have. Neither judgmental nor a pushover, but easygoing and low-maintenance.

He stepped in some gum. At first thinking that good fortune had deserted him, he noticed that a hundred-dollar bill was stuck with it. He peeled it off. The gum came off easily, too. Things were looking up.

A squirrel scampered before him. The odd animal was dark red with black spots. It had big blue eyes. Unusually large, it seemed. But Phil didn't know enough about squirrels to know for sure.

It batted its eyes and cocked its head at a lovable angle.

"Hi, little fella. Aren't you friendly?"

The squirrel stood, leaning against his leg. Its ears

tilted forward. He reached down to scratch its head. The squirrel nipped at his finger, drawing blood. Phil jumped back, and the tiny spotted predator crouched. Its ears flattened. Its tail bristled. It snarled, showing razor-sharp yellow teeth. Its body tightened in preparation to spring.

Lucky stepped out of the pizzeria. The squirrel narrowed its eyes and hissed like a snake. Phil may not have known much about squirrels, but that had to be unusual. The god transformed into a two-hundred-pound timber wolf, retaining his raccoon head and tail, although his snout was elongated and canine. The squirrel turned and ran. Lucky gave chase.

"It's okay!" shouted Phil. "It was just a little bite!"

The squirrel darted under a car in the parking lot, and Lucky scrambled after it. Phil jogged down the row of cars, trying to keep pace with the pursuit. The lot wasn't very full. There was nowhere for the squirrel to hide. It ducked and weaved, avoiding Lucky's snapping jaws. The squirrel veered off and headed back toward Phil.

"Oh, crap."

The squirrel charged. Its narrow eyes focused on either his throat or his crotch. He couldn't tell for sure, but either possibility seemed unpleasant. The rabid rodent leaped.

It was the throat. Phil was simultaneously relieved and terrified.

Lucky grabbed the squirrel by the tail and whipped it away. The rodent landed on its feet and whirled to continue the attack. Lucky transformed into a raccoon-headed bear. He stepped between the squirrel and Phil.

The rabid creature backed away.

Lucky clapped his paws, and a crate fell out of the sky. It missed the squirrel by several yards, striking a car and crushing its roof. The crate burst apart, sending shards of wood and jelly beans flying like shrapnel. Phil was fortunate enough not to have anything hard hit him, but he was pelted with candy.

Lucky clapped again. A recliner plummeted like a bomb. His aim was better but still off by a few feet.

"Damn it."

The squirrel bolted in the opposite direction. With each clap of his paws, Lucky dropped miscellaneous bombs of divine wrath. He smashed a sportscar with a refrigerator and pulverized a pickup engine with a bathtub. An anvil missed both the cars and the squirrel, but it did leave a big dent in the pavement.

"Aw, screw it." Lucky reverted to his casual raccoon shape. He snapped his fingers, and a midsize boat found its target. The boat wasn't quite a yacht, but it was large enough to pulverize the animal and several automobiles.

The god scratched his head. "I guess it's true what they say. If you don't keep up the smiting practice, you get rusty."

Phil gawked at the debris littering the parking lot.

Lucky scooped up a handful of jelly beans and popped a couple in his mouth. "Want one?"

"No, thanks."

"Are you sure? They're pretty good if you pick out the gravel."

He noticed Phil's stunned expression.

"You okay, buddy? That squirrel didn't hurt you, did it?"

Phil held up his wounded finger.

"We better get a Band-Aid on that. Maybe some antiseptic. Just because you're hanging out with a god of good fortune, that doesn't mean we can't use a little common sense, right?"

Phil nodded. "What was that?"

"Nothing," said Lucky. "Feral squirrel. See them all the time in the city." He rocked back and forth on his toes and heels. "Hey, whatever it was, it's dead now, right? It'll never nip another finger again, and that's a promise. I smote it good. Just consider it one of the many fine services I offer my followers. Now aren't you glad I'm around?"

Onlookers were gathering to view the damage.

"This scene is getting crowded. Do you want to get out of here?"

"But what about all the cars you destroyed?"

"Not our problem." Lucky enveloped them in the globe of light. "According to the Divine Intervention Concordat of 1845, a god or goddess is not responsible for any incidental damages resulting from the execution of his or her wrathful obligations. The squirrel bit you. I exacted my rightful divine retribution. It's as simple as that. Now let's bolt before things get complicated."

They lifted into the air. Phil surveyed the shattered remains of the boat.

"Why did it attack me?" he wondered aloud.

"I wouldn't worry about it, kid. As long as I'm around, everything will be turning up roses from now on."

"But—"

"Do you like burritos, Phil?" asked Lucky.

Phil lost his train of thought. "What?"

"Burritos? Not a big fan, myself, to be honest, but sometimes, I still get a hankering. I think tonight is a burrito night. What do you think?"

Lucky smiled, and a warm, comforting feeling passed over Phil.

"Uh, yeah, burritos sound good."

Lucky snapped his fingers. "Excellente."

"Excellente," agreed Phil in a bit of a fog.

6

By noon, Teri had ripped her skirt, gotten several runs in her stockings, and broken a heel, and there was a wrinkle in her collar that refused to go away. Her computer had eaten her presentation, and she'd lost the index card with her backup notes and the backup backup notes. And she was fairly certain she was coming down with a cold, too.

When lunch rolled around, she was all too eager to get out of the office. She usually ate at the deli tucked in the building's ground floor. Teri found her regular table and sat quietly. She wasn't moving unless she absolutely had to.

A tall brunette sashayed her way to the table and had a seat. "Geez, hon, looks like you've had better days."

"You have no idea."

"You stay here," said Janet. "I'll go and order for the both of us."

"Thanks."

When Janet returned with her tray, Teri's iced tea

tipped. The lid popped off, and tea spilled across the table. She pushed away from the table to avoid getting splashed. Her chair tilted, and only Janet's quick hand on Teri's sleeve stopped her from falling.

Janet offered to buy Teri another drink, but Teri turned her down. Instead, she took a bite of her soggy sandwich, chewing very slowly to avoid biting her tongue.

Janet's sandwich had somehow escaped the flood. "I don't know, hon. Maybe Phil's right. Maybe you should get a god."

"We have one."

"Oh, really?" Janet raised an eyebrow. "Is he hot? Or is he even a he? Did you go the goddess route?"

"No, he's a he."

"Cool. So is he hot?"

"He's a raccoon."

"Like with the striped tail and the cute little paws?"

Teri nodded.

"Very retro."

"Well, he does seem to like Hawaiian shirts," replied Teri. "The kind that were in fashion... actually I don't think they were ever in fashion."

"Kitschy. And a bit surprising. I always pictured you as more of a traditional gal. Well, actually, I thought you'd talk yourself out of it at the last minute."

"I wish I had."

"Not going so well, is it? What's his gig?"

"His what?"

"His schtick. His game," said Janet. "His specialty?"

"Good fortune." Teri's sandwich dripped cold tea and mayo on her blouse. It was already ruined, so she didn't think much of it.

"Looks like he's broken."

Teri shrugged. "I think it's my fault. He wanted to move in, and I wasn't crazy about the idea. I think he picked up on that."

"He wanted to move in?"

"He says it's part of his personal touch," said Teri.

"So what's the problem?"

"I don't know." Teri added more napkins to her improvised dam on the table. "I keep going back and forth on this."

"You really need to make up your mind," said Janet.

"I know."

"And if you ask me, you already made up your mind when you signed up, right? Too late to back out now."

"I guess you're right. But I circulated a petition to keep a temple of Athena off my college campus. I marched for the Deity Restriction Act. Hell, my generation was going to change things. We were going to break the chains of thousands of years of divine codependence."

"Hate to break it to you, but that movement died a long time ago."

"I know." Teri sighed. "Did you know that according to the latest polls active tribute has risen by 20 percent in the last ten years?"

"Can't say that I did," Janet replied.

Teri set down her soggy sandwich. Her appetite was gone. "You don't think I'm compromising my ideals?"

"Oh, you're selling out, all right. If it makes you feel any better, I thought about getting some of that divine favor once myself. I even answered an ad in a newspaper."

"How'd that work out?" asked Teri with mild interest.

"Didn't. Turns out that AFG stands for African fertility

goddess. Said she could guarantee me fifty kids." Janet shuddered. "I like rugrats, but not that much."

Teri lost her appetite.

"Don't be so hard on yourself," said Janet. "You're compromising your principles a little. That's just the way it works. This is real life, after all. It's great to be a college kid with ideals, but you have to live, right?"

"Yes." Teri sounded unconvinced.

"It's not like you chose a big god, is it? It's not like you're sacrificing bulls or giving up eating dairy or anything weird like that, right?"

"No, I suppose not."

"He just wants to live with you. So let him live with you. I don't see what the big deal is."

"Now you sound like Phil."

"You should listen to us then," said Janet. "Anyway, you can follow without putting your heart into it. Most gods don't care that much. They just want a little brownnosing, and they're happy."

Teri said, "You're suggesting I follow half-assed."

"Why not? Just treat it like a job you don't care that much about. Keep your head down, do the minimum, and don't worry too much about it. Your god will probably move out in a few weeks. Then you won't have to do much more than maintain an altar. How hard can that be?"

Teri perked up. "Do you really think he'll want to move out that soon?"

"I'd bet on it. You know gods. They get bored pretty fast. And I've seen you and Phil, hon. You aren't exactly the most exciting couple. In a week or two, three tops, your raccoon god will be climbing the walls."

Teri had never been so happy to be labeled boring.

Her appetite returned. She was able to finish off half of her soggy sandwich. After her lunch with Janet, Teri felt better, even though bad luck continued to plague her. But she'd brought it on herself. And the fact that Lucky didn't crack open the earth and throw her into eternal hellfire showed that he wasn't such a bad god. She could weather the storm of misfortune until Phil fixed the problem.

She was relieved when his call finally came. Lucky did all of the talking. He was so busy selling himself that it was three minutes before she was finally able to find an opening to say yes.

"Great," he said. "I'll see you tonight then. We'll hang out, get to know each other. It'll be fun."

"Yes, I'm sure it will be."

"Terrific. See you then."

As soon as Lucky hung up, she felt relieved. She looked terrible, and there was no time to find her notes. With each step to the meeting, her confidence grew. Now she had a fighting chance. She pushed her way into the conference room.

It was empty.

Janet tapped Teri on the shoulder. "Rescheduled. Didn't you get the e-mail?"

"My computer has been having problems," said Teri.

"That's a bit of good luck then, isn't it?" Janet smoothed Teri's wrinkled collar, and it stayed in place. "I take it then that your god problem is worked out."

Teri nodded.

"Cool," said Janet. "So when do I get a chance to meet him?"

"You want to meet him?"

"Are you kidding? You know I love gods."

"First of all," said Teri, "I didn't know that. You never even brought up the subject until I mentioned Phil and I were talking about it."

"I don't advertise it, but I'm a huge deiphile."

"I hear they have pills for that now."

"You're a riot." Janet mimed a laugh. "So can I meet him?"

"You really want to?"

"Hell, yeah."

"If you're so into gods, why don't you have one of your own?"

"I decided years ago that I was a fan, not a follower," said Janet. "So can I meet him?"

"I don't know..."

"Oh, come on. You can tell him I'm a potential convert." Janet said, "You'll score some good little follower kudos. I'll get another signature for my autograph book."

"You have an autograph book?" asked Teri.

"I have two. And a photo album. And I haven't added anything to either since I saw Tekkeitsertok."

"Tekkeitser—"

"Inuit god of hunting, master of caribou. Met him at a charity event. Real nice god. So what do you say? You can't turn me away, can you? I've never met a raccoon god before. It'll be fun, and it'll take some of the awkwardness off of your first night with him. Let me be your wingwoman."

It was plain that Janet wasn't going to drop this. She'd keep bugging Teri until she agreed. Better to get it out of the way. And it would be good to have someone there who was actually excited to meet a god.

"You can come," she said. "But don't wear anything

too slutty. I don't need my new god thinking I'm hanging with a loose crowd."

"Whatever you say, but trust me, there's no such thing as too slutty when it comes to dressing for gods. I had a ten-minute conversation with Moritasgus and he didn't once look me in the eyes."

"Morita—"

"Celtic sun god."

"Like Apollo?" asked Teri.

"There's a lot of overlap among the gods," said Janet. "FYI: it's a sore spot with some of them actually so it's usually smarter not to bring it up."

"You are a groupie," said Teri.

"Hon, you have no idea." Janet lowered her voice to a guilty whisper. "I didn't even mention the scrapbooks."

7

Civilization had taken the bite out of the divine powers, regulated and tamed them aside their mortal followers. The heavens could offer a boost, but they no longer built empires or razed continents. The good ol' days of sacking and pillaging a village and offering up the souls to your god were gone. Roger Worthington suspected he would be lousy at sacking and only a modestly talented pillager at best so he didn't mind. But he also knew that, aside from being somewhat handsome (emphasis on the some-what), he wasn't exceptional in any way, and if he was going to get ahead, he'd have to offer blood, sweat, and sacrifice to do it.

If it didn't have to be his, so much the better.

There were still real gods out there, untamed powers that both mortal and immortal authorities wanted forgotten. They'd been forced underground, worshipped by secret cults in hidden temples tucked in darkened corners.

Their influence had faded, but they still knew how to get things done. And they didn't care where their blood came from.

Worthington's first cult had been a complete waste of time. They followed an obscure wisdom goddess who promised to open their minds. In the end, it'd just been an excuse to get high and talk about the secrets revealed when you played Beatles records backward. Harmless fun, but Worthington wasn't in it for fun. He was in it for power.

The next god was more promising. They met in the storeroom of a Pancake Hut, after hours. It wasn't much of a temple, but it got the job done. There he joined in paying tribute to an exiled volcano god who promised to split the earth and devour civilization, placing his followers on top in the new world order. It sounded promising, and the tremors accompanying every blood offering were a nice show. The peak came when someone managed to get hold of an elephant. That was a lot of blood, all right. Their god slurped it down with gusto, and a quake in Singapore killed a few thousand people. But it was a far cry from the fall of nations, and Worthington found himself wondering if maybe his god was taking credit for someone else's divine wrath or, even more annoyingly, possibly just an ordinary earthquake. Even if it had been the work of his god, it would take a hell of a lot of blood to bring about the end of civilization. Worthington wasn't willing to put that much effort into it.

He abandoned the cult. A tremor split the earth and devoured the Pancake Hut a week later. The untamed powers were outlawed for a reason. Even compared to the capricious nature of gods, they were unpredictable and dangerous. The cult could've been destroyed because of some perceived sin. Or perhaps out of boredom. Or quite possibly by accident. That was always the risk.

Worthington was undeterred. He found two kinds of gods in his quest. Impotent deities who promised much but never delivered and powerful forces who refused to act because they feared the wrath of the other gods. It was four years before he caught his break.

In China, he discovered a death god cult. Tribute was easy. Once a month, all the members were required to draw straws. The loser was fed to the god. By then, Worthington had grown inured to such risks. He climbed the ladder of leadership by submitting to the sacrifice lottery twice a month, then once a week. Then two or three times a week. Eventually, every day of his life was decided by a flip of a coin. The others were impressed by his dedication. As was his god. And when he finally drew the short straw and was placed on the altar, he suggested that perhaps a god would do better to sacrifice his less enthusiastic followers rather than his most devoted servant. And the death god agreed with him.

With all the power of his god focused on him after that, he made a small fortune. It was more work. And messier. His god needed blood, and Worthington was the only one to make sure he received it. But Worthington developed a relatively risk-free system, and his prosperity continued. He could've remained comfortable the rest of his life. After five years, he realized it wasn't enough.

He needed more.

His god was a jealous god, and all too eager to devour any offending souls. But Worthington had learned something in his dealings with the temple underground. There were civilized gods. And there were untamed gods. And, hidden away, nearly forgotten, with names whispered in fear by mortal and god alike, there were savage gods. Their powers were enormous, but their demands were of the most primitive variety. Blood and souls, chaos and madness. They wanted the heavens and Earth to run thick with gore, to see mortals and gods tear each other to pieces. To revel in a single moment of boundless, primeval terror. They weren't above a little sacrifice either, but it did take something bigger than an elephant to get their attention. Fortunately, Worthington had the power and influence to provide it.

His old god wasn't happy with the transition, but he didn't make a fuss. And when the god of ugly death meekly backed down from Worthington's new master without so much as a whimper, Worthington knew he'd made the right decision.

He could make the President disappear with a single phone call or destroy cities with a three-word e-mail. Any woman he desired could be in his bed by tonight and out of his way by morning. No indulgence, no matter how ridiculous or absurd, was denied him. And though he didn't actually indulge because, aside from his ambition, he was a very dull sort, he still appreciated having the power for power's sake.

The only downside was his very cranky roommate, but Gorgoz usually stayed in the basement.

Worthington was in the middle of dinner when Gorgoz rang his bell. At first, Worthington ignored it, expecting the butler to take care of Gorgoz's demands. The clang of the bell grew more insistent after five minutes.

He pushed away from the table and walked through his

exquisite and tastefully decorated house. He'd paid enough
for the decorator's services to know, even if he didn't get it
himself. But it wasn't for him. He didn't ever have guests.
But if he did, he was sure they would be impressed. There
were a dozen or so rooms he hadn't visited, that he'd seen
only as sketches a few years ago.

Along the way, he almost stepped on a spotted roach
and a mottled, crimson serpent. He was accustomed to
the steady stream of felines, rodents, reptiles, and insects
coming in and out of the house at all hours. He'd had pet
doors installed to accommodate Gorgoz's spies, souls
drafted into the god's service. It was part of Gorgoz's
price. Servitude didn't end with death. The lucky minions
were transformed into shape-changing spies, scouring the
world as the eyes and ears of Gorgoz. Worthington had no
intention of spending his afterlife as a spotted housecat.
He wasn't keen on mortality and had plans in motion to
avoid death. Nothing specific at this stage, but anything
was possible for a man willing to take the right chances,
make the right deals.

The ringing bell and the snake guided him, keeping
him from getting lost in his own house.

"Coming!" shouted Worthington. "I'm coming!"

He descended the stairs. Gorgoz kept the basement
dark with only a single hanging bulb and a big-screen TV
lighting the dinginess. He sat slumped in his recliner. He
rarely left the comfort of its five-speed massage settings.
He even more rarely changed his clothes and never bathed.
The room smelled of formaldehyde, seaweed, and nachos.

"What took you so long?" he asked, never turning his
twisted face away from the television. Its light reflected
off his bulbous fish eyes.

"I was all the way on the other side of the house," replied Worthington.

Gorgoz snorted. A glob of neon blue snot rocketed from his nostrils and splattered the television screen. He held up his bell and shook it in annoyance. "Beer me."

"Yes, Master." Worthington paused. He already knew the answer, but he had to ask anyway. "You haven't seen Montoya around, have you?"

"Who?"

"The butler. The one I pay to...beer you."

"Oh, him." Gorgoz tapped his long black claws on his tusks. "I ate him. Is that a problem?"

"No, no. Not really. It's just...Montoya was actually a pretty good butler, and good help can be hard to find."

"I've had better," said Gorgoz. "That one we had a couple of weeks ago, the Chinaman—"

"They're called Asians now," interrupted Worthington.

"The Asian was crunchier." Gorgoz crushed his empty beer can and added it to the mound on the floor. "I like 'em crunchy."

"Yes, yes."

"Do you dare question my judgment, Roger?"

"No, never."

"Such insolence deserves swift retribution. You're lucky Mary is on." Gorgoz's long tongue snaked out and licked the snot off the television screen. He swallowed it with a gulp, revealing the smiling image of Mary Tyler Moore. "If this wasn't the clown funeral episode I'd get out of this chair and break your spine."

Worthington suppressed a smile. Gorgoz talked a big game, but he needed Worthington. He'd made sure of that. Dealing with gods wasn't any different from any other business contract. It all came down to leverage. Gorgoz had many followers, but none could equal what Worthington had to offer. Secretly dedicated slaughterhouses offered a steady tide of blood. Millions of dollars a year were burned in his god's name. And millions more were used to support smaller cults scattered across the world. But Worthington made sure that none of these cults were self-sufficient, and that without his money, they would disappear. Without Worthington, there was no Temple of Gorgoz.

The savage god had existed, mostly forgotten and without influence, for thousands of years before Worthington had taken him in. He could always start over, but that would require him to get his butt out of the recliner.

"By the way, Roger," said Gorgoz, "have you seen Lenny anywhere? Usually takes on the form of a squirrel."

"There are a lot of squirrels coming in and out of here every day," observed Worthington.

"Lenny was one of my favorites, you know. He served me well in life, but even more so in death. Always reliable."

"I'm sure he's just running a little bit late."

"Let's hope." Gorgoz growled, not at Worthington but just in general annoyance. He held up his bell and rang it vigorously. "I don't see my beer, minion."

At the kitchen, Worthington discovered a bloodied and broken squirrel pulling its way across the linoleum. It should've been dead, but supernatural will compelled it to return, even if it had to drag itself with its one functioning limb.

"You must be Lenny."

The squirrel held up its head and gasped, spitting up blood.

"He's down in the basement. Where else would he be?" Worthington dropped several beers into a plastic bag and tied it to Lenny's tail. "Don't keep him waiting." The creeping squirrel dragged its carcass across the kitchen floor, leaving a smear of blood and fur across the tile. Someone would clean up the mess. He didn't know who, but he didn't care about those details. He had more pressing concerns.

Worthington was willing to make many sacrifices for his god. Cold veal was not one of them.

Teri's day turned around after she talked to Lucky. It wasn't as if everything corrected itself, but her bad luck faded. And some of that bad luck turned good. The technician sent to check on her computer said it was shot, and that it would have to be replaced. The outdated computer had always been temperamental. She'd been low on the replacement list, but now management had no choice but to move her to the top.

One of her bosses (she had several) noticed her disheveled appearance as the two of them shared an elevator ride. When Teri explained all the misfortune that had befallen her of late, they shared a chuckle. It wasn't much, but it was an opening, a chance to make an impression.

She kept finding loose change underfoot, under desks, in drawers. Pennies and nickels, quarters and dimes, and several silver dollars. By the end of the day, she had twenty bucks' worth of change jingling in her pockets.

A golden woman approached Teri's desk around quitting time.

"Ms. Teri Robinson?"

A closer look revealed that the woman wasn't just gold in color. She was actually made of the precious metal. Her skin, her hair, her eyes, and even her clothes all gleamed.

"Yes, that's me," said Teri.

"Hello, I'm Veronika, your Hephaestus Motors personal liaison. Veronika with a *k*."

A handshake confirmed it. Veronika's hand was smooth and cold as polished metal.

"Your car is ready, Ms. Robinson. Shall we take a look?"

"Already?"

Veronika's beautiful face remained aloof, almost unreadable, but she raised a delicately sculpted eyebrow. "Yes."

"What about the broken axle? The shop said it would take at least a week to fix."

"Perhaps for mortal mechanics," said Veronika. "Shall we go and inspect your car to see if it meets with your approval?"

Teri followed Veronika. Teri's bare arm brushed against a golden sleeve. The metal "cloth" was cold but supple. Teri wanted to touch Veronika's hair, but it seemed a little presumptuous.

The coupe was parked out front. It was Teri's car, but polished and waxed. It didn't look brand-new, but it was pretty close.

Veronika said, "Along with the axle, we took the liberty of some basic maintenance. Tune-up, oil change, spark plugs, and while we were at it, we added some improvements. The usual low-level package. I'm sure you'll be very

pleased with the results. We don't usually work on automobiles with this much...character." Veronika frowned.
"Someone must have called in a big favor."

"Lucky?"

"Indeed, you are fortunate. Mortals used to sacrifice
droves of livestock for an improvement package like
this."

"No, I meant Lucky. My god Lucky."

Veronika glanced at her work order. "Doesn't say." She
paced the coupe, allowing Teri to inspect it. "We did what
we could to increase fuel efficiency to a thousand MPG."

"A thousand?"

"Yes, dreadful, I know, but the best we could manage
with what we had to work with. We also coated the chas-
sis with a high-quality adamantite-based glaze to protect
against future dings, dents, and stains. The tires are an
organic form of rubber very recently developed. Nearly
puncture-proof and self-repairing, as long as you remember to water them regularly and allow them to get a few
hours of sunlight a week."

"I park in the garage," said Teri.

"Might I suggest purchasing a sunlamp then."

The car's door swung open on its own and Veronika
stepped aside to allow Teri to get in. The seat was warm
and soft.

"Genuine faux gryphon hide," said Veronika. "Finally,
we threw in a navigation charm at no extra charge." She
pointed to the clear vial of green liquid hanging from the
rearview mirror. A large yellow eyeball floated within it,
and when Teri looked at the eye, it looked back.

Veronika thrust a clipboard before Teri. "If you'll just
sign here, Ms. Robinson, the car is all yours."

"And that's it?" asked Teri one more time, just to be sure. "All this is absolutely free?"

Veronika flashed a patronizing smile. "Yes, Ms. Robinson."

Teri signed. Veronika sprouted a pair of solid platinum wings. They didn't flap, but the golden woman rose into the air.

The door closed and locked, and the car started spontaneously.

The big eye bobbed, staring at her.

Veronika descended to earth. She tapped on the glass with a slender finger, and the window rolled down.

"I almost forgot. If you have any concerns or complaints, feel free to give me a call, day or night." Veronika handed Teri a card. It, too, was gold in color, though made of paper. "We've also included a complimentary year of roadside assistance, so you'll want this." She gave Teri a small velvet bag that smelled of mint. "Just burn a leaf or two should the need arise."

"Thanks." Teri tried the door, but it didn't open. "Not that I'm complaining, but how do I get out?"

Veronika reached into the car and flicked its eye. "Behave yourself now."

The doors unlocked.

"I'm afraid the navigation charm can be a touch over-eager. Just be firm with it."

Veronika disappeared into the clouds.

Teri put her hands on the steering wheel. The car responded by moving her seat back so that she could barely reach the pedals. She tried adjusting it, but it didn't budge.

The eye stared at her.

"Come on, now. I've had a long day, and I just want to go home." She tapped the vial, not too hard. "Please?"

The car pulled into the street. She wrestled with the wheel and strained to hit the brakes. The car ignored her. It traveled a few blocks before having to stop at a red light.

"Stop!" she shouted.

The car killed its engine. The eye sank to the bottom of its vial, reminding Teri of a dejected puppy. Or at least a giant dejected puppy eye.

"I'd really like to drive myself. If that's okay with you."

The eye bobbed in resemblance of a nod as the seat slid forward to a comfortable position and the engine started just as the light turned green. She tested the gas and brake pedals. They were responsive.

She thanked the eye and started driving.

The radio came on and flicked to a country-and-western station.

"I'm not into country music."

The charm picked another station playing the biggest hits of the seventies. Teri wasn't crazy about that either, but the charm was trying so hard, she decided to let it go. Though by the time she made it home, she had absorbed enough disco to last a lifetime.

She parked in the driveway, deciding to wait until sunset to pull into the garage. Phil's car was in good shape, too, with the same polished sheen and navigation charm hanging from the mirror.

Phil was in the kitchen. She slipped up behind him and gave him a hug.

"Hey, baby," he said. "How was your day?"

"Better now." She glanced down at the counter, where

he was busy pinning cucumbers and bologna to crackers with toothpicks. "What's that?"

"Hors d'oeuvres. Lucky wants to have a few guests over."

"A party? Already?"

"It's not a party," said Phil. "Just some friends."

Teri glanced around. "Where is Lucky?"

"He's out picking up some decorations."

"Decorations? For the not-party? The not-party with hors d'oeuvres?"

Phil hesitated. "Yes."

"I thought he wanted to spend his first night here getting to know us better."

"Change of plans, I guess." He kept his back to her, working on the hors d'oeuvres. "This isn't going to be a big deal, is it?"

"What's that supposed to mean?" she asked.

"Teri, he's a god. They change their minds a lot, and our job is to keep him happy. So if he wants a not-party with hors d'oeuvres and decorations then we should probably give it to him."

"You know what? You're right." She opened the fridge, found it stocked with a case of beer. She grabbed a long-neck and twisted the top.

"Those beers are for the not-party," said Phil.

"We paid for it, right?"

He nodded.

"Then I get the first one." She took a swig. Then she stuck out her tongue. She wasn't a beer drinker.

He offered her a cucumber sandwich. She nibbled on it. "How old is this bologna?"

"It's still good." He double-checked the package. "Doesn't expire for another two days."

She jammed the sandwich in her cheek and washed it down with more beer. "By the way, Janet is coming over tonight."

He gave her a look.

"She invited herself," Teri said. "She's a deiphile. Couldn't wait to meet our new god."

"One more doesn't hurt," said Phil.

"I'll go change and then help with the not-party preparations."

"Thanks. You're a peach, you know that."

"Oh yeah. I know."

She gave him a hug and a peck.

"Hey, now," said Lucky. "I'm not interrupting anything, am I, kids?"

Teri and Phil parted.

"How long you two crazy mortals been married?"

"Two years," she replied.

"We dated two years before that," Phil added.

"And you still have the passion. That's beautiful. It really is. Can one of you lovebirds do me a favor? I left a couple of bags on the porch."

Teri volunteered. Along with the bags of decorations, a tall gray figure in frayed, dusty robes stood on her porch. The shadow of his hood hid his face. He held a small potted plant in his hands. The plant was dead.

"Hello," he said. "Is this the right address? I'm here for the housewarming."

She nodded.

"This is for you then." The gaunt man held out the dead plant. She took it. A chill passed through her as she brushed his withered hands.

"Charon, old buddy!" shouted Lucky. "You're early.

Didn't think you'd make it. Surprised Hades was willing to take that stick out of his ass and give you the night off."

A wide-shouldered god in a black-and-red suit stepped into view behind Charon.

"He's my ride," said Charon.

"Hades, my man." Lucky chuckled. "You know I just kid because I love."

The lord of the underworld cracked a smile. "Forget it. I'm just here for the beer."

"Fridge is thataway." Lucky jerked his thumb over his shoulder, and Hades headed toward the kitchen.

"By the way, I'm in front of a hydrant," remarked Hades. "Could you direct my driver to the designated parking?"

"Geez, that guy is a cheapskate," whispered Lucky. "Owns half the real estate in the underworld, and you still can't keep him away from free booze."

He and Charon chuckled. Dust and ash rose off Charon's robes. Teri inhaled it and fell into a short coughing fit.

"Sorry," he apologized. "I came straight from work. Didn't have time to change."

"You can borrow something from Phil's closet. I'm sure he won't mind, right, Teri?"

She nodded while struggling to clear her sticky throat.

"Charon and I will grab a shirt while you take care of Hades's ride and start on the decorations."

She tried to protest but Lucky and Charon had already vanished into the bedroom.

Hades's ride was a black chariot adorned with silver skulls and twisted thorns. The wheels were aflame, and it was drawn by a pair of muscular beasts, vaguely horselike except for the snorting of fire and the slavering jaws.

The driver was a specter in a chauffeur uniform. He opened his skull and howled at Teri.

"Uh, yeah," she said. "Just park it over there, I guess."

The driver cracked the reins, and a clap of thunder shook the sky. The beasts roared, stamped their hooves hard enough to crack the asphalt, and pulled the chariot away. Its flaming wheels left a trail of bubbling tar.

The neighbor across the street threw Teri a dirty look. She didn't know his first name. Or his wife's. Or those of their two or three kids. She'd never actually talked to any of them, only nodded politely.

Within an hour, the house was overrun with gods, demigods, and legendary creatures. The gods and their entourages turned out to be first-class mooches. After they drank all the beers, they devoured everything consumable in the refrigerator. They even ate the steaks in the freezer. Didn't even bother to cook them. It still wasn't enough. A harpy and her lizard-creature boyfriend eyed Teri and Phil hungrily.

A blue djinn in an equally blue leisure suit defused the problem. Teri wished for more food, and he snapped his fingers, creating a magical tablecloth that produced as many beers, fruits, and cheese crackers as the gods could consume. The harpy and her boyfriend pounced on the table. Teri thought about reaching for a cracker, but figured it was a good way to lose an arm.

"Normally, I don't do this without throwing in a little curse, too," said the djinn, "but what the hell? You guys throw a helluva party." He slipped off to flirt with a woman with horns growing out of her forehead.

Teri scanned the party. So far, it was a casual affair. The gods and demigods were all behaving themselves.

She'd been worried about the guy with the smoking head, but once they removed the batteries from the smoke detectors, he wasn't any trouble. The snail god wasn't nearly as slimy as she'd first expected, and he'd given her a voucher for a free carpet shampooing. Phil was having a good time. He'd arranged an impromptu video game tournament, and was currently beating down Hades in a round of Death Ninja 3. The lord of the underworld snarled as Phil's digital samurai executed his finishing move.

Janet called out to Teri from across the crowded room. Teri motioned for Janet to follow her into the backyard so they could talk.

"Wow," said Janet. "I didn't know you were throwing a party! Why didn't you tell me about this?"

"It was spur-of-the-moment."

"I am so glad I brought my camera. How do I look?"

Teri had known Janet was attractive, but she'd never realized just how attractive. With her hair down and in a form-fitting red dress, she was beautiful. It wasn't made-up beauty either, that sort of prettiness that comes from having the right clothes and the right hair and makeup. It was just a natural appeal. The low neckline emphasizing her breasts didn't hurt either.

"You look fabulous," said Teri, feeling a little self-conscious about her own appearance.

Lucky and a large serpent with sparkling rainbow scales and feathered wings stepped into the backyard. The serpent held a beer in the clawed fingertips at the end of his wings.

"There you are, Teri," said Lucky. "Been looking all over for you. I'd like to introduce you to my good buddy Quetzalcoatl."

"Call me Quick." The serpent tipped his party hat, letting the elastic snap back into place. "Everyone does."

Janet elbowed Teri and cleared her throat.

Lucky smiled. "And who might this lovely mortal be?"

Before Teri could introduce her, Janet pushed her way forward, knelt down, and introduced herself. Lucky took her hand in his paw and mimed a kiss.

"Any friend of Teri's is a friend of mine. Care for a beer?"

"I'd love one."

"If you'll excuse us, gang. Watch out for this guy, Teri." Lucky poked Quick. "If you're not careful, he might get you drunk and strap you to his altar."

Lucky and Janet went back inside.

"So..." Quick ran his long tongue around a fang. "...Cool party."

"Thanks."

Awkward silence passed between them.

"How long have you known Lucky?" she asked to make conversation.

"A while now," replied Quick. "He helped me out when I was going through a rough time." He flapped his wings. "I mean, I only turned my back for a second. Who'd have thought a few conquistadors could cause so much trouble?"

"Yeah, that was a helluva thing," she agreed.

"Y'know, he was only joking about the altar thing," said Quick. "I was never into human sacrifice, even when it was legal."

"Oh, I know. Conquistador propaganda."

"Damn straight."

They tapped their beers together and shared a swig.

A dryad stuck her head out the door. "Excuse me, but where are your facilities?"

Teri excused herself to give directions. She showed the dryad the line to the bathroom. An ogre lumbered up to Teri. He spoke with a dry, cracked voice. "Are you Teri Robinson?"

She nodded.

"There's a fury looking for you." The swung his arm toward the front door. "And she looks pissed."

The fury invoked by the homeowners association was a cruel, pale woman in a crimson pantsuit. She'd been called down to enforce the code, and she did so with all the dedication with which her other sisters might chase down murderers and tax evaders. She could detect the smallest violation ranging from improper lawn ornamentation, loose shingles, and birdhouses with an improper motif. Teri considered passing her off to Phil, but he was still in the middle of his tournament and having a good time. So she decided to handle it.

The fury glared with deep red eyes. "Mrs. Robinson, you are aware you are in violation of several important regulations."

"Can I offer you a beer?" asked Teri.

"No." The fury's frown deepened. "Thank you, but I'm on duty." She clicked a pen and began filling out a citation. "You are aware that all parties require two weeks' notice?"

"It's not really a party."

"Any gathering that involves more than five cars or eight nonresident guests is defined as a party according to the code. You'd know that if you read the regulation book."

"Yeah, I've been meaning to do that, but I've been really busy lately and—"

"Ignorance of the code is no excuse." The black veins on the fury's skull-like face throbbed. She ripped the citation from the pad and thrust it accusingly at Teri. "I've issued a warning this time, as per homeowners association guidelines." The fury smiled, revealing sharp teeth perfect for ripping out the throats of murderers, traitors, and those damned souls who dared to stick plastic pink flamingoes on their lawn. "Don't let it happen again."

Lucky appeared beside Teri. He hopped up and intercepted the citation.

"Edna, is that you? You're looking scarier than ever."

"Lucky, you ol' son of a bitch."

"Hey now, what's this?" He scanned the citation. "You're not raining down wrath on my girl Teri here, are you?"

"Just doing my job," said Edna, sounding a bit guilty. "She's not one of yours, is she?"

"Yep. But more importantly, she's a good kid."

"Rules are rules."

"We're celebrating, and it got a little out of hand. My fault, not hers. Can't we look the other way just this once?"

"Well…" The fury's fury faded. The citation disappeared in a flash of white flame. "I could never say no to you, Lucky."

"Come on in. Have a beer."

"One can't hurt, I suppose." She pulled out the stiletto knives keeping her hair in a bun. The black curls cascaded down past her shoulders as she joined the party.

"Thanks," said Teri.

"Don't mention it, kid." He winked. "All part of the service, right? Do yourself a favor, Teri. Relax a little. Have a good time. Mortal life is too short to be worried all the time."

Janet showed up, handed Lucky a fresh beer. "Didn't you promise to introduce me to that fox-eared demigoddess?"

He led her away.

Teri found Phil in the kitchen.

"So how did the tournament go?" she asked.

"You are now looking at Red Ronan, reigning Death Ninja 3 champion of Heaven and Earth."

She put her arms around him and gave him a kiss. "I think we made the right decision."

"Are you sure? No more doubts?"

She shrugged. "Maybe a little bit of doubt. But not very much."

"All I can ask for at this stage, I suppose," said Phil.

She kissed him again.

Charon poked his head into the kitchen. "Hades is burning for a rematch, Ronan. Dare you accept?"

"You're on."

9

Bonnie had horrible dreams. They weren't like ordinary
nightmares, neither vague nor surreal. More like an edited
playback of her life, as if someone had shot a movie, cut
out all the good parts, and left only a parade of tragic,
painful, and humiliating moments. She awoke, feeling as
if she hadn't slept a wink.

Syph, head bowed, sat in the corner of the bedroom.

"Oh, Jupiter," groaned Bonnie. "What are you doing?"

The goddess raised her head. Her hair fell across her
face, but she gazed at Bonnie with one colorless eye.

Bonnie covered her head with the blanket. She turned
over and tried to go back to sleep. But she could feel the
goddess still looking at her. Bonnie just wanted to get
some sleep, to find refuge in unconsciousness. But even
asleep, there was no escape from Syph.

"I'm sorry," said the goddess. "About the dreams. In
time, you'll get used to them."

"That's what you think," mumbled Bonnie from under the blanket. She had no intention of getting used to any of this, and she wasn't about to surrender to the goddess's influence. She hadn't asked to follow Syph, and there had to be a way of getting out from under her.

The alarm blared.

She didn't want to get up. She just wanted to lie here and wither away. But that was the goddess, not her. Bonnie was a happy person. She tried to stay positive no matter what. It wasn't always easy. Not after her mom died. Or when she broke her leg and lost her dance school scholarship. Or that time her dog was hit by a car. And there was that car accident when she thought she might've had whiplash. And that other time when—

Bonnie sat up and blocked the negative thoughts seeping into her mind.

"Sorry." Syph stood. "Would you like some breakfast? I can go make some eggs, if you'd like."

"That'd be nice," replied Bonnie insincerely. She wasn't hungry, but it'd get Syph out of her hair.

After the tattered goddess left the room, Bonnie felt a little better. She was able to drag herself out of bed and get dressed. She couldn't make herself take a shower, but she did run a comb through her hair and find the energy to brush her teeth. It was important to keep going through the motions, despite the weight bearing down on her. Bonnie couldn't give in to the hopelessness.

Syph had a plate of runny eggs, burned toast, and a bowl of cereal sitting on the table.

"Don't eat the cereal," she said. "The milk has soured."

"I just bought that milk," said Bonnie.

Syph shrugged. "Sorry."

"Do me a favor, will you? If you're not going to leave me alone could you at least stop all the apologizing?"

It might've been a trick of the light, but Bonnie thought Syph almost smiled.

"Your eggs are getting cold."

Though the scent of cooking was still fresh in the air, the eggs were ice-cold. Bonnie could tell just by looking because ice was forming on the plate. She didn't eat them, didn't even touch them. Accepting a gift from a goddess of heartbreak would only compound her problems.

"Thanks," said Bonnie, "but I'm running late. I'll grab something on the way."

"No, you're not," replied Syph, "but thank you for bothering to make an excuse."

Bonnie took the bus to work. Syph didn't follow her out of the apartment, but the goddess still managed to beat Bonnie to the bus. Syph even saved her a seat.

A burly man with a permanent scowl occupied the seat behind her. His radio blasted out hard-core speed metal, where the guitarist played so fast the notes bled together and the vocalist roared. Thirty seconds after she boarded the bus the radio started playing twangy country songs about broken hearts and shattered lovers. He fiddled with the knobs to try to tune in another station and even changed the CD with no effect. Eventually he gave up and turned it off.

Syph didn't get off the bus with Bonnie, but when she reached the bookstore, the goddess was already there, perusing the magazine section. Bonnie decided she would do her best to ignore Syph. Maybe if she was offered no acknowledgment Syph might push off and bother someone else.

Bonnie went to the break room and clocked in. Ms. Carter, the assistant manager, pulled her aside.

"I trust you are feeling better today, Bonnie."

There was an accusation there. Carter was a stickler. Bonnie had been working at Books N' More for four years now, and she'd missed only one other day. It had just happened to be Carter's first day as assistant manager. Now Bonnie was branded as a slacker. Her nose piercing probably didn't help, and she was pretty sure that her short hair qualified her as a potential lesbian in Carter's estimation.

"Much better," Bonnie replied.

It was a bit of a lie. She wasn't herself, but she was adjusting. The goddess had been right. Yesterday had been rough. Last night, even rougher. This morning wasn't so bad. She still felt the weight on her chest, the desire to surrender herself to oblivion. But that wasn't her. That was the goddess's influence. Knowing that helped her to work around it.

Carter frowned, but she was always frowning. "Good, Bonnie. I hope we can trust you to be a reliable member of the Books N' More family."

"Yes, Ms. Carter."

Her boss walked away in her standard kick-step mode of walking.

Bonnie discovered it wasn't so easy to ignore Syph. The tattered goddess didn't speak to Bonnie, didn't follow her around. She merely lurked in the store, walking down the aisles, having a latte at the in-store café, browsing the magazine rack, and otherwise killing time like any other customer. But there were problems.

A customer threw a stack of bridal magazines on the counter while Bonnie was working the register.

"I need to return these," the woman said.

"I'm sorry, we don't take returns on magazines," Bonnie replied. "It's store policy."

"But they're defective." The customer opened the top magazine and pointed to a random page. "Look!"

At first glance, the photo seemed fine. A closer inspection revealed the anomaly. The beautiful bride wasn't quite so beautiful. She had the perfect dress, the perfect hair, the perfect bouquet. But she was snarling, and the mascara around her watery eyes was smudged.

Bonnie flipped through the pages. It only got worse. Article headlines reading "How to Poison That Cheating Bastard" and "Top 10 Reasons You'll End Up Dying Alone" filled the magazine. Perfect photo brides frowned, then in later pictures became slouching withered figures in frayed, stained dresses. The very worst was a two-page spread of a wedding where the groom had decided to forgo his bride-to-be in favor of the maid of honor. Bonnie could understand that, but she did think it was a bit much for the happy couple to consummate their love in the middle of the aisle while the guests looked on.

Modern Homes magazine was full of photos of burning and crumbling houses. All the plants in the gardening magazines were dead. Bonnie wisely chose not to open the *Kitten Fancier* magazine.

"I want my money back," said the customer. "I don't care what your policy is."

"Yes, I see what you mean," said Bonnie. "Just give me a moment."

"Hey, Bonnie," said Vince, "have you seen Carter?"

"I think she's in her office."

"Not there. I checked." He leaned over the counter and

rifled through the drawer beside her. "Have you at least seen the key that unlocks the store radio station? I'm getting sick of listening to 'Copacabana' over and over again."

Barry Manilow's crooning tragic tale was stuck on permanent replay. Although it seemed that every ten minutes or so Lola's end was a bit more tragic. Bonnie didn't think that in the original version an earthquake opened up, swallowing the heartbroken showgirl, the Copacabana, and a troop of orphaned Boy Scouts who just happened to be in the nightclub asking for directions to a charity campout jamboree.

"Somebody at that radio station is going to lose their job," said Vince.

She feigned ignorance.

After refunding the customer's money and throwing the magazines away to dispose of the evidence, Bonnie sought out Syph, sitting at the café.

Bonnie spoke through clenched teeth. "What are you doing?"

"I'd say I'm sorry, but you asked me not to do that anymore."

The café clerk placed a cup of coffee before the goddess. "Here you go, ma'am. I'm afraid that all our dairy products have spoiled, so it's free."

"Why, thank you. I prefer it black actually. Black like the endless night that inevitably engulfs and devours all mortal souls."

Bonnie glanced around before leaning closer. "You can't do this," she whispered. "I work here."

"What do you expect me to do?"

"Go away. Go home. If you can't leave me alone then at least go back to my apartment and wait for me there."

"There's nothing to do there." Syph sipped her drink. She frowned. "More bitter than I expected, but then again, it always is."

"May I speak with you a moment, Bonnie?" asked Carter. "If you're not too busy chatting, that is."

Bonnie plastered on a fake smile and turned from Syph.

"Have you seen this?" Carter held up a romance novel titled *Love's Empty Promises*. The art was traditional except that the subjects weren't particularly attractive. The long-haired hero was flabby and the redheaded heroine was cross-eyed and hunchbacked. They had their backs turned to each other, and the real shame was that this prevented them from noticing the cattle stampede rushing toward them.

"I think there's something going on here." Carter pointed over Bonnie's shoulder at the goddess. "And I think it has to do with that customer there. I don't think she's an ordinary woman."

"Probably just a homeless person," said Bonnie. "She could be dangerous. Let me take care of her. You're far too valuable to the store to risk—"

Carter pushed past Bonnie. "Excuse me, miss. I'm afraid I'm going to have to ask you to leave the store."

Syph took another sip. "I can't do that. Not without her."

Carter followed the goddess's gaze to Bonnie.

"I can explain, Ms. Carter. I can. This is all just a misunderstanding."

"No misunderstanding. I'm her goddess."

"No, she's not. She's not! I didn't solicit her, didn't ask to be her follower."

"You said hello," observed Syph.

"I keep telling you that doesn't count!"

The goddess shrugged.

Carter's frown deepened. "Bonnie, the law prohibits Books N' More from discriminating against anyone simply for their choice of god or goddess—"

"She's not my goddess!" said Bonnie with a bit more force than she'd intended.

Carter's brow knit in a disapproving glare. The outburst would probably find its way into Bonnie's employee file.

She pulled Carter closer and whispered, "This is only temporary. I'm taking steps to get rid of her."

Carter's jaw tightened. "The policy of Books N' More is to foster a spirit of tolerance toward its employees and whatever divine powers they choose to align themselves with, providing said alignment does not negatively affect their job performance." She held up the romance novel. "Does this look as if it is not affecting your work, Bonnie?"

"Look, I'll take my break now," said Bonnie.

Bonnie grabbed the book from Carter. It immediately burst into flame. She dropped it and beat it out with a defective magazine.

Carter cleared her throat.

"I'll take an early lunch now," said Bonnie with a smile. "She's coming with me, and when I get back, I'll come back alone. It'll all be fine. I promise!" She grabbed Syph's hand, ignoring the chill passing through her, and dragged the goddess toward the door.

There was a Burger Town just down the street. Bonnie ordered her lunch, then sat Syph down at a table.

"We need to have a talk," said Bonnie. "I know you're

a goddess, and that by myself, I can't get rid of you. But I think we both know that I have a slam-dunk case for a restraining order with Divine Affairs. So why don't you save me the trouble of having to file with the court and—"

"It won't save you. You don't think you are the first to turn to Divine Affairs, do you?"

"But you have to follow the rulings of the court," said Bonnie.

"You don't get it, do you? Yes, if the court decreed it I would have to release you as my follower. But it takes time to bring a case to the court, time for a ruling to be handed down. Several months at least. And none of my followers have ever lasted that long."

She sighed. A dove flew into the window beside them and broke its neck.

Bonnie stuffed a handful of fries into her mouth. Under Syph's influence, they were cold and soggy. This was what Bonnie's life was going to be like for the foreseeable future. A constant barrage of metaphorical soggy fries. Not a single drop of joy. Only unhappy endings. An endless depression that would eventually consume her soul.

"How many months do I have?" asked Bonnie.

"Four, perhaps five," said Syph. "One lasted almost six before losing the will to live. His heart just stopped beating, and he turned to stone. Shame about that one. I rather liked him."

Bonnie put her head on the table and almost cried. Almost.

"No!" She sat up and slammed her palms on the table. "I'm not giving in! I'm not going to sit here and let you kill me!"

Syph opened her eyes in startled surprise. It was the

first time Bonnie had seen Syph appear anything other than depressingly resigned.

"There has to be a way to fix this," said Bonnie. "Mortals have defied the gods successfully before."

"Not in a very long time. The Age of Legends has long passed. A shame. They were brighter days."

Syph smiled and sighed wistfully. Bonnie braced herself for another dead bird or icy wind or symbolic spontaneous combustion. Instead, the dark cloud hiding the sun moved to one side and allowed a few warm rays to shine down on Bonnie and her goddess. The moment didn't last. The cloud jumped back into its solar-interception duties, and a roach crawled out from under Bonnie's burger bun.

She flicked it away. "What just happened?"

"Hmmm?"

"I felt better all of a sudden." Bonnie took a bite of a fry. It was still tasteless, but there was a little crispiness. "And so were you. Don't deny it. I saw you smile."

"Maybe I did. Aren't I allowed a smile every so often? Must I always be dour?"

"I don't know. Mustn't you? You are a goddess of tragedy and hopelessness, aren't you?"

"I wasn't always." Syph spoke in a low embarrassed tone. "A long time ago . . . well, I suppose that's not important anymore." She slouched, and a crack split the window. "It's not worth talking about."

Bonnie wasn't so sure about that.

"Gods can change their province?" she asked. "I didn't think you could do that."

Syph nodded.

"So why don't you just change then? You obviously aren't happy as the goddess of tragedy."

"It doesn't work like that. I can't choose to change. It's not something I control."

"How?"

"It's not important. I'd rather not talk about it."

"Oh no. You don't get off the hook that easy."

Syph arched her eyebrows in surprise.

"It was such a long time ago, I hardly remember it, when I wasn't what I now am." A reluctant smile crossed Syph's face. The cloud scooted over to allow half the sun to shine.

Bonnie bit into her burger, after checking for roaches, and discovered it wasn't absolutely terrible. It wasn't good, but she didn't want to spit it out. She was grasping for any possible solution to her goddess problem. At the very least, it eased her suffering to get Syph to talk about it. That had to mean something.

"You dragged me into this," said Bonnie. "You owe me."

"I don't see how it's relevant."

Bonnie smiled mirthlessly. "Indulge me."

Syph thought about this a moment, and it must have brightened her day because the cloud vanished from the sky in a puff.

"It's funny. No one has ever asked me about this before. No one ever cared."

Bonnie didn't care either. Not about the goddess anyway. But if it made Syph feel better about herself and made Bonnie's life better in the process, she was perfectly willing to play along. She reached across the table and patted Syph's hand. It was cold, but not as cold as before.

"You wouldn't know it to look at me," said Syph, "but I was once the goddess of love. I brought only joy and hope to all around me, made the world a more beautiful place.

Everything I touched was brightened by my presence, and my favor was coveted by king and peasant alike.

"But my influence didn't end with mortals. I was courted by all the best gods. The most powerful of deities sought my company. There wasn't a god I couldn't seduce with merely a demure smile and a coy glance."

Bonnie studied the colorless, icy goddess sitting across from her. It was hard to imagine.

"And I dated them all," said Syph. "From the most insignificant mortal to the most powerful of the divine. I gleefully spread my joy across the heavens and Earth without care, and should have done so until the end of time."

"So what happened?"

Syph sighed. The cloud came back, bigger and blacker than ever.

"I fell in love."

Bonnie waited for further explanation, but Syph just sat there. She bit her lower lip as a single bloodred tear ran down her cheek.

"I don't understand," said Bonnie. "Shouldn't that have been a good thing?"

Syph chortled. Or tried to. But all that came out of her tight throat was a strangled grunt.

"Would it serve a goddess of death to die herself? Or a goddess of war to see the world of mortals consumed in nuclear holocaust? The needs and welfare of gods don't rely solely on a singular motivation."

"Hadn't thought of it like that," admitted Bonnie.

"Few mortals do. You think it's easy to be a god. But we are as fallible and foolish as mortals. Perhaps even more so, since our immortality often leads to boredom, and boredom leads to recklessness. And it's easy to be reckless when immortality usually keeps us from having to deal with the consequences of our actions." She laughed again, bitterly. The cloud rumbled, growing to cover half the sky.

"At first, it was wonderful. I, the goddess of love, had discovered love. Genuine love. My powers increased, and for a while, I thought I might even be able to usher in a new golden age in Heaven and Earth."

"What happened?"

Syph lowered her head and mumbled into her shoulder.

"What?" asked Bonnie.

Syph pulled her hand away and studied her fingernails. "He dumped me."

A rolling storm materialized over the Burger Town. People ran for cover as tiny heart-shaped pieces of hail rained down. Each piece shattered exactly in half upon impact.

"And?" asked Bonnie.

Syph looked Bonnie in the eye. "And what?"

"And what else? Something else must have happened to change you."

"You still don't understand, do you? I was dumped."

"Hold it," said Bonnie. "Don't you gods and goddesses leap out of each other's lives all the time? Don't you have brief infatuations, followed by hollow relationships? You're always cheating on each other, right?"

"Not always."

"Uh-huh," said Bonnie skeptically.

"Okay, so usually that is true. Although there are true and long-lasting marriages among the gods. Though not many, I'll admit. Immortality and boredom are rarely healthy for a long-term relationship."

"What's the big deal then?" said Bonnie. "You got dumped. Business as usual among immortals, isn't it?"

"No. Not business as usual. The right thing to do would have been to marry me. Even if he didn't love me, he should've wanted to possess me only because I was desired by others. Or he could've waited until enough time passed that we would've naturally drifted apart. But he dumped me. Me. The goddess of love, rejected by her first true love. I was in my heyday, and he was only a minor god. But I chose him, despite the dozens of proposals from much more influential and desirable deities. Zeus himself was among my suitors."

"You almost married Zeus?"

"Married? No, not married. Hera wouldn't have been very happy about that. But he did offer to buy me a condo on Mount Olympus along with a generous allowance."

Bonnie cracked a smile. "You're telling me you were almost a kept goddess?"

"It was a very generous offer. I didn't consider it. Not seriously. But it was nice to be asked."

The storm dissolved. The sun beamed. As much as Bonnie hated to ruin the goddess's mood and the weather, she still needed answers.

"Why don't you tell me about this guy?"

She braced herself for the worst, but it wasn't as bad as she expected. That small cloud covered the sun, and her remaining fries were suddenly covered in a fuzzy orange fungus.

"Why do you want to know?" asked Syph.

"Maybe because it will make you feel better to talk about it." And when you feel better, Bonnie added to herself, I feel better.

She spent the remainder of her lunch hour listening to Syph reminisce about her lost love. When the memories were good, the sky was clear and the birds sang. When they were bad, those same birds would fall silent and car accidents would happen in the nearby intersection. Nobody was seriously hurt, though at one point a blind man had his foot run over. Bonnie felt bad about that, but she encouraged Syph to continue.

The not-party went until three in the morning, but Teri and Phil went to bed around midnight. They didn't get much sleep, but she awoke refreshed to the smell of frying bacon.

Phil was in the shower.

"Honey, who's cooking?" she asked.

"I don't know. Lucky?"

She doubted that. He didn't seem the type.

Phil was half-right. It wasn't their new god but one of his friends. The giant rainbow serpent puttered around their kitchen.

"Hi, Teri. I hope you don't mind. I borrowed a couple of bucks out of your wallet and found a twenty-four-hour market. Thought I'd whip up some of my special sun god omelets. Just my way of saying thanks for letting me crash on your couch last night."

"Yeah," she said. "No problem."

"It'll just be a minute," Quick said. "I hope you like 'em spicy. I couldn't find any reasonably priced human flesh, so I had to substitute ham."

"Uh-huh," said Teri as she poured herself a cup of coffee.

"That was a joke," said Quick. "I realize it's not always easy to tell with gods."

"No, that's fine. It was funny." She forced a smile and took a sip.

"Loosen up, Teri. I promise I'm not going to swallow you whole. I'm not that kind of god anymore. Plus, you're Lucky's follower, and I wouldn't do that to a friend."

He smiled, and it was ingratiating. Surprising, considering sharp fangs filled his maw.

Phil, toweling dry his hair, appeared at her side. "Shower is ready. What smells so good?"

"Eggs à la sun god," she said, "minus the human flesh."

Quick chuckled.

Teri excused herself, but she heard the shower running. The door to Lucky's room was open a crack. He must have been an early riser. She hadn't seen him as that type. Raccoons were nocturnal. Then again, Quick was a giant serpent monster, and he didn't eat people. Or so he claimed.

Teri went back to the dining room. Quick urged her and Phil to have a seat as he served them breakfast.

"What's the verdict?" asked Quick.

"A little spicy," said Phil, "but thank you. They're good."

"De nada. I'll get some milk." Quick slithered into the kitchen.

"Why is he still here?" asked Teri.

Phil shrugged. "Lucky said he's in a rough spot right now."

"When I agreed to this," she said, "I agreed to one god. One." She held up her index finger to illustrate the point.

"He's not really our god," replied Phil. "It's not like we owe him any tribute. I don't see what the big deal is."

"The big deal is that there's a giant snake serving us breakfast."

"A good breakfast," said Phil.

She glared. "Doesn't he have a human form, at least?"

"Lucky said he doesn't like to wear it anymore."

Before she could ask why, Quick slipped out of the kitchen and laid two tall glasses of milk before them.

Teri excused herself again. The shower wasn't running, so she knocked on the bathroom door. "I hate to be a pest, but I really need to get ready for work." She added a hastily mumbled, "M'lord."

Janet opened the bathroom door. "No problem, hon. Though you can ease up on the titles. It's your bathroom after all."

By the time Teri took her shower, Janet had already left. Work was hectic, so they had to put off any confrontation until lunch. Teri wasn't sure if Janet would be waiting at their usual deli table, but she was there, looking innocent.

"Hi, hon."

Teri slammed her tray onto the table. "You had sexual intercourse with my god."

"Yeah?" said Janet. "So?"

"Sex. With my god."

"Is that a problem?"

Teri's jaw dropped.

"I don't see what the big deal is," said Janet.

Teri tried to verbalize it, but she realized she didn't know what the problem was.

"It just seems like a bad idea," she finally said.

"Why?"

"Because he's my god. It could make things complicated."

Janet laughed. "Oh, hon, you really are new to this, aren't you? It's not complicated. That's one of the things I love about god sex. It's no strings attached."

"Wait a second." Teri lowered her voice. "You've done this before."

"Sure. All the time."

"All the time?"

"Well, not all the time." Janet counted off on her fingers. "Six times."

Teri leaned forward. "Isn't that dangerous?"

"I'm careful. I use protection. I don't care if Xochipilli himself appeared to me, all oiled up and ready for a night of sensual delights, no glove, no love. That's my policy.

"If it'll make you feel better, I promise not to see him again," said Janet.

"Thanks."

Teri struggled to wrap her mind around this.

"What if he wants to see you again?"

"You don't have to worry, hon," said Janet. "Gods mastered the art of casual sex thousands of years ago. Lucky was a one-night thing. He said he'd call, but they never do."

Her cell phone rang. Janet excused herself to take the call. She returned two minutes later and had a seat.

"Well...this is awkward."

"What?" asked Teri. "What is it?"

Janet sucked on her soda with a guilty look.

"Oh no," said Teri. "That was him. It was him, wasn't it?"

Janet averted her eyes and nodded.

"You just said they never call. You just said that. They never call!"

"They don't."

Teri glared.

"They don't. Not normally. Not ever before." Janet smiled. "I'm just as surprised as you are."

"Whatever. It's not important," said Teri. "What did you tell him? I hope you came up with a good excuse."

Janet chewed her lip.

"You told him you couldn't see him again, right?" asked Teri. "Right?"

"About that..."

"You agreed to go out with him again?"

Janet nodded. Once. She slurped her empty soda.

"I don't believe you. You promised you wouldn't see him anymore. You promised."

"And I meant it," said Janet, "but I thought about it. Wouldn't it be better for me to go out with him one or two times more and let him get bored with me rather than risk insulting him? Look what happened to you yesterday. I couldn't be responsible for another curse of lousy luck again, could I?"

"This doesn't have anything to do with me," said Teri. "If you'd been thinking about me you wouldn't have slept with Lucky in the first place."

"Hey, now. Let's not start saying things we could end up regretting. In fact—and I wasn't going to tell you this—I slept with Lucky to put him in a better mood after you insulted him. You really should be thanking me. I don't think some gratitude is uncalled-for."

Teri and Janet locked stares.

"That's bullshit, and you know it," said Teri.

"Okay, so it's bullshit. You got me, hon. But the way I see it we have two choices now. I can either call Lucky back and tell him that I have to wash my hair and hope that there's no wrath, either intended or incidental, raining down on our heads. Or I can go out with him for another date or two and let him get bored." She pulled out her cell. "He's your god. I'll go with whatever you decide."

Teri silently mulled it over as they finished their lunch and rode the elevator back to work.

"All right, you can go out with him again. I guess."

"Great. You won't regret it. I'll show him a good time, put him in a fantastic mood, and before you know it, you'll be covered in fortune and prosperity."

"Just make sure it's not too good a time," said Teri. "We want him to get bored, remember?"

"So we're cool then?"

"Yes, we're cool."

The door opened, and they prepared to part ways to their different departments.

"When you were sleeping with my god," asked Teri, "did he keep the raccoon head the whole time?"

Janet grinned slyly.

"You know what?" Teri waved her hands to silence Janet. "Forget I asked."

The gods lounged on the couch, watching telenovelas.

"I'm confused," said Lucky. "Is the dude with the eye patch a bad guy or not?"

"He's a cop," replied Quick.

"And that hot hostage in the low-cut dress is his wife?"

"Right, but he's undercover, so he can't let the other bank robbers figure that out." Quick scratched his head. "Or maybe he has amnesia and doesn't remember either. I'm not sure."

"Amnesia. Where do they come up with this stuff?"

He held up his soda can, and Quick tapped it with his glass of tomato juice.

"Do you think I made a mistake with Janet?" asked Lucky. "I probably should've waited a couple of days before calling."

"Three days," said Quick. "Calling the next day can be construed as a bit needy. Two days after is okay. But three days means you're interested but not desperate."

Lucky chugged his soda.

"Three days, huh?"

"Just what I've heard through the grapevine. Last time I went on a date it was still acceptable to send out warriors to abduct a virgin."

"Simpler times," said Lucky.

They clanked their glasses together again.

"You think I came across as needy then?" asked Lucky.

"Oh, yeah."

"Crap."

"I like the new followers, by the way," said Quick. "Good folks. Though I don't think Teri likes either of us very much."

"I wouldn't worry about it," said Lucky. "She's won't be the first reluctant mortal I've had to win over."

"So are you going to tell them?"

"Tell them what?"

Quick ruffled his feathers. "They really should know."

"I don't think it's important. I'm sure it's all water under the bridge by now."

"And if you're wrong?"

"I have hundreds of followers. There's nothing very special about these two."

"Except you're living here. To an outside observer with a grudge, that might make them seem important."

"Well, of course, they're special," said Lucky. "All my followers are special. But I lived with Tom for years and nothing happened. And Rebecca before that. And Gary before that. It's been just over a hundred years since the last...incident."

"You've been hanging around with mortals too long, Lucky. A hundred years is a blink of an eye. But the world of mortals changes faster than ever. It's not so easy for a god to lay low anymore. How did Teri and Phil find you?"

"Internet," said Lucky.

"The information age," said Quick. "If he wants to find you, all he has to do is click a few buttons."

"He doesn't operate that way. I doubt he even knows what a computer is. He never could adapt. Stupid bastard got left behind in the Middle Ages. Did I ever tell you that during our last civil conversation, he predicted the long-bow was just a fad."

They chuckled.

"I'm not saying he's the smartest god," said Quick, "but you have to admit he's persistent. And he knows how to hold a grudge. And he may not have adapted to the new world, but that just means he's more dangerous."

"No, it just means that he's faded into obscurity.

Most of his power disappeared with the last of the Philistines."

Quick said, "Just because he went underground, that doesn't mean he disappeared. Or that there aren't plenty of mortals out there willing to follow him."

"Mortal losers," mumbled Lucky, "following a loser god. Do you know that he's still using transfigured souls as personal agents? Who does that anymore?"

"How do you know that?"

Lucky gritted his teeth.

"I might have run into one."

Quick turned off the television.

"No shit?"

"Just one," added Lucky hastily. "It wasn't even a big one. And I smote it. End of story."

"They deserve to know. For their own safety."

"They're not in any danger. Anyway, aren't mortals supposed to die in service of their god? Isn't that the way it's supposed to work?"

Quick squinted hard at Lucky.

"Don't blame me." Lucky picked up a magazine and pretended to read it. "Blame the system."

The serpent god drained the last of his tomato juice and slithered into the kitchen to refill it. Lucky thumbed through the magazine until Quick returned. He turned on the television, and neither of them said anything until the show ended.

"I used to think like you," said Quick. "I used to think mortals were disposable commodities, to be used and discarded at my whim. You lose a couple, you gain a couple. What did one or a hundred or even a thousand here or there really mean in the end?"

"Hey now," said Lucky. "I'm not advocating strapping anyone onto an altar and cutting out their still-beating heart."

Quick shot him a dirty look. "That's not fair. That was a different time."

Lucky shrugged. "I'm just making the observation. That's all."

"I never asked them to do that," said Quick. "They just started doing it on their own."

"You didn't stop them, though, did you?"

"No, I didn't stop them. I should've, but I didn't."

Lucky tossed aside the magazine. "Aw, crap, Quick. I'm sorry. That was a cheap shot."

"No, you're right. I wanted the blood. I didn't ask for it, but when they offered it, I didn't complain."

"Different time. Like you said."

"Did you ever wonder how a handful of conquistadors managed to topple an empire? How I let that happen?"

"You always said you were on vacation when that business went down. By the time you came back, it was already over."

"Come on now. What kind of god would I be if I didn't check in on my followers now and then?" Quick blew a raspberry. "That story was bull, and you always knew it. Everyone always knew it. We just play along because if there's one thing we gods excel at it's avoiding responsibility."

Lucky said, "Mortals kill each other. It's not our job to solve all their problems."

"Bullshit!" roared Quick. A clap of thunder shook the house. His glass of tomato juice spilled across the carpet, and the sofa fell over, sending Lucky sprawling.

Quick transformed into his human shape. He stood

twelve feet tall and had to hunch under the ceiling. Symbols in fresh blood were painted on his flesh. In one hand, he held an onyx spear. In the other, he dangled a collection of skulls. He bared his pointed teeth and glared with bloodshot, raging eyes.

"Take it easy, buddy," said Lucky.

Quick glowered. "I saw it happening. I knew what was going on." He lowered his head and wiped a tear from his cheek. "I watched them die.

"They prayed for my intervention. But I thought, screw 'em. Not my problem. If they couldn't take care of a handful of Spaniards with blunderbusses then why the hell should I bother? Let the weaker followers perish so that the stronger should thrive. And if I lost them all, so what? I'd just start again. There were always more mortals, more followers. So I stood by and did nothing. Nada. I just let them die. They offered rivers of blood in tribute that I gladly accepted, but when it came time to do my part, I just walked away."

Quick shrank into human proportions, and helped Lucky right the sofa.

"But you want to know the worst part about it?" asked Quick. "The worst part is that after it was all over, I still didn't care. Do you want to know when I started caring?"

"No," said Lucky.

"It was about fifteen years later. I had a handful of followers, but nothing to get excited about. I couldn't figure it out. Here I was, the grand and revered Quetzalcoatl, and I was mostly forgotten. A few hundred thousand dead mortals didn't mean much to me, but they sure as hell made an impression on any potential followers. Guess they decided that if ol' Quick wasn't powerful enough to save an empire, they'd be better off looking for divine intervention somewhere else. And damned if I didn't agree after I had a century to think about it."

He transformed into his slouching serpent form.

"By then it was too late, of course. I'd blown my reputation. I'd lost all credibility. End of story. Game over."

"Don't be so hard on yourself, Quick. You'll get back on your feet . . . er, tail."

"No, I'm finished. Just an old used-up god, a remnant from a different era, more of a novelty than a deity. Don't make the same mistakes I did, Lucky."

Quick sighed and ran his tail around the tomato juice stain. "Teri is not going to be happy about that."

"I'll tell her I did it," said Lucky. "It'll be easier for her to take."

"Thanks."

Lucky slapped Quick on the shoulder. "I get what you're saying about Phil and Teri."

"So you're going to tell them?"

"I'll let them know. When the time is right."

Quick shot Lucky a glare.

"I need some time to show them the benefits of my company. You can't expect me to spring this other teeny little mostly unimportant detail on them out of nowhere, can you?"

"No, I guess not," agreed Quick. "But you should tell them. And tell them soon."

"Oh, absolutely. Next week or the week after that. A month at the very most. In the meantime, I'm sure everything will be fine."

With a sigh, Quick slipped off the sofa and slithered away.

11

Phil stopped at a convenience store to buy a lottery ticket on the way to work. He didn't normally waste his money but decided it wouldn't hurt to check the benefits of his new god. He figured that a lottery ticket was a good test for a minor prosperity god, and Phil wasn't taking anything on faith.

He won twenty bucks.

In the interest of science, he bought another five tickets. Three of them were winners, and one broke even. He ended up with an extra hundred dollars. Under ordinary circumstances, he would've walked away, but he continued the experiment. He spent the winnings on tickets. Some won. Some lost. And he ended up maxing out at the hundred-dollar threshold.

Phil would've purchased another round of tickets, but he had to get to work. His understanding of the god/ follower relationship told him there was a limit to the good fortune Lucky could provide. There was only so much prosperity to go around, and until he earned more favor to raise his share, he figured a hundred bucks wasn't bad. Just a little help. Exactly what Lucky had promised.

There was a traffic jam on the expressway, and the navigation charm pulled off on its own. He didn't fight it. The eyeball hanging from his rearview mirror seemed to know what it was doing. It guided him down side streets and alleyways on a route he would never have picked on his own. But it worked. Whatever lane he was in was the fastest. Every light was green. And his car merged so smoothly, it was almost as if the other drivers had all signed an agreement to let him pass. Phil's only complaint was that the charm did such a great job that he found himself a little bored by the end. He'd remember to bring some reading material tomorrow. Maybe he could get a DVD player installed.

There was a new computer waiting in his cubicle. He ran his hands along the monitor.

Elliot's head appeared over the cubicle. "They found it in the back of a storeroom. Nobody even knew it was there. Must've been misplaced. They offered it to Bob, but it's kind of old so he turned them down. So lucky break for you, huh? And since my car showed up at my apartment yesterday, all polished with a full tank of gas and a two-for-one coupon for Applebee's pinned under the wiper, and your shirt is devoid of jelly doughnut stains today, I can only assume that you've straightened things out with your new god."

"Yup. From now on, it's smooth sailing."

Phil leaned back. His chair collapsed, and he fell on the floor.

Elliot couldn't stop laughing.

"That's priceless," he wheezed between guffaws.

Phil inspected the chair. The screws had all fallen out.

"That's weird," remarked Elliot needlessly. "You didn't do anything to anger your god, did you?"

"Not that I know of."

"Eh, probably just a prank. They'll do that sometimes. Or it could only be a coincidence. Things like that happen, even with luck on your side."

Phil inserted the screws back into place. He rattled the loose chair.

"Here, dude, this might come in handy." Elliot reached over the cubicle wall and held up a screwdriver.

"Thanks," said Phil. "Where did you get this?"

"Had it in my desk drawer. It was there when I moved into the cubicle. Funny coincidence, huh?" Elliot smiled devilishly. "Or is it?"

Phil smiled as if amused, but the smile was accompanied by the dawning realization that perhaps life wasn't so simple when you followed a luck god. The idea kept popping into his head. It was easy to ignore at first, but as the day progressed it started occupying more of his thoughts until it proved to be a distraction noticeable not just to him but to those around him.

Without a god watching over you, it was safe to assume that things just happened. Finding twenty bucks on the sidewalk was good luck, and having a pigeon crap on your shoulder was merely ill fortune. There was an advantage to being subject to the whims of an indifferent universe. You didn't have to interpret every little thing that happened to you during your day.

If Phil had picked a patron of gardening then it would

be a lot easier to blow off these little occurrences unless they involved making sure the tomatoes grew properly or keeping gophers from eating the carrots. If his deity's domain had been automobiles, Phil could know a leaking radiator was probably a sign he'd fallen short in his tribute and a lack of bugs on his windshield was a divine thumbs-up. In either case, it would be easy to ignore a sprained ankle or a cracked foundation as just a random event.

Phil's god was a god of luck, and everything was in his province. All the little things, anyway. And Phil was beginning to understand that life often hinged on those moments.

The support of the gods wasn't absolute. At least once a year a foolhardy disciple of Zeus was struck by lightning on the assumption that he was immune to thunderbolts. The truth was that with Zeus on your side, the odds of getting zapped went down significantly, but no god, not even a big leaguer like the King of Olympus, could immunize all his followers against every stray bolt of lightning from the sky. And Lucky couldn't protect Phil from every possible bit of bad luck.

But Phil couldn't help but see a conspiracy of heavenly disapproval behind every touch of ill fortune. The supreme irony was that with Lucky at his side such moments were rare, and that just made them more obvious. And it wasn't Phil's imagination that those unlucky moments were a bit more unusual now.

For five minutes, he couldn't find a working pen. Even the pens given to him by coworkers were inexplicably dry once he took them in hand.

At lunch, the waiter dropped Phil's food three times

and had to send it back to the kitchen. The waiter apologized. The restaurant waived the check. But Phil wasn't certain their incompetence was the problem.

For about an hour, his shoelaces kept coming untied. He tried knotting and double-knotting, but nothing could stop them from hanging loose. He didn't trip, but he came close a few times.

He ignored the pen incident, and he tried not to make too much of the dropped food. But after the shoelace problem he nearly called Lucky. Phil didn't follow through on that impulse. He did not want to be one of those people who saw the work of divine powers in every little thing. Or even worse, one of those other types of people who appealed for divine intervention at the slightest inconvenience. Favor was supposed to make his life easier, but only an idiot expected it to solve all his problems.

He resolved to stop thinking about it. He couldn't quite succeed, but he did manage to stop focusing on it so much. By quitting time, it occupied only a little corner of his mind, and he was able to ignore that corner for the most part.

Elliot and Phil were leaving at the same time. They ascended the stairway to the top level of the parking garage, where they parked out of habit. They weren't really friends so much as two guys who spent eight hours beside each other five days a week. Neither disliked the other, but they never saw each other outside the office.

"One more day closer to death," remarked Elliot with a grin. "At least when I get to Tartarus, I'll be used to the grind. Pushing a boulder up a hill for eternity almost sounds relaxing compared to another boring meeting on"—he shuddered—"teamwork dynamics."

Phil chuckled as they exited onto the garage roof. Half

the spaces were empty, leaving the place wide open. The fading heat of the day rose from the black asphalt. A flock of finches perched on Phil's car. And only Phil's car.

Every bird was red with black spots and bright blue eyes. They were eerily silent and almost unmoving. They'd also caked his car with bird crap. Elliot's car, right beside Phil's, was untouched.

As one, the birds turned their blue eyes in Phil's direction. Then, without a screech or a warble, the flock launched itself in Phil's direction. It whirled around Phil and Elliot like a cyclone. The chirping grew into a ghastly chorus. Phil covered his ears. But it wasn't the sound that drove a wedge into his brain. It was something supernatural underneath it, a psychic assault. The static made it hard to think, but it didn't stop him from pondering just how painful it would be to be pecked to death by a hundred little bird beaks.

Phil and Elliot made a break for it. Phil's car was closer, and it obligingly opened its doors for them. They jumped inside, and the doors slammed shut again. By a stroke of luck, none of the birds made it in with them. The car shielded them from the birds' deafening chirps.

Phil slouched in his seat and exhaled.

"Thanks," he told the navigation charm hanging from the mirror.

The eyeball bobbed at him.

The finches settled in a circle around his car. They went silent again.

"Thank you, Lucky." He turned to Elliot. "Are you okay?"

"Yeah. You?"

Phil checked himself for any cuts or bruises, but miraculously, the birds hadn't laid a beak on him.

An especially large finch glared at him through the windshield. Then, in an instant, they were gone, launching themselves skyward and disappearing.

The navigation charm hanging from Teri's rearview wasn't perfect. It had trouble parallel parking. And while it was pretty good at avoiding traffic jams, it wasn't able to perform miracles.

A series of fender benders, a serious accident, and a tractor trailer jackknife had reduced traffic to a crawl. There was nothing to do about it but sit it out. The charm made it easier. She didn't have to pay attention and could while away the time reading.

It was probably why she never saw the truck coming.

Her car was passing through an intersection when a cement truck barreled along and smashed into the rear half of her coupe. She spun out like a top and bounced off another automobile, coming to a stop across two lanes.

It happened so fast that it was over before she even realized. But it was only the first part of the accident.

Brakes squealed as another car plowed into the coupe. She was knocked a few feet more and into the path of another truck. She yelped as it moved forward. Its bumper was higher than her hood, so the truck bounced onto the coupe. Its huge front tire rolled across the hood and right toward the windshield. Teri ducked into her seat, as if that would prevent her from being crushed.

But the coupe didn't crush. Even as the large vehicle came to a halt with its tire resting on her roof.

It took her a few seconds to realize she wasn't hurt. Another few seconds to remember that she was riding in an invulnerable car. There wasn't even a crack in the wind-shield. She was a little shaken up, but even that seemed minimal. Maybe there was some kind of enchantment that protected the passengers from the worst of a collision.

Lucky had saved her life.

She rolled down her window and peered upward at the truck perched above her. Cautiously, she exited the coupe and moved to a safe distance. The intersection was a pileup of automobiles. The cement truck that had caused the chain of vehicular carnage had plowed into a store-front. The driver peeked from the open door. He glanced around the scene. His eyes met hers, and he frowned.

He jumped to the sidewalk and ran away. She lost sight of him in the crowd.

A trio of red spotted pigeons landed on the truck. They were strangely un-pigeonlike in their movements. Their heads didn't bob, and they just perched on the truck, star-ing down at her. And just her.

A shiver ran through her, but that had to be because of the accident, the noise, the chaos. The pigeons were just something weird for her to focus on. But she had a winged serpent sleeping on her couch and her best friend was dat-ing a raccoon, so Teri's definition of notably weird had changed over the past few days.

Still, the oddly colored pigeons qualified.

A siren drew her attention, and she glanced away. When she looked back, the birds were gone.

But she couldn't get them out of her mind.

Bruce made it back to his home without getting caught.

It'd all seemed so simple. Steal a truck, wait for the

right opportunity, and then crush Teri Robinson under his bumper. He'd picked Teri rather than Phil because she was a woman, and that had made her less threatening in his mind. Irrational, he knew, especially since his weapon of choice was a twenty-ton vehicle. But this would be his first human sacrifice to Gorgoz. He'd slaughtered a small menagerie in his dark god's name, but humans were a big step. Still, when the order came down, he was ready for it. This was his chance to prove himself to Gorgoz, to rise up in the ranks.

And he'd blown it.

But he was safe. Nobody had seen him. Except maybe Teri, and it was a fleeting glance at best. She'd see him again. And next time, there would be no miracles to save her.

"Hello, bug."

He jumped at the voice.

The spotted rat on his sofa stared at him.

Bruce knelt. "Master, I have failed you."

"Yes, you have."

"It won't happen again," said Bruce.

"No, it won't."

The scampering of dozens of tiny rodent feet filled the room. And Bruce knew the time had come to pay the piper. He regretted that it was going to end like this, struck down before he even had a chance to rise up in the ranks, before he'd gotten his chance to at least get something worthwhile from all the blood he'd spilled in Gorgoz's name. But, honestly, he wasn't surprised.

The swarm of squirrels, rats, and one ravenous, red-speckled wombat pounced on him and devoured him, and Bruce's career in Gorgoz's temple came to a bloody end.

"I challenge," said Lucky.

"You challenge?" Quick tapped the table with his clawed fingertips. "But it's a word. S-O-M-B-R-E-R-O. A wide-brimmed hat."

"I know what it is," said Lucky. "But it's not an English word and the rules say very clearly that all words must be in English."

"No, the rules say words must appear in the dictionary."

"So I challenge. Check the dictionary."

Quick picked up the pocket dictionary resting beside the Scrabble board and flipped through to the S section.

"Is it in there?" asked Lucky with a wry grin.

"No, it's not," replied Quick, "but that's not fair. The page is missing. Just like every other page that would contain every other word that you've challenged."

"It's not my fault the only dictionary we could find was defective."

"Then whose fault is it?"

"Hey, it's just my nature. I can't help it." Lucky laid out all his tiles, reading as he went. "Z-E-O-L-I-T-E."

"That's not a word," said Quick.

"Do you challenge?"

"What's it mean?"

"Do you challenge?" asked Lucky.

"You don't know what it means, do you? You just laid out the tiles at random, didn't you?"

"I know what it means," replied Lucky after a moment's hesitation. "Do you know what it means?"

"Why don't you tell me then?" asked Quick.

"Why don't you tell me?" said Lucky.

"Just admit it. You don't know what it means."

"Okay, so I don't. But I don't have to know. That's not in the rules."

The gods stared at each other across the coffee table of honor.

Lucky smiled. "Do you challenge or not?"

Quick scooped up the dictionary and flipped through it. He slammed the book onto the table. "I hate playing games of chance with you."

"Scrabble is not a game of chance. It is a game of skill with an element of chance. There's a difference. And don't be such a sore loser. Come on. You're due! Nobody wins all the time. Not even me. I think I saw an old copy of Clue in the closet."

"Don't you need three for Clue?"

Phil walked through the front door.

"Phil will join us," said Quick. "Won't you, Phil?"

"Uh, sure," said Phil. "What are we doing?"

"Playing Clue." Lucky bounded to the other room to get the game.

"It's been forever since I played that game," said Phil. Quick shook his head.

"What?"

"You'll see."

"You have a little something there." Quick pointed to a spot of white bird crap on Phil's shoulder.

"You should see my car."

"Uh-hmm." Quick grinned. "Let me guess. For the most part everything was going great today, but sometimes, odd moments of improbable bad luck hit you out of nowhere."

Phil nodded. "How'd you know?"

"The universe is a chaotic place by nature. Gods of fortune can curb that, even bend it in the favor of their followers, but they can't completely prevent bad things from happening."

Lucky returned with the game and started setting it up.

"Want to explain about entropic balance?" asked Quick. "You're the luck god."

"It's not that complicated," said Lucky as he laid out the miniature pewter murder weapons. "In the old days, we usually just ignored it and all that ill fortune gathered up in a giant clump of negative karma hanging over our followers' heads. Eventually, it would fall and fall hard. Whammo, a lifetime of delayed entropy would hit them all at once." He punched his fist into his palm. "The results...not very pretty.

"But you don't have to worry about that anymore," said Lucky. "We eventually figured out that if we allowed small bits of random chaos into our followers' daily lives we could defuse the big whammy. Entropy isn't picky. It just doesn't like being ignored. So a few odd misfortunes here, a little bizarre luck there, and everything works itself out just fine."

"I didn't think you had to worry about stuff like that," said Phil. "I thought you just did whatever you wanted."

"Oh, we have rules we have to follow, too," said Quick.

"Are you allowed to admit that in front of me?" Phil asked. "Isn't there some kind of rule against it?"

Lucky and Quick chuckled.

"Some gods think we should present an all-powerful image to mortals all the time," said Lucky. "But they're humorless pricks."

Phil laughed. He was becoming used to this. Not just talking with gods and living with gods, but actually liking them despite himself. But Lucky and Quick weren't immortals as he knew them. They weren't aloof or terrifying or wrathful. They were just a couple of working stiffs scraping by with a handful of followers and hoping to get ahead. Even if he would have preferred not having a reformed Aztec sun god sleeping on his sofa, he could relate.

They picked their pawns, and Lucky won the roll to see who would go first.

"Imagine that," mumbled Quick.

"Oh don't be such a spoilsport."

Lucky picked up the die just as the front door opened. Teri stepped in, a little disheveled and with a slightly dazed expression.

"Teri, what's wrong?" asked Phil.

"There was an accident."

Quick threw a glare at Lucky, who stared nonchalantly at the die in his hand.

"What happened?" Phil asked. "Are you hurt?"

"No, there were some injuries, but nothing serious. I got hit by a truck. It was a real mess. I could've been killed." She absorbed the thought. "I should've been killed."

Phil put his arm around her and guided her to the sofa. "Are you okay?"

"I'm fine. Lucky's car saved my life."

Quick cleared his throat while Lucky straightened out the line of miniature murder weapons.

Teri gave a brief account of her accident. She mentioned the strange speckled pigeons at the end.

"That's weird," said Phil. "I was attacked by spotted birds today, too."

"Are we going to play this game or not?" asked Lucky. "This murder isn't going to solve itself. Didn't a great mortal once remark that justice delayed is justice denied?"

"I got it." Phil snapped his fingers and pointed to his god. "This is all because of you."

"These things happen," said Lucky. "I don't think there's anything to be gained by overanalyzing random events like this."

Quick grunted. "—Says the luck god."

Lucky's smile faded. "Well, now, I can explain—"

"It's more of that entropic rebalancing, isn't it?" Phil said. "The pressure valve to keep the really bad stuff from happening."

"Yes! Karmic necessity. No big thing. A little inconvenient, sure, but not really a problem."

"Getting run over by a truck is not an inconvenience," said Quick.

"Hey, I'm thirsty," said Lucky. "Anybody else thirsty?"

"I could use a soda," said Phil.

"One soda, coming up!" Lucky grabbed Quick by the wing. "Want to help me with this one, buddy?"

"Help you grab a soda? Does that really require two gods?"

"Excuse us." Lucky pulled Quick into the kitchen.

"Will you cut it out?" whispered Lucky as he grabbed a beverage.

"They need to know," said Quick.

"They're my followers. That's for me to decide. So why don't you mind your own business?"

Quick flapped his wings in exasperation.

Lucky poked the serpent god in the chest. "If you find it too hard to shut up, you're always free to find another place to crash."

Quick snarled. "You're an asshole."

Lucky's ears fluttered. "All part of my charm."

They returned to the living room.

"One soda for my newest follower," announced Lucky boisterously. He tossed the can to Phil.

"I was just explaining how it works," said Phil. "The way that weird things have to happen to keep chaos in check. It's not going to always be like this, is it?"

"Oh no," said Lucky. "It'll balance itself out eventually, and you can trust that while you're under my influence even vicious squirrels and nasty birds are little more than an inconvenience."

Quick bit his lip hard enough that his fangs drew blood.

"So are we going to play or not?" asked Lucky. "If I recall correctly, I'm first. And I think I will try to solve the crime."

"You haven't even eliminated any suspects yet," said Phil.

"Can't hurt to take a guess, can it? I think it was Professor Plum in the conservatory with the lead pipe." Lucky opened the envelope and spread out the cards for everyone to see. "Must be my lucky day."

Quick sighed. "This is why I only play checkers with gods of fortune."

"Are you sure this is the right place?" asked Bonnie.

"I'm sure," said Syph.

Bonnie studied the house across the street. It was nice but unremarkable. Difficult to imagine that a god called it home.

"Are you sure?"

"Yes, I'm sure."

"How do you know he's in there?" asked Bonnie.

"I just know."

"Okay then. Do you want me to go in with you or do you think you can handle it on your own?"

Syph slouched in her seat.

"I can go in with you if you want," said Bonnie.

Syph sighed, and the rearview mirror fell off. Bonnie had long since moved past commenting on things like this. She'd almost stopped noticing them. She waited for Syph to say or do anything, but the goddess just sat there.

"What's wrong?" asked Bonnie.

"I can't do it."

"What?"

"I've changed my mind. I can't go in there."

Bonnie tightened her grip on the steering wheel.

"Do you want to stay a goddess of heartbreak forever?"

"No."

"Well, the first step to changing that is to confront the lousy bastard whose rejection turned you into...this."

"I guess that makes sense," said Syph quietly.

"You're damn right it makes sense. This guy rejected you. He treated you like crap. You, the goddess of love!"

"He wasn't as bad as all that. Really, it was more my fault than his."

Overwhelming gloom filled the car. Even knowing it was a foreign despair forcing itself upon her didn't help Bonnie resist entirely. She rolled down her windows in hopes of letting the negativity escape.

"You have to stop doing this to yourself. And to me. And to people like me. Being divine doesn't give you the right to go around destroying people's lives."

Syph raised her eyebrows questioningly.

"So maybe it does," admitted Bonnie. "You can keep doing this until the end of time, jumping from mortal to mortal, crushing hopes and joy one victim at a time. We can't stop you. I know I certainly can't. But you keep saying you're sorry about this. That doesn't mean anything. Not unless you try to prevent it."

Syph said nothing. Bonnie wrung the wheel, trying to read the inscrutable goddess.

"What if he doesn't like me?" asked Syph softly.

"Do you care if he likes you?"

"I don't know. Should I? Is it wrong that I care what he thinks?"

"You were dumped. It's not weird to have mixed feelings. You resent him for rejecting you, but you also want him back because you weren't ready for it. And maybe underneath that, you feel like because he rejected you that you have something to prove by showing him he made a mistake. And if you can get him to take you back it'll be vindication, show that you are worth something."

"You seem to be an expert on this," said Syph.

"No more than anyone else," replied Bonnie. "We mortals have to deal with this a lot. Most of us anyway."

"How sad for you. To have your short lives burdened by such complications."

"Yeah, it sucks," agreed Bonnie.

She surrendered to the ennui and just slumped in defeat. She didn't even cry. Not because she wasn't terminally depressed. But it was such an overwhelming hopelessness that she just felt numb.

"So if I go in there and talk to him, it'll make me feel better?" asked Syph.

"Yes, it will." Bonnie half-smiled. "Absolutely, it will. Maybe." She tried looking Syph in the face and lying to her, but she couldn't. Whether this was due to her honest nature or the draining effects of the goddess wasn't clear. It took energy to lie. Energy Bonnie didn't have.

"Probably not," said Bonnie. "Some people will tell you that it's good for closure, but I think they're fooling themselves. It's not like you're going to knock on that door and have a twenty-minute discussion that'll fix all your problems. Usually, the conversation is either ugly or awkward or both and you walk away feeling worse about yourself or just pissed off at the whole world."

"Then why do it?" asked Syph.

Bonnie thought about it a moment.

"Because you have two choices. Choice number one: get over it and move on with your life. That's the healthy thing to do, the best way to handle it. Considering that you've been nursing this depression for a few thousand years, I don't think that's an option."

Syph lowered her head as ice formed on the dashboard.

"Odin's missing eye," grumbled Bonnie. It was hard enough keeping herself from giving up, but the goddess of tragedy was even more easily discouraged. And when Syph felt down, that negativity transferred to Bonnie. It was a vicious cycle.

"Oh, for Olympus's sake, snap out of it." She smacked Syph on the shoulder. "Go up and knock on that door and confront this guy. It probably won't make you feel better, but it's just something you have to do. Don't you think two thousand years of misery are enough? This isn't unrequited love anymore. It's not even unhealthy obsession. It's just pathetic."

"No mortal has ever dared talk to me this way." Syph's face reddened.

"Does it make you mad?" asked Bonnie. "Does it piss you off? Good. That means that you're not an entirely lost cause. Now get in there and give this god some of that divine wrath everyone is always talking about."

"I would, but he has company."

Syph pointed to a car pulling into the house's driveway. Bonnie ducked down, though she wasn't sure why.

"You don't have to worry," said Syph. "I've made the car invisible."

Janet exited the car and rang the doorbell. The door was answered by a raccoon.

Syph ducked. "Get down."

Bonnie did so. "I thought you made us invisible."

"It doesn't work on other gods."

Bonnie raised her head just enough to see the raccoon. "Wait a minute. You're not telling me that...that's the god that broke your heart?"

"Yes," said Syph.

"That god?"

"Yes."

"With the fuzzy tail and loudest Hawaiian shirt I have ever seen? The god who is wearing sunglasses even though it's eight in the evening."

"Yes."

"The god who stands maybe three feet tall at—"

"Yes," said Syph. "That god!"

Lucky took Janet's hand and placed his muzzle against it.

"What was that?" asked Syph. "Was that a kiss?"

"I don't think raccoons have lips capable of kissing," said Bonnie. "That seemed like more of a nuzzle."

He said something, and Janet laughed.

"Are they flirting?" asked Syph.

Janet knelt down and playfully ruffled the fur on his head.

"She is flirting with him." Syph didn't shout, but only because she spoke through clenched teeth. "Is this a date?"

"It looks like a date," said Bonnie as Lucky and Janet climbed into her car.

Bonnie started her car.

"What are you doing?" asked Syph.

"I'm following them," replied Bonnie, still slouching behind her wheel somewhat.

"Why?"

"Because…"

Something was different about Syph now. Maybe it was jealousy. Or rage. Or maybe just unpleasant discomfort from seeing the object of her obsession getting on with his life before her. Whatever it was, it was better than the constant ennui radiating from her. Either way, Bonnie was worried that if she told Syph any of this it might go away.

"Why not?" said Bonnie.

Janet wasn't usually intimidated by the gods. She had enough experience with powers to remove most of the mystery and romance from the divine. She'd mingled with gods. Flirted with a few. And screwed several. But she'd never been on a date with a god. Not a real date.

She realized this on the drive to the restaurant, and for the first time ever, she wasn't sure what to say.

"So…" She started without having any other part of the sentence mapped out. Her improvisational skills abandoned her.

"So…" replied Lucky.

They didn't say anything for a few minutes. The radio didn't even have the consideration to fill the silence with music. Instead, it played commercials. Janet flipped through the channels, but the radio refused to cooperate and she finally gave up, stopping on an Oracle Friends' Network ad.

Lucky snorted. "That is such a scam."

"Really?"

"I'll let you in on a little secret." He leaned closer. "Nobody has had a destiny in a thousand years. Not an official destiny anyway. Things got too big for that a long time ago. It was a lot easier to preconfigure the paths of fate when there weren't so damn many of you mortals running around. Now it's pretty much impossible. I think the last guy the Fates tried to guide was Gary Hamelin. And we all know how that worked out."

"Never heard of him," she said.

"Exactly."

"Well, my mom swears by them. Said they helped her find some lost keys one time."

"Oh, yeah, they're good for stuff like that, I suppose. Just don't expect them to be infallible. It's a good way to end up doing life in a Peruvian prison."

"Gary Hamelin?" she asked.

"Trust me. You don't want to know."

They shared a light chuckle, and for a moment, Janet thought the ice was broken. They'd already hung out, already slept together. But there was still an uncomfortable aura around this date.

"Why did you ask me out?" It'd been on her mind for a while now, though she hadn't intended on inquiring. But she was desperate for any conversational thread, and this one just sprang spontaneously.

"Oh, no reason. Why did you say yes?"

"I had a choice? I thought if I refused you'd transform me into a spider or a flower or something like that."

"Fruit basket."

"What?"

"I usually transform people into fruit baskets."

She studied him from the corner of her eye, noticing the slight smirk on his muzzle.

"Oh, you are so full of shit," she said. "You don't do that."

"You got me. And you're full of it, too. You didn't say yes because you were worried about being smote by a disappointed god."

"Okay, so you got me," she admitted. "So you would've been disappointed if I'd said no?"

"Of course."

"I'm just surprised. I didn't think gods dated mortals much anymore. Not like official date dates. If you know what I mean."

"Kind of fell out of fashion," he admitted. "Mind if I turn up the radio?"

"No, no. Go ahead."

"Dancing Queen" came out of the radio. Lucky's ears fell flat. "Oh, Tiamat, I hate this song."

"Go ahead and change it."

"Thanks." He fiddled with the tuner until he found a song that pleased him. "That's better."

"'Waterloo?'"

"Yeah," said Lucky. "Great song."

"But isn't 'Waterloo' by ABBA?"

"That's right."

"And isn't 'Dancing Queen' by ABBA?"

"Correctamundo."

"And don't they sound almost identical?" asked Janet.

"What's'a matter? Don't you like ABBA?"

"Who doesn't like ABBA?" said Janet.

"Hecate," said Lucky. "Huge Bee Gees fan. But what can you expect from a goddess of darkness?"

"Don't change the subject. You were just telling me that you like 'Waterloo' but not 'Dancing Queen.' Even though, by and large, they're the same song. At least stylistically."

"Oh, sure, stylistically," agreed Lucky. "But 'Dancing Queen' is a vapid little emptiness. 'Waterloo,' on the other hand, is a noble study into humanity, a continuation of the great Greek tragedy tradition. Yet it's also a triumph of the mortal spirit, an unwillingness to surrender against the inevitable darkness, and even an ability to find comfort in defeat." He snapped his fingers along with the tune. "She can't refuse, but at least she feels like she wins when she loses. Think about it."

"Oh, I will," said Janet with strained sincerity.

"Music has always been the greatest expression of mortal philosophy," continued Lucky. "The path to enlightenment is found in the lyrics of Spinal Tap."

"That's not even a real band. Next you'll be extolling the virtues of the Monkees."

"Nah. Every ounce of the Monkees' artistic merit left with Peter Tork."

"Tell me you're joking."

He flashed a devilish smile. "You'll just have to figure that out on your own."

"You're so full of shit," she said with a chuckle.

"Usually, but most mortals are either too awed or too afraid to call me on it. Take Phil and Teri. They're good kids, but they're always walking on eggshells around me."

"But I don't," she said.

"No, you don't. You're a rare breed of mortal, Janet. You aren't afraid and you aren't disdainful. No pressure. No expectations. You have no idea how attractive we gods find that in a mortal."

"Thanks."

"Plus, you've got a great ass."

Janet gave him a light slap on the shoulder. "I do believe you're going to make me blush, Mr. Luck God."

Bonnie tailed Lucky and Janet to an Italian restaurant. The god and his date went inside while Bonnie and Syph waited in the parking lot for a few minutes.

"What now?" asked Syph.

"Now, we go in."

"Isn't that a bit rude?"

Under ordinary circumstances, Bonnie wouldn't have considered it. But she was fighting for her life here. Good manners were a restriction she was willing to ignore. She was actually hoping for an ugly scene. Anything to snap Syph out of her funk.

They were in luck. The place was busy and the hostess offered them the only available table, which was within view of Lucky, who sat in a booth with his back to them. It gave her time to think this through.

The waiter, Steve, spilled out tonight's drink specials. Bonnie didn't pay attention. She cut him off, ordering a beer.

"And you, ma'am?" Steve asked Syph.

The goddess offered no reply. Her unblinking stare focused on Janet.

"She'll take a water," said Bonnie.

"Great. Can I interest you in some appetizers?"

"Just the drinks right now. Thanks." Bonnie nudged him aside to get a better view. He took the hint and went to the kitchen.

Lucky and Janet shared a laugh.

Syph scowled. The wax bubbled on the small candle in the center of the table, and its flame turned black.

Bonnie fanned the flames, metaphorically.

"They certainly seem to be having a good time."

The goddess tore ten long slashes in the tablecloth and wood with her fingernails. A spiderweb of black and blue veins darkened her face and neck. She literally hissed.

"That bitch."

"Hold on," said Bonnie. "Don't you think you're aiming your wrath at the wrong target?"

"Who does she think she is?"

Steve returned with their drinks. Syph ran her finger along the edge of her glass, and the water boiled.

"Can I take your order now?" asked Steve.

"Two specials," said Bonnie quickly.

"Ma'am, we don't have any specials."

"We'll take the enchiladas then."

"We don't serve—"

She grabbed his pad. "Steve, we are in the middle of something important. I don't know if you're really that oblivious or you haven't noticed that this is a goddess of tragedy and she's in a really, really bad mood. Either way, why don't you just bring us whatever you like best?"

"Actually, I don't eat here. Confidentially, I hate Italian food. And the cook doesn't wear a hairnet."

Bonnie ground her teeth. "Spaghetti. We'll take two orders of spaghetti."

"Meat sauce or marinara?"

"You're screwing with me."

"A little bit," admitted Steve.

Janet flipped her hair and scratched Lucky's ear.

Syph slammed her fists on the table and the entire restaurant rattled. Every candle on every table erupted, sending up geysers of flame, melting the plastic holders, and scorching the ceiling.

Everyone in the restaurant, including Lucky, looked in Syph's direction.

"Spaghetti," said Steve. "Got it." He bolted for the kitchen.

Lucky stood and started walking over to the table.

Bonnie whispered to Syph, "Be strong."

He stood before them.

"Hi," Bonnie said and immediately regretted it.

Syph pushed forth a smile. "Oh, hi, Lucky."

He took a seat at the table, steepled his fingers, and frowned. "What are you doing here, Syph?"

She fiddled with her fork. "Nothing."

Bonnie wondered if she should say something, but she decided to let the situation unfurl on its own. She would've excused herself, but she had a vested interest in how it turned out.

Lucky's ears fell flat. "Syph…"

"We're just having dinner," replied the goddess lightly, unable to look in his direction. "This is Bonnie. She's my follower."

"Syph…"

"We're allowed to have dinner!" said Syph a bit too eagerly. "I don't care what that restraining order says."

Caught in mid-drink, Bonnie sputtered and choked.

"We've been over this," said Lucky. "I get North and

South America, Asia, and Antarctica. You get Africa, Europe, and Australia."

Syph spoke into her chest. "Australia is barely a continent."

"Fine. I'll trade you Antarctica for Australia if it bothers you so much."

"Whatever. I've been thinking. We're two mature, immortal beings. We should be able to work this out in a reasonable way without all the drama, right?"

"We should," said Lucky suspiciously.

"Honestly, I don't even see what the big deal is. Maybe I overreacted a bit at first, but that was before I realized that you'll come to your senses. Eventually. All I have to do is be patient."

"Fine. Be patient. Just be patient somewhere else."

Syph laughed. She tried to pass it off as casual and light, but it was forced and high-pitched.

"You always were a witty one." She nodded at Janet. "Who is that?"

"Nobody," said Lucky.

"Is she your date? Are you dating a mortal?"

"That's none of your business."

"I can't believe you'd actually stoop to dating a mortal." Syph chuckled coldly and elbowed Bonnie in the ribs. "What century is this anyway?"

Bonnie made a noncommittal gruntish sort of noise.

Lucky forced an impatient smile. "She's nice."

"I'm sure she is," said Syph. "She's also doomed to dust."

"Syph..."

The goddess threw up her hands. "It's true, isn't it? She is mortal, after all. They all find their way into the grave sooner or later. Usually sooner."

Lucky stood on the chair, put his hands on the table, and leaned forward. "You'll leave her alone."

"Of course, of course. She seems lovely, doesn't she, Bonnie?"

Bonnie stuck her beer in her mouth by way of reply.

Lucky's fur bristled as an electrical crackle passed between the god and goddess. The dim lighting flickered.

The manager, a tall woman in a pantsuit, approached the table.

"I'm sorry. Is there a problem here?"

Bonnie expected the manager to be blasted to atoms by a withering glance from the god and goddess. Lucky and Syph both smiled.

"No problem." He hopped off the chair. "Just a couple of old friends catching up. Nice to see you, Syph. Sorry you couldn't stay longer." He walked away, and all the divine energies dissipated from the atmosphere.

The manager exhaled, wiping a bead of sweat from her brow. She made an offering of complimentary bread sticks to the goddess, but Bonnie turned them down. She grabbed Syph by the arm and dragged her out of the restaurant. Syph protested, but Bonnie ignored her. She knew it wasn't at all wise to manhandle a goddess, but she didn't care. She shoved Syph into the car and didn't say another word until she'd driven a few miles away.

"I was actually looking forward to the spaghetti," said Syph.

"What just happened in there?" Bonnie tried to keep the edge from her voice, but it didn't work.

"I talked to him. Just like you wanted me to."

"That wasn't what I wanted."

"It wasn't?"

Bonnie was so distracted, she ran a red light and was nearly hit by a truck.

Syph suggested, "You might want to drive carefully when your passenger is a goddess of tragedy. You never know when a bus full of orphans is nearby."

Bonnie pulled into a supermarket parking lot.

"What was that thing he mentioned? Something about a restraining order?"

"Oh, that." Syph folded her arms and shrugged. "That's nothing. Just a little misunderstanding, that's all. I did some things, some embarrassing things. Maybe I overreacted when we had our problems. I admit that. Anyway, it's not a restraining order per se. It's more of a voluntary territorial division arbitrated by the Court of Divine Affairs." Syph turned her head away and mumbled, "More silly than anything else."

"What did you do?" asked Bonnie despite herself.

"Oh, I just kept him from making any mistakes until he realizes he really does love me. Lucky always did fancy the mortals a bit too much. I just helped him to understand how fleeting their affections were."

"You've done this before, haven't you? To him. That's why he wasn't surprised to see you."

"It was your idea to talk to him," said Syph. "Really, it's your fault."

"I notice you didn't mention the restraining order—"

"Voluntary territorial division," corrected the goddess.

"This is what you do? You follow this god around, ruining his love life, along with whatever random mortals you come across?"

"You make it sound so..."

"Pathetic?" interrupted Bonnie.

"The pursuit of love is never pathetic."

Bonnie laid her head on the wheel and laughed for a solid minute.

"And to think that I was actually feeling sorry for you earlier tonight. Now I find out you've devoted your endless life to making everyone as miserable as you are."

"You don't understand, Bonnie. The path to true love is never easy. Not even for immortals. He loves me. I know he does, even if he doesn't. If I can help him to realize that then everything will work out the way it was always meant to."

"Okay, you're creeping me out now. Do you have any idea how unbalanced that sounds? You can't make someone love you."

Syph chuckled lightly. "Don't be absurd. Of course I can. I'm the goddess of love."

"More like the goddess of stalkers," replied Bonnie. "Did you ever stop to think that if you'd just let this go, stop fixating on this one rejection as the defining moment of your unending life, that you might be able to leave this trail of doom and gloom behind you? Maybe what happened to you has nothing to do with Lucky. Maybe it's your own damned fault for refusing to move on."

Syph's brow furrowed. Her jaw clenched.

"You just don't get it, do you? But you'll see. I'll show you."

She stared straight ahead at a little old lady carrying a bag of groceries in front of the parked car. The bottom of the sack fell out, spilling oranges, a carton of eggs, and a jar of jelly that shattered on the pavement.

"Oh for cryin' . . ." Bonnie exited the car and helped the woman salvage what groceries she could. When she returned to the car, the goddess was gone. Gone, but not forgotten. The heaviness still weighed on Bonnie's heart. And three words were burned into the pleather cushions of the passenger seat.

I'll show you.

14

Over the next few weeks, things fell into place for Teri and Phil.

Lucky spent less and less time at the house. His dates with Janet grew more frequent, and he usually slept over at her place four or five times a week. They spent more time with Quick than with their own god. Sometimes they would go days without seeing Lucky at all, with only rumpled Hawaiian shirts in the hamper to tell them he'd popped in for a visit and grabbed a shower and something to eat before heading back to Janet's place.

When they suggested that Quick use the guest room, he refused. The room was more than just a closet full of Lucky's clothes and an unused bed. It was the shrine to their god, the sacred space devoted to his appeasement. Even if he didn't use it for much, it still counted as tribute.

Quick was stuck on the sofa, but he was quiet and a

decent cook. And he was considerate enough to leave the house every so often to give them their privacy. Usually, he'd just go for a slither around the block for a few hours or sit in the backyard with a glass of tomato juice and a book. It wasn't very godlike behavior, but he had long ago abandoned the ways of tribute and favor.

"I'm just trying to get my head together," he'd explained. "I don't really need to mess around with that game right now."

Both mortals knew that Quick was just making excuses, but they saw no need to push things. He was immortal. He had plenty of time to "find himself." It really was none of their business. They just chalked up the serpent god living in their midst to more tribute for Lucky, and as long as Quick was willing to do the dishes every now and then, they didn't feel too put out.

Janet and Lucky's relationship changed from infatuation to genuine affection much faster than either was willing to admit, but Teri noticed. At her lunches with Janet, she'd catch Janet smiling wistfully and wouldn't have to guess what or who she was thinking about. More and more, the discussions became about something "cute" Lucky did or some romantic gesture or just something funny he'd said. Teri considered putting in a discouraging word, but she didn't see the point in throwing cold water on it just because it was most probably doomed to an ugly end. Most relationships were, when she really thought about it.

It was hard to be negative, though, when good luck was in their hip pocket. Everything started going right. It wasn't big or obvious, but it was noticeable. Aside from the twenty to thirty bucks of loose change Phil and Teri found every day, there were other subtle benefits. Any supermarket line they chose was always the fastest. Even the most crowded restaurant just happened to have a table available upon their arrival. They were always the twentieth caller to the radio contest, found things on sale just when they needed them to be, and rarely had to deal with traffic jams. Lucky didn't fix their lives, but he did remove all those little annoyances that made the bigger problems harder to focus on. Phil took advantage of this to just relax while Teri found she could accomplish so much more.

There were still the quirks of luck. Phil stepped in gum at least once a day, and Teri found that her shower would inexplicably blast her with cold water about once a week. But these were just annoyances, and nothing compared to the frustration that a single bad day could create.

The strangest thing was the animals: the birds, squirrels, stray dogs and cats that appeared around them. Always red. Always speckled. Always with the large blue eyes.

Lucky told them it was nothing to worry about and that the animals would go away eventually. They just needed to give it some time.

But the animals kept coming.

Phil and Teri grew used to seeing them. In the end, they seemed less threatening than the daily gum on Phil's shoe, so after a while, both mortals stopped really noticing.

And life, blessed by good fortune and serendipity, was good.

Phil had seen the Supervisor walking the office before. He'd nodded to her a few times. And once, he'd even shaken her hand while passing by as introductions were being thrown around. But she was too far above him on the corporate ladder to have any deeper interaction on those few occasions when she descended from the seventh floor. She usually appeared like a phantom from a special elevator, spoke to one of the fourth-floor department heads, and disappeared whence she came. Which was why it was surprising when she took a sharp right down Phil's row of cubicles. Everyone kept their eyes on their work as she proceeded down the aisle.

He bent over his keyboard and squinted at the screen as if his life depended on it. It was several moments before he realized she had paused by his cubicle.

He glanced from the corner of his eye to be sure, not willing to look away from his work for fear of getting caught slacking off. In his peripheral vision, she was a blurry shadow, the living embodiment of all the nebulous dangers that lurked, barely seen and never spoken of, waiting to devour careless members of lower middle management who revealed just how redundant their positions were.

The Supervisor didn't say anything. She just stood there.

He slowed his typing and turned his head. She wasn't nearly as terrifying as he'd assumed, but he'd never looked at her directly before. She was a short, stout woman. Her plain gray suit was wrinkle-free, and her hair was pulled back in a ponytail. She didn't smile, but she wasn't frowning either. She was inscrutable.

"Phillip Robinson." It wasn't a question, but there was a pleasant lilt in her voice, even if her face remained uncommitted. "I'd like you to come with me."

He suppressed a gulp.

She gave him just enough time to save his work before turning and marching away. He ran after her. Elliot shot him a questioning, vaguely frightened glance, and Phil shrugged. She led him to the special elevator. It wasn't different from any other elevator, but it still filled him with dread.

He didn't ask what this was about, and she didn't say. He watched the floor numbers light up until the elevator reached seven. Not all the way to nine, but closer than he'd been before.

"This way, please."

He ended up in an office. A secretary guarded the door, but she made no attempt to stop them from entering. The office was more like a small apartment with all the amenities of an art deco living space. Not to Phil's tastes, but impressive if only because he knew how others valued something like this.

The Supervisor vanished without another word. She closed the double doors behind her and left him to his fate.

A heavyset man sat behind the large desk. He was big, but not fat, brimming with physical power. His haircut probably cost more than Phil made in a month. Phil didn't know who he was, but he assumed this was someone important.

The man stood, spread his arms wide, and offered a boisterous greeting. "Phil, so good of you to make it! Welcome, welcome!"

Phil ventured closer with visions of the giant desk rolling over and crushing him beneath it. He decided to invoke the first rule of corporate survival. Humor the boss.

"Hello"—he read the nameplate on the desk—"Mr. Rosenquist."

"Oh, please. Why so formal? Call me Van." Rosenquist smiled, revealing perfectly white teeth. Everything about the man, from his tan to his trimmed mustache and square jaw, was a model of the subjective perfection that so many spent thousands of dollars achieving.

Rosenquist began the journey around his desk. By the time he rounded the second corner, a nameless dread had fallen on Phil. He didn't expect the boss to pounce and devour him, but his gut reaction was much the same as if he had. These were dangerous territories for an employee of his position, and not everyone who ventured into these lands made it out intact.

The boss seized Phil's sweaty hand and squeezed.

"Can I interest you in a cup of coffee? Great stuff here. Imported. I think it might even be from a country we have a trade embargo with, but I don't ask. Plausible deniability."

Phil drank coffee only in the morning, and that he liked strong and black. Anything else didn't interest him. But Rosenquist was already pouring the cup from an hourglass-shaped carafe. He handed it to Phil, who held the mug in both hands, unsure of what to do with it.

"Smell that," said Van. "Isn't that wonderful?"

Phil went through the act of inhaling the aroma. He found it unpleasant, but he kept that to himself.

"I suppose you're wondering why I called you up here."

"Yes, sir ... Van."

Rosenquist poured a cup of his own, sniffed it, then set it down on his desk. "The truth of the matter is that you're doing a hell of a job for us down there, Phil." He slapped Phil's shoulder. "Just one hell of a job."

Phil braced himself for the next part. The ". . . but we're making layoffs" part or the ". . . but corporate restructuring renders you redundant" part.

"We could use a man like you on the seventh floor."

"Me?" Phil tried not to sound too surprised.

"Yes, you. We have a new position opening soon. Executive vice president in charge of complicated government paperwork. Not the final job title, but that's the gist of it. And you've made the short list of candidates."

"Me?" This time he utterly failed to hide his disbelief.

Rosenquist chuckled. "It's not guaranteed at this stage, you understand. We're feeling out some others. But I don't think there's any harm in telling you that you're the front-runner at this point."

"But why me?"

"Why not you? Can I be honest? Sure I can. You look like the kind of man who appreciates honesty. Am I right?"

Phil nodded. As if he could answer no to the question.

"If you get this position, it really won't be much different than what you're doing now. But our lawyers tell us that we need someone in a more official position. Legal reasons. Don't ask me to explain it. So we sent down a memo asking for each department to send us possible candidates based on paperwork error ratios."

"They keep track of how many mistakes we make?"

"Oh, it's all monitored somewhere. The list was sent up to us, and it was quite a long list. We trimmed it to the top ten candidates via a selection of PER reports and seniority indexing. It was still a fairly long list. Then a computer error ate most of the data and only four were left. So it looks as if you had a stroke of luck there."

Phil smiled. Lucky had come through again.

"It's not glamorous. You'll move out of your cubicle, but your office won't be much better. You'll be an executive in pay only. Can you accept that?"

"Same job," paraphrased Phil, "more money."

"A lot more money," added Rosenquist.

"I can live with that."

The intercom buzzed. The boss had a short exchange with his secretary. "I'm afraid you'll have to excuse me a moment, Phil. Have to put out some fires. Make yourself comfortable. I'll be right back."

Phil put his coffee down and walked to the window. The equally tall building across the way obscured the view, but if he stood close enough to the glass, he could almost see the street below.

Movement on the outside caught his attention. A red pigeon with black dots perched on the ledge. The bird stared back with its bright blue eyes and pecked the window twice. Hard enough to leave a long crack in the glass. He was worried it might break through and dive-bomb his eye. Instead, it flew away.

He backed away but kept watching for it to return. It didn't, and after a minute, he was comfortable enough to take his eyes off the glass. Though he kept it in his peripheral vision.

He reached for a mug, but since his attention was split, he ended up knocking it off the desk. He scrambled to pick it up, but the coffee had all spilled out on the carpet. He found some paper towels in the wet bar and tried dabbing up the spill with only mild success.

"Son of a..."

There wasn't enough in the carafe to refill the mug all the way. Phil took the half-filled beverage. That way, his boss still had a full cup and Phil would have less to drink. He congratulated himself on his cleverness when Rosenquist returned.

"Van, I'm sorry, but I spilled some coffee on—"

"Don't worry about that. Housekeeping will take care of it." Rosenquist slapped Phil between the shoulder blades hard enough to put a permanent bend in his spine. "You're an executive now."

"I have the job?"

"Practically." He picked up his mug and waited for Phil to do the same. He obliged, and they tapped them together.

Rosenquist took a hearty gulp of his beverage while Phil took a sip. It wasn't very good, but right now, it tasted like nectar from Olympus.

"Now it'll take a few days to get everything in order," explained Rosenquist. "All the normal bureaucratic hoop-jumping. But I am confident in saying, unofficially, welcome to the seventh floor."

"Thank you, Van."

The boss seized Phil in another painful handshake. He caught Phil glancing over his shoulder at the window.

"Something wrong?" asked Rosenquist.

"No," said Phil. "Everything's great."

"Good to hear it." He glanced down at his cup. "Hey, didn't I give you the red mug?"

"I don't know, Van. Did you?"

Rosenquist's smile fell. "Did you switch mugs?"

"I might have. I wasn't really paying attention when I refilled—"

Rosenquist poured his coffee on the floor and peered into the cup.

"Something wrong, Van?"

The boss threw his mug aside. Beads of sweat poured down Rosenquist's face. He released Phil and grabbed his chest.

"Van, just stay calm. I'll get a doctor."

Rosenquist lurched forward. Phil moved to catch the toppling executive. Rosenquist was heavier than Phil expected and they ended up on the floor together, the boss on top. Phil had trouble breathing, and it wasn't just the weight bearing down on him. The pair of hands wrapped around his throat had something to do with it, too. Phil gasped for a few strangled gulps of air as he stared into Rosenquist's bloodshot, twitching eyes.

Rosenquist's body went stiff as he sucked in one last strained breath. He collapsed. Phil rolled Rosenquist to one side and caught his breath. Rosenquist wasn't breathing, and his face was frozen into a ghastly rictus. Phil had never seen a rictus before, but he was pretty sure this qualified.

The next few minutes were a blur. He remembered alerting the secretary, who called the paramedics. They arrived quickly, but by then it was obviously too late. Phil sat in a chair in the lobby, trying to figure out what had happened.

A heart attack at that particular moment in time seemed unfortunate. A lousy bit of luck. He wondered, several times, if this would hurt his chance for promotion. Then he felt guilty that he was thinking like that while a man had just died.

He kept wondering. Was it luck?

Or was it Lucky?

*   *   *

Phil left work early so he could beat Teri home. He found Lucky sitting on the sofa, watching television. It seemed as if that was all Lucky did with his free time. Phil had come to realize that gods, for all their awesome power, were deprived of the one thing that made life worth living.

A time limit.

Silently, Phil turned off the TV and sat across from Lucky.

"I was watching that," said Lucky.

Phil took a moment to compose his thoughts. He didn't have long before Teri walked through that door.

"My boss died today."

"Sorry to hear that, buddy."

Phil held up his hand, and a surprised expression crossed Lucky's face.

"Did you kill him?"

Lucky sat up. "Excuse me?"

"I'm not judging," said Phil. "I just need to know. Did you kill him?"

"I don't kill people."

Phil sucked in a long breath.

"You can tell me the truth."

Lucky tossed out a chuckle, but when Phil didn't join in, the god frowned.

"I'm only going to say this once more, buddy." Lucky removed his sunglasses and looked Phil in the eye. "I. Don't. Kill. People." He reached for the remote. "It's not my thing."

He turned on the television. Phil rose and pushed the OFF button on the set.

"I'm not saying you killed him intentionally. But maybe you got him by accident."

"Oh, I don't know. Been a long time since I killed anybody by accident." He laughed as if telling a joke, but Phil couldn't tell.

"All right, all right. Something obviously has you on edge, Phil. Sit and we'll get this straightened out."

Phil did most of the talking. He described the incident at the office in rapid detail, partly because he wanted to get this sorted before Teri walked through the door, partly because his mind was racing. He mentioned the spotted red animals that kept popping up. Not everywhere, all the time. Not always in obvious ways. But still there, still haunting him from the corner of his eye.

"Is that it?" asked Lucky in his usual offhand manner. This once, it came off as dismissive. "This is all perfectly normal, Phil. Happens all the time. It's called central cog syndrome. You're still adjusting to the benefits of divine favor. And right now, you're starting to feel like the whole universe revolves around you."

Phil didn't like the sound of that, and it must have shown on his face.

"Don't sweat it," said Lucky. "Your ego isn't getting out of control. You're just trying to figure things out. Now, I might have no small influence on the way your life is going, but I'm not all-powerful. You and me, we're just a couple of guys in the grand scheme of things. We don't rule the universe. Things are going to happen. Good things and bad things that have absolutely nothing to do with either of us."

Phil's doubts softened.

"You've had people die in your life before I moved in, right?" asked Lucky.

Phil nodded.

"And you've had weird luck before, too, right?"

He nodded again.

"So there you have it."

"But what about the animals?"

"That might have something to do with me." Phil thought he noticed a guilty glint in Lucky's eyes, but he couldn't be sure as Lucky had put his sunglasses back on. "But I'm sure it's nothing to worry about."

Teri came through the door.

"Hi." She gave him a hug and noticed his distant response. "Something wrong?"

"One of my bosses died."

"Oh, that's horrible." She hugged him tighter. "Want to talk about it?"

His head resting on her shoulder, he studied Lucky, who was back to watching television. He didn't think Lucky was telling him everything, but he didn't want to press it. If Lucky was right, if this was all in Phil's imagination, then sharing his concerns with Teri would just get her worked up again. She'd finally gotten comfortable with this arrangement.

Lucky had a point. It was absurd to believe that everything around him had something to do with a grand cosmic conspiracy. Had he really gone that far around the bend that the lives and deaths of others seemed only to be omens meant for his own interpretation?

Thinking about it made him feel a bit embarrassed.

Teri came as a much-needed distraction from his thoughts. "Are you sure everything is okay?" she asked.

"It's fine. Just a weird day." He forced a smile. "But I'm sure it's nothing."

Syph might have vanished, but her influence remained. Bonnie still had the unpleasant dreams and still felt as if she were walking around with an anvil strapped to her head, weighing her down, making her sluggish. The effects were diminished and her resistance to it was growing, but she still could sense the impending approach of crippling depression.

She took a shower. The hot water wasn't working. She had some burned toast. She had to eat it dry because her butter had gone rancid. Then she drove to Lucky's house and rang the doorbell.

Teri answered the door.

"Hi," said Bonnie. "I'm sorry to bother you, but can I speak to Lucky?"

"I don't think he came home last night, actually," said Teri.

"Oh."

Teri waited for Bonnie to say something else, but Bonnie had trouble slogging through her thoughts. She hadn't developed a contingency plan. She hadn't developed much of a plan at all.

"Can I help you with something?" asked Teri.

"I'm Bonnie. Bonnie Weinstein. You don't know me, but my goddess is stalking your god. And she's ruining my life. And I just wanted to talk to him because... well, I don't really have a clear reason for that. But I didn't have any better ideas, so I thought I'd give it a shot."

Bonnie glanced over Teri's shoulder and noticed Quetzalcoatl sitting on Teri's sofa.

"How many gods do you have living here?"

"Just two," said Teri.

"And they get along?" asked Bonnie.

"Maybe too well," replied Teri. "Would you like to come in?"

Bonnie hesitated, studying the giant serpent in their living room. She leaned in and whispered, "He's not going to eat me, is he?"

"Him? Oh, he's harmless."

Sensing Bonnie's discomfort with the feathered serpent on the couch, Teri led Bonnie into the dining room. That plan failed, though, when Quick slithered in to join them.

"Let me grab my husband," said Teri, leaving Bonnie alone with Quick.

"Hi, I'm Quick."

He extended his wing, and she gingerly shook it.

"You don't have to worry." He offered a sharp-toothed grin. "I filled up on waffles at breakfast, so you're perfectly safe."

Both were quiet until Teri returned with Phil.

"Bonnie is having some goddess problems that she says have something to do with Lucky."

Quick's colorful plumage fell flat. "Not Syph again."

"You know about this?" asked Phil.

"Oh, sure. It's been a thing she's had going for quite a while now. He was hoping she'd moved on this time."

Bonnie filled Teri and Phil in on the dangers of being an unwilling follower of a heartbreak goddess. Quick offered his own insight.

"It's something of an anomaly," he explained. "We gods don't fixate romantically. Not usually. It's just not in our nature to have long-term relationships. It's why we used to obsess over mortal lovers. Even if it's a lifelong commitment, it's only a mortal life. Over before you can get bored with it. Then again, most of us get bored long before that. But Syph is different. She just can't let it go.

"It's become her nature now. She can't help it. Every time Lucky starts dating, Syph just shows up. I don't think she even plans it. It just happens."

"Can't you stop her?" asked Bonnie. "Don't you gods have rules you have to follow? Isn't there some sort of peer pressure you can throw at her? Maybe an intervention?"

"I guess it's possible. But she's not doing anything serious. She's just killing a few mortals. Nobody is going to notice."

"I noticed," said Bonnie.

"You're right. It's important. I wasn't implying that you aren't a victim in all this, and that nobody should care. But the gods, most of them anyway, are far too irresponsible to get involved."

"What about you?" said Phil. "Can't you do something?"

"I wish I could. But I'm not Bonnie's god. There are rules in place to keep divine infighting to a minimum. And the most important is that a god will not directly intervene in the lives of another god's followers. Or even in the lives of those who have chosen to remain unaffiliated. Hands off. It's damage control. Too much bad press in the old days came from just doing whatever we wanted. So now we wait to be invited before we do anything. Most of us, anyway."

"But I didn't invite Syph," said Bonnie. "She chose me."

"That's kind of a gray area," admitted Quick, "but any sensible god will probably err on the side of caution. Better to let a few unfortunate mortals perish than get our hands dirty."

"That's terrific."

"There has to be something we can do," said Teri.

Quick smiled.

Bonnie scowled, thinking the god was getting off on her predicament. "What's so damned amusing?"

Quick said, "It's amazing. It really is. You mortals live such inconsequential lives, confined in tiny bodies, bound in tiny universes. Your time is so brief, and who could blame you if you decided to indulge your flicker of existence on every hedonistic impulse that entered your minds? But you still find time to care about each other, even strangers. It's inspiring."

"Does that mean you'll help me?" asked Bonnie.

He hesitated.

"You just said that gods live without consequences."

He flapped his wings in a shrug. "I'm just a minor deity at best. If I overstep my bounds, they'd probably make an example of me. I feel bad for you, Bonnie. But—"

"Just not enough to stick your neck out," said Bonnie.

He folded his wings and studied them rather than look at her. "Prometheus threw you a little fire and look what happened to him."

"I get it. Just another mortal screwed by the system. Why should you care?"

He mumbled an apology. The mortals stared across the table at each other for a few moments.

"That's it then. There's nothing we can do. I'm sorry to have bothered you." Bonnie stood. "I'll let myself out."

"Wait." Teri said, "We can at least talk to Lucky about this. He may not be your god, but he's mine, and this does involve him. And he's dating a friend of mine, too, so—" She turned to Quick. "You said this happens every time Lucky starts dating someone?"

"That's right."

"What happens to the mortal he's dating when this goddess enters the picture?"

Quick didn't answer.

"What happens?"

"What you think happens."

"You knew about this?"

He nodded.

"And you didn't warn us?"

"You're not my followers," he said.

"That's pretty low, Quick. I expected more from you."

The serpent god laid his head on the table and covered his eyes with his wings. "I wanted to tell you, but Lucky's my friend. I didn't think it was my place. I talked to him about it, and I'm pretty sure he was going to let you know."

"When? After my friend was blasted by a bolt of lightning?"

"Lightning isn't usually Syph's style," he replied.

She glared. The glitter went out of his scales and his rainbow feathers paled.

"I told you this god thing was a bad idea," said Teri.

That was only half-true. While Phil had been the one to come up with the idea, she'd been the one to convince him to go through with it. She stormed away before he could say anything, though that was just as well as this would probably be a bad time to remind her.

"I'm sorry, Phil," said Quick. "I thought about telling you, but it's complicated. There's a code of ethics."

"It's fine," replied Phil. "I get it. Lucky's your friend."

He deliberately avoided sounding judgmental. He couldn't blame Teri for being upset, but he couldn't help seeing it from Quick's perspective. Phil knew secrets about his friends and coworkers that he kept in confidence. And they knew things about him. There were secrets he even kept from Teri. Embarrassing bits from his past that he didn't deliberately hide but never mentioned. None of those bits were earth-shattering, but it was all a matter of scale.

"You're a good guy, Quick. Teri's just upset now. She'll get over it."

Quick smiled. "Do you really think so?"

"Sure."

Phil didn't qualify his statement by adding that he wasn't quite so positive that would be true if anything happened to Janet. He didn't see the point in saying it. It was just another thing left unsaid to make someone feel better. The irony didn't escape him.

Teri tried Janet's cell number. There was no answer. She tried Janet's home number next. Still no answer. She left messages, not saying too much, fearing Lucky might listen in on them.

She tried not to think the worst, but she couldn't stop thinking of Janet lying smote somewhere. And Lucky, that inconsiderate bastard, running off to Valhalla to pick up chicks without giving her a second thought.

Teri dialed again.

The doorbell rang. She thought of Lucky, coming home from an all-night bender after casually discarding another mortal life for his own amusement. She'd let him know just what she thought of that. Screw the consequences of a rebuked divinity. She didn't care. It was time to stop being pushed around by the whims of the gods. It was time for mortals to take a stand.

Her face twisted into a righteous scowl, she threw open the front door. Two men in dark blue suits greeted her. One of them was tall and balding with a pockmarked face, vaguely sinister. The other was unremarkable except for a pair of thick glasses.

"Hello, ma'am," said the taller one in a slow, deep voice. "We have a special offer for you from the temple of the lord of sunken dreams."

"No, thanks," she said. "I gave at the office."

She tried to close the door, but the tall one pushed it open. They shoved their way inside. The eyeglasses man pulled a pistol. He didn't point it at her, but its mere presence was enough to make her raise her hands.

"Are you alone?" he asked.

The taller one said, "Why are you asking her that, Eugene? We know she's not alone. We've been watching the place."

"I was testing her honesty, idiot. And you aren't

supposed to use my name, Rick." He waved his weapon at Teri. "Okay, miss. Where is everyone else?"

Teri didn't answer.

"I told you this was a bad idea," said Rick. "We should've waited."

The gunmen tried to hide their squabbling by whispering. They still didn't point their weapons directly at her. She could've possibly jumped the smaller one and taken away his gun. It might not have been that hard. But his partner wasn't likely to just stand aside and watch.

The men ordered Teri into the dining room. The serpent god sitting at the table didn't surprise them, but Eugene waved his gun at Bonnie.

"Who's this? Who the hell is this, Rick?"

"I dunno. Some lady?"

"You didn't mention her."

"So?"

"So you were supposed to be watching."

"She must've gone in when I wasn't looking."

"You were on lookout. Do you know what lookout means?"

"She's just one lady. I don't see what the big deal is."

"She's an unknown quantity." Eugene pointed. "We have the two followers and the serpent god. And that was supposed to be it."

"Excuse me." Quetzalcoatl raised a wing. "I hate to interrupt, but you do know who lives here, right?"

"You're not allowed to interfere," said Rick. "That's against the rules. Tell him, Eugene."

Quick said, "I know the rules. They aren't my followers. Not my problem."

"That's right." Eugene smirked. "So shut up. This doesn't concern you."

Quick shot across the dining room. He doubled in size, rearing up before the gunmen. His gold and silver scales sparkled, his plumage spread out like a rainbow-colored cobra's hood, and he opened his jaws wide enough to swallow a human whole. They fell to their knees, cowering before the terrifying deity.

His voice grew rough and rumbling. "You really have thought of everything, haven't you? I bet you even know that Lucky didn't come home last night."

They nodded.

"I can see you're a couple of sharp guys," said Quick. "You'd have to be sharp to try something like this. Or stupid. Sharp is keeping a watch on the house before making your move and knowing the rules. But stupid is taunting a god with your overconfidence. Stupid is not understanding that if you smirk at a god who doesn't have much to lose, he could easily forget the rules and devour two arrogant mortals who are threatening a group of people that he has grown fond of.

"I swore off human flesh a few hundred years ago." He licked his lips with his long, purple tongue. "But I'm feeling a bit peckish, and I think I just might fall off the wagon. Maybe an apology would help me curb my appetite."

"We're sorry," said Eugene while Rick whimpered.

Chuckling, Quick shrank to his normal human size. "Still got it." He helped the thugs get to their feet. "If anyone needs me, I'll be watching *Oprah*."

He offered Teri, Phil, and Bonnie a wink. They guessed it was meant to be reassuring, though it would've been more reassuring if he'd swallowed the thugs in two bites. He left the room instead.

All the mortals exchanged puzzled glances.

"Okay, then." Eugene waved his gun in a generally threatening manner. "You can put your hands down."

"What are you going to do?" asked Phil.

"Quiet!" growled Rick.

Eugene shot him a dirty look, and he shrugged.

"This is nothing personal," said Eugene. "You seem like nice people. But Gorgoz says you're supposed to die. And it's a great chance to earn a few extra points of favor."

"Pawns of the gods," added Rick, "carrying on their petty feuds. And if we don't do it, somebody else will. I know it's not a great consolation, but the order came down, and we're just trying to get a jump on this before someone else beats us to it."

"Showing a little initiative." Eugene pointed his gun at Teri.

"Wait!" Rick put his hand on his partner's weapon and pushed it down. "Who is going to shoot who?"

"I thought we discussed this. There are two of them and two of us. We each get one. That's the only fair way."

"But what if one is worth more than the other?"

"Gorgoz wants them both dead."

"But what if he wants one more dead than the other? I need more favor than you. I'm behind on my mortgage."

Eugene said, "The order didn't specify a preference."

"What about that one?" Rick pointed at Bonnie. "Do we have to kill her?"

"I guess. She is a witness, after all. We'll offer her up as a sacrifice to Gorgoz."

"Who gets to do it?" asked Rick.

"You do, okay? Happy?"

Rick smiled. "Yes."

Eugene rolled his eyes, raised his pistol, and cocked the hammer.

Phil stood and stepped between Eugene and his wife. "Kill me. But don't shoot the women."

"That's some misogynistic bullshit." Teri pushed him aside. "Kill me but let them go."

"This isn't a good time for feminism," he replied.

"Says you." She turned her eyes away from the guns trained on them. "You know how I feel about women and children first. It puts women in the same category as children. And I am not a child."

"I wasn't saying that. I was just trying to be noble."

"Because it's the man's job to be noble," she said, "and the woman's job to—"

"Dammit, this is not the time to be having this discussion!"

Bonnie stood. "Shoot me. I'm the one who is going to die anyway. Might as well get it out of the way."

"Excuse me," said Eugene. "But this is an assassination, not a negotiation. You're all going to get shot. There's no way around that."

"Although, for the record, miss," said Rick, "I agree with you that it's chauvinistic nonsense."

Teri slapped Phil on the shoulder. "See?"

Rick's cell rang, and he answered it. "Uh-huh. No, we haven't done it yet. No. Okay, okay. You're right. No, I haven't forgotten about the mortgage. Yes, I take this seriously."

Eugene cleared his throat loudly.

"Honey, I have to go." Rick hung up. "She said the

raccoon god just left that woman's apartment. We better do this fast."

Eugene pointed his gun again. Things were complicated by the three hostages each jostling to be in front of the bullet. He decided to just pull the trigger and let destiny pick the first victim.

His gun didn't fire.

"What's wrong?" asked Rick.

"It's not working."

"Is it jammed?"

"I don't know. I've never used one of these before."

"Try the slidey part on top. Isn't that what they usually do in the movies?"

Eugene fiddled with his weapon. It made a loud clack, and he yelped as it pinched the flesh of his palm.

"Is the safety on?" asked Rick.

"No, the safety isn't—"

The dining room echoed with the pop of a gunshot. Phil, Bonnie, and Teri checked themselves for holes. After a few seconds, everyone noticed a new hole in Rick's thigh and a red stain spreading across his slacks. He, oddly, was the last to notice.

"Oh, shit. You shot me!" It was a needless observation. The kind only made by someone who had never been shot before, who expected to just keel over in agony when struck by a bullet, when it rarely worked that way. "You asshole, you shot me!"

"It was an accident!" shouted Eugene. "I told you we should've bought revolvers. And taken that course on gun safety."

Rick leaned against the wall. "What kind of idiot points his gun at the one person in the room he doesn't want to shoot? You shouldn't need a class for that." He gingerly pinched the wound. "Gods, I'm going to bleed to death now."

"It doesn't look so bad. Did the bullet hit the bone?"

"How the hell should I know?"

"Did it feel like it hit the bone?"

"You want to know how it feels? It feels like some idiot shot me in the leg. That's how it feels!" Rick started to slide down the wall.

Eugene moved to brace his partner. Without thinking, he jammed his pistol down the front of his pants. There was another pop of gunfire.

"Oh gods, oh gods!" He fell to his knees. The bullet had missed his groin by less than an inch. It had drilled a bloody trench in his leg and the flash had burned some highly sensitive areas.

"You gods-damned moron!" shouted Rick, too obsessed with his own wound to notice the hostages sneaking out of the dining room.

Quick lay across the sofa. "Hi, gang. Just in time for *Family Feud.*"

"You knew that would happen," said Phil.

"This is the current residence of a god of good fortune and prosperity. Anyone who really understood the rules would know that trying to kill two of Lucky's followers in the house where he hangs his hat would be a bad idea."

Another gunshot echoed from the dining room, followed by more swearing.

"Sometimes initiative is a bad idea," said Quick with a smile.

Gods were lazy. It was their nature, the design of divine metaphysics. The most successful and influential of gods weren't the ones who had the most followers. They were the gods who did the least for the most and convinced everyone to overlook it. Zeus and Svarogich, the biggest divinities in North America, were also the two biggest clients of every reputable PR agency on the continent. It was no coincidence.

Janet knew all this. So she also knew that it was a pretty big deal when Lucky brought her breakfast in bed. It didn't require any divine power to pour milk over Cheerios (and they were her Cheerios and milk), but the mere act of offering a mortal anything without asking for something in return wasn't a casual act among gods.

"You're out of orange juice," said Lucky.

"Funny," she replied. "I was sure I had enough for one more glass."

"Nope. I checked."

He sat on the bed.

"So things are going pretty good between us, aren't they?" he said.

"Pretty good," she agreed.

"It's been a long time since I knew anyone I could just hang out with."

"What about you and Quick?"

"He's cool," said Lucky, "but it's different among mortals. Just more interesting."

"So that's what I have going for me? I'm mortal? Just a little slumming."

"I didn't mean it like that."

She rubbed his ear. "I know, baby."

He smiled. "I'm just saying that so far these last two weeks have been the highlight of this century."

"Mine, too," she said. "So far," she added with a grin.

He put his hands together and opened them, revealing a golden necklace with a silhouette of a raccoon head.

"Nice," she said.

"I want you to wear it."

"I don't know, Lucky. I'm not into jewelry. I know I'm a woman and I'm supposed to be, but I have enough trouble keeping track of earrings. And isn't this dangerously close to a talisman of fealty? Are you trying to make me into one of your followers?"

"Fine. Forget it." He tossed it away with an exaggerated motion, and the necklace disappeared. "No big deal."

Janet had been on the mortal end of more than one immortal fling. They were fun, casual, a chance to hobnob with immortals, have a few laughs, without any risk of getting serious. She liked it that way.

It didn't feel the same this time. She hadn't expected his reaction. He tried to pass it off, to hide it behind a devil-may-care smile. But she could tell by the way his whiskers drooped that he was disappointed. She wasn't sure how she felt about any of this herself. But she did want the necklace. Not because it was pretty. It wasn't. Or because it came from a god.

It was because it came from him.

"I was just kidding around," she said. "I'd love to wear it."

Lucky reproduced the necklace and put it on her.

"Are we going steady now?" she asked.

"I don't know. Are we?"

They shared an awkward smile. She playfully tweaked his ear.

Lucky glanced at his wrist, though he didn't have a watch. "I really should get out of here. Check on Phil and Teri."

"Sure."

"Uh, so I had a great time."

"Me, too."

She took a spoonful of cereal, chewing very slowly to force Lucky to carry the conversation. She wasn't sure what to say herself, and he was so cute when he stammered.

"Yeah. Okay." He hesitated, searching for the right words to end the conversation. "You did have one last glass of juice. I, uh, drank it."

"Oh, I know." She winked and imitated his trademark finger snap/gun point.

Lucky laughed.

He left. As soon as she heard the front door close, Janet

released a long sigh. This was getting complicated. She ran her fingers along the cool necklace.

"Damn."

Someone knocked on her front door. She jumped up, hoping it was Lucky but grabbing a robe just in case. Cinching up the robe, she answered the knock. Syph fixed Janet with a cold stare. The leaves of a nearby tree wilted and yellowed.

"Hey, you're that goddess," said Janet. "That one Lucky was talking to at the restaurant the other day."

"Yes, Luka and I are old friends," said Syph, "and we need to talk."

"You just missed him."

"No, I don't need to talk to him. I need to talk to you."

Janet leaned against the doorjamb. She appraised the goddess neutrally before grinning slightly.

"Sure. Come in. Want something to drink?" asked Janet. "I'm all out of juice, but I can make some coffee."

"Thank you. That would be lovely. That's a charming necklace, by the way."

"What? This old thing?" Janet chuckled. "I think it's a bit tacky, but it was a gift, so I wear it."

She puttered around the kitchen, rinsing out the coffeepot and starting the machine. It took a few minutes, and Syph said nothing. Janet almost thought the goddess had left. She didn't care enough to check until the coffeemaker beeped. She briefly debated pouring only one cup, but she took the chance. Syph sat on her couch.

"Want some milk?" asked Janet.

"I prefer it black," replied Syph. "I have a feeling your milk has gone sour anyway."

Janet sniffed the carton. "No, it's good."

She poured some into her coffee while Syph glared.

"So a little talk, huh? Just between us girls?" Janet sipped her steaming cup of coffee.

Syph frowned at her own cup. The liquid had frozen into a single block of brown ice. Janet didn't comment but couldn't resist stretching out her contented sigh a bit. She pushed forth her brightest smile, knowing it would irritate the hell out of Syph.

"What's up?" Janet added an extraneous lilt to the question.

"Enjoying your little tryst with a god, are you?"

"Sure. Lucky's cool."

Syph suppressed her snarl with only mild success.

"I'm glad you're having fun. It's nice for mortals to find some joy, considering how miserably short and meaningless your lives are. No offense."

Janet didn't drop her smile. "None taken."

Syph's displeasure manifested in a scowl. That was it. Nothing else changed. There was no drop in temperature, no broken glass, no cracks in the plaster or exploding lightbulbs. Aside from her own frozen coffee, the goddess had no effect, conscious or unconscious, on the environment.

"Lovely place you have here," said Syph. "Very... lived in."

"It's not much, but it's home."

"Luka was always enamored of the common mortal. Do you know, I don't think he ever abducted a nymph in his life. Even when it was all the rage. No, for Luka it was always about the peasants, the milkmaids, the mud-covered maidens toiling in the fields. Hardy stock with sturdy limbs and firm hips, but rarely the waifish type."

Syph made a show of appraising Janet. The goddess smiled wryly.

"I beg your pardon. I wasn't trying to insult you."

"Are you kidding?" said Janet. "I work very hard on these thick limbs. Do you know how many curls it takes to get this toned?"

Syph's face went blank.

"My, aren't you the pleasant little mortal?" she said with an icy tone.

"I try. I figure if I'm going to live a miserably short and meaningless life, I might as well make the most of it."

"An excellent philosophy," agreed Syph. She walked around the room, pretending to look around, but inwardly fuming. "But I do sometimes marvel that since your lives are already all too brief you don't take more care with them. So many foolish decisions to be made, and you always seem determined to make as many as you can."

"Eh, when you're mortal you know you're going to die," said Janet. "Most of us don't try to overthink it. I wouldn't expect you to understand, of course. You get to live forever and ever and ever."

Somehow, she made it sound like an insult.

"Long after you are moldering in the dirt and your bones have withered to powder, Lucky and I will still be walking this earth," said Syph. "Providing you mortals haven't blown it up by then."

"Or you gods haven't smote it to dust ahead of us," said Janet.

Syph and Janet dropped their polite smiles and locked stares.

"Very well," said the goddess. "Let's be direct, shall we?"

"Oh, let's," agreed Janet.

Syph said, "You're a smart woman. You've read your history. You know how this works."

"How does this work?" asked Janet with feigned wide-eyed curiosity.

A few red veins darkened the goddess's flesh. Her left eye twitched, but she otherwise maintained her composure. Though when she spoke there was an edge to her voice.

"You're a trifle, a momentary indulgence. You can't honestly believe he cares for you. You aren't that naïve."

"And how naïve am I?"

Syph set down her cup and walked to a wall. She pretended to adjust a hanging picture frame and caressed a fern. It didn't wither.

"Do you think you're the first hapless mortal he's seduced?"

Janet laughed. "Jeez, I hope not. Thoth knows he's not my first god. Although I admit you're my first jealous goddess."

"Luka is mine. He will always be mine."

"Okay. And what's that got to do with me?"

Syph said, "I'm giving you an opportunity to walk away. Before I am forced to intervene."

Janet laughed again.

"You find this amusing?"

"Sure. Why not? So you have a thing for Lucky. I get it. What I don't get is why you should care if he sows some wild oats along the way. Isn't that how it's usually done? I'm only mortal, right? You can have him back when he gets bored."

"Presumptuous cow, you dare dictate terms to me?"

Syph's skin paled, and her glowing red skeleton flashed.

She pointed at Janet with a twisted finger and unleashed a mournful howl. The goddess focused her displeasure on her romantic rival.

Syph's divine wrath battered against Lucky's affections with the effectiveness of a rubber ball thrown against a mountain. Sensing all her power metaphorically rolling limply to her feet, Syph ground her fangs.

The fangs were new.

"Well, this has been a barrel of laughs," Janet said, oblivious to the dark powers being focused against her. "But you should probably leave now."

The goddess burned, but Lucky's power kept her from mussing a single hair on Janet's head. It also prevented any changes in her apartment. Anything that would cause the slightest discomfort to this mortal trollop was held in check. The moods and desires of gods reached out to affect their environments, but Syph's were bottled up by Lucky's superior power. Her jealousy and anger built up inside her in the form of godly constipation. The tightness in her guts put her in a worse mood, which triggered more rage, which continued to build up in a nasty cycle.

The most irksome detail was the bizarre revelation that Lucky must really care for Janet. Syph could feel the fortress of divine protection built from Lucky's affections. And as long as that was in place, there was nothing Syph could do to Janet.

"The door is this way," said Janet, without fear of the raging goddess.

Syph fantasized about pouncing on Janet and strangling the life from this mortal the old-fashioned way. But she hadn't fallen that far yet, and direct smiting of that sort was prohibited in this day and age. Divine Affairs allowed her to ruin one mortal life at a time as long as she did so subtly. Bashing mortals over the head with her own hands, even if it was justified, would have consequences that even a fallen goddess should consider.

Syph had to leave this stifling apartment before all her bound-up wrath caused her to implode. She knew she wouldn't explode because that would make a terrible mess, and Lucky's protection would never allow that.

"I'm glad we had this little talk," said Janet as she showed Syph out. "I'll let Lucky know you dropped by."

She slammed the door before Syph could say anything else.

Syph's power surged outward. The earth rumbled. The sky darkened. Burning hail pelted the ground, setting the plants ablaze and scorching the grass. The foundation of a neighboring building in the complex collapsed, causing the structure to lean dangerously close to toppling.

None of these manifestations had any effect on Janet's building. And though the sidewalk was broken and shattered, Syph was certain that Janet hadn't felt so much as a tremor while nestled in her sanctuary.

It wouldn't last. Lucky was a god, and the affections of the gods were fleeting. When Lucky finally grew bored with her, she would be vulnerable. Of course, then Syph's jealousy would be meaningless, but she would still smite this arrogant mortal when that day came.

Syph was about to transmute into a molting dove and fly away when she sensed something, a disturbance in the metaphysical ether. She followed it to its source, a woman banging on an apartment door.

"Come on, Scott! I know you're home! I just want my DVD player! It's mine! You know it's mine!"

Syph observed the woman for a few moments as she kicked the door and unleashed a torrent of vulgarities. Eventually, she smacked her head against the door and grumbled.

"Excuse me," said Syph, "but is something wrong?"

The woman turned around. "Oh, sorry. I didn't mean to cause a racket. It's just that I broke up with this asshole a few weeks ago. Well, he broke up with me..." She shrugged. "Never mind. I'm sure you don't care."

"Actually," said Syph, "I do care. Perhaps you'd like to tell me about it."

The woman hesitated. "I don't know. I'm sure you mean well, but I'm not really looking for—"

"You've been wronged."

"It's just a DVD player," said the woman.

"No, it isn't. It's the way he used you, the way he tossed you aside when he was done, the lies, the wasted time, the hundreds of little concessions you made to make it work that didn't make one bit of difference in the end except to make your life harder." Syph swallowed her own rage and forced a smile. "It's never *just* a DVD player, is it?"

"No, I guess it isn't."

"I sense in you a lover wronged, a soul in need of divine aid. And I offer my services without obligation. Merely as a favor from one wronged soul to another. I'm the goddess of heartbreak and tragedy. But why don't you just call me Syph?"

"I'm Christine."

They sat on the front steps, and Christine told her story. It wasn't unique. She'd met a guy, dated awhile. Then he'd dumped her. Syph knew that there was nothing tragic or noteworthy about Christine's failed romance. That didn't prevent the goddess from empathizing.

"That's it," said Christine. "It wasn't a big deal. Wasn't like we were planning on getting married or anything. We weren't even very serious. All I want is my DVD player back. Is that too much to ask?"

"No, it isn't."

Syph approached the apartment door.

"It's locked," said Christine.

"No earthly lock can prevent the rightful wrath of the scorned lover."

Syph could've blown the door off its hinges or evaporated it or something equally dramatic. But she went the subtle route and turned the handle. The door opened.

Scott was in there, sitting on the couch, watching television. He looked up, potato chip crumbs nestled around the corner of his mouth. Before he could speak, Syph waved her hands to silence him.

"Foolish mortal!" she bellowed loudly enough to shake the walls. "You have wronged this woman, and I come bearing justice in her name and the name of all wronged lovers everywhere! Prepare to be cast into the pits of endless despair where unfathomable horrors shall tear at your flesh and nibble at your genitals beyond the end of time!"

Syph felt invigorated, energized. This was what she was meant to do. She gestured and opened a tear in the time/space continuum. The portal glowed bright green, putting a lime tint on everything in the apartment.

"And now...you..." She turned to Christine. "What was his name again?"

"Scott."

"And now, Scott. For your transgressions against love, the most heinous and unforgivable act any mortal or god can perform, I cast you into oblivion!"

Syph seized him by the T-shirt and dragged him to the portal. He was still too stunned to respond aside from gaping.

"Wait!" said Christine. "I didn't think you were allowed to do things like this."

"Technically, no," said Syph. "But who is going to tell?"

"I didn't want this."

The goddess paused. "But he wronged you."

"It was just a bad relationship. They happen all the time. Wasn't even really a relationship."

"But what about your DVD player?" asked Syph. "Doesn't it make you mad?"

Christine said, "Well, yeah. It is *my* DVD player. But I don't know if that warrants being thrown into Hell. Heck, it's not even that good a DVD player. Sometimes, it has trouble reading discs."

"It's true!" shouted Scott. "That thing is a piece of crap! Never worked right!"

Syph glared. The beasts in the pit howled for his blood.

"Okay, so I should've given it back," he replied. "I'm sorry. I really am. And I'm sorry about that time I got drunk and made out with your sister. Or that time I missed your birthday to go to Atlantic City with the guys so I lied and said my grandma was sick and I needed to fly out of town to see her. And I know I shouldn't have borrowed two hundred bucks for car repairs when it was really to put the down payment on a big-screen TV, and I can't blame you for hating me for that time I ran over your mom's cat and threw it in the garbage before anyone noticed, and—"

He paused to catch his breath.

"You didn't know about any of that, did you?" he said.

"How long did you date this guy?" asked Syph.

"Three months," replied Christine. "The sex was really good."

Scott couldn't suppress his satisfied grin.

"Toss him," said Christine.

Syph threw Scott into the swirling vortex. It sealed shut with a satisfied shriek.

"Vengeance is served," said Syph.

"Wait." Christine went to the kitchen and grabbed something to drink. "I can't do that. I can't send him to Hell just because he was a bad boyfriend."

"But what about all his sins? Don't you deserve vengeance?"

Christine shrugged. "I kind of knew he was a loser before we even started dating."

"But you offered him love, the greatest gift in all of Heaven and Earth—"

"Actually, I never loved him. I'm not sure I even liked him."

"But you could have," said Syph. "You could have loved him if he had given you a chance."

"Not really. I was just looking for a fling when we started dating. Kind of why I asked him out in the first place."

Syph stammered.

"That DVD player is a piece of crap," added Christine. "He can keep it."

Syph snapped her fingers. The portal opened and spat Scott back into the apartment. He was battered, bruised, and scratched, and his clothing was torn, but no serious injuries had taken place.

"You can destroy the TV," said Christine to the disappointed goddess.

The television fell into the shrieking portal. The unknowable horrors were audibly disappointed not to have a soul to rend, but they satisfied themselves by switching on a baseball game before the portal closed.

"Justice is served." Syph leveled an accusing finger at Scott, who was too dazed to pay much attention. "May you learn the errors of your ways, heartless mortal. Love is a blessing from above and any fool who spurns it shall face the wrath of the heavens themselves."

She filled the apartment with absolute silence as she stared deep into his eyes.

"Pray we do not meet again."

Syph and Christine left the apartment.

"Thanks," said Christine. "What do I owe you?"

"Oh, it was no problem. I couldn't take anything."

"I've never actually done this before. Is tipping allowed? Or is that frowned upon?"

"It's not necessary."

"I insist. Is five dollars okay?"

Christine handed Syph some cash. The second Syph touched the money, she sensed a surge in the cosmic balance. It wasn't the money itself, but the act of offering tribute. It had been centuries since Syph had been offered a willing tribute, ages since she'd met a mortal who wasn't unhappy to know her. She'd forgotten what it felt like.

That was the secret to a god's power and why she was unable to harm Janet. Lucky was a minor god, but he did have his followers. More than Syph had. It was all about tribute, and she couldn't match his because she'd spent the past thousand years moping, neglecting her followers.

No wonder Lucky didn't respect her. She wasn't much of a goddess at all anymore. Any god in the universe could thwart her power.

"Oh," Syph said to the departing Christine, "if later tonight you feel like pouring a bottle of wine down the sink in my name, I wouldn't complain."

"Sure."

"The good stuff," added Syph. "Preferably something that doesn't come in a box."

"Okay." Christine skipped away quickly.

Syph was in mid-transformation when Scott poked his head out of his apartment.

"Uh, excuse me."

"Yes," she replied coldly.

"You're a goddess of scorned lovers?"

"More or less."

He approached tentatively. "Do you help guys, too? Or do you strictly work for chicks?"

Syph pondered the question. She hadn't thought about it.

"See, there was this chick named Stella," he continued, "and she totally screwed me over. She keyed my car. And she faked a pregnancy to get some extra bucks out of me. And she took my dog."

"Your dog?" repeated Syph thoughtfully. "In all of Heaven and Earth, there is nothing so embodied of unconditional love as that of our loyal canine companions."

Scott perked up. "So you'll do it? You'll help me out?"

"I might." Syph examined the crisp five-dollar bill in her hand. "It all depends on what you are willing to do for me."

Teri and Phil weren't happy to discover they were in the middle of an illegal holy war. They were even more upset to be informed of this by a pair of Divine Affairs agents on their front lawn.

A gray sedan, an ambulance, and a police cruiser were parked outside their house. Curious neighbors gawked from their own front porches or peeked out their windows. Neither Phil nor Teri was the kind to be overly concerned about their neighbors, but it was a hell of a commotion. Especially the sedan and the two Divine Affairs agents who came with it. Divine Affairs made people nervous, and rightfully so. Most gods played by the rules. But not every god. And the rogue gods were just as dangerous as in the history books. Even a little bit more so since the hubris of mortals only made these untamed gods more wrathful.

The agents operated in pairs, one mortal and one immortal. Agent Watson, the mortal, was a lanky man in standard Divine Affairs gray. The immortal agent was a muse named Agent Melody. Her suit was bright purple and her every gesture seemed as if it should have been set to music. Wagner would've been inspired to write a four-second symphony just by watching her remove a pen and paper from her coat pocket.

Phil was slightly more artistic than his wife. Just enough that being near Agent Melody, he found himself distracted, composing haikus in his head and having difficulty concentrating.

The ambulance sirens blared as it pulled away from the curb, taking the two failed assassins with it.

"How are they?" asked Teri.

Watson replied, "They seem to have suffered a total of five self-inflicted gunshot wounds. Also, one of them somehow managed to burn himself on your stove and got a corkscrew stuck up his nose."

Neither Teri nor Phil could remember ever even buying a corkscrew.

"According to the paramedics," said Melody, "none of the injuries should be fatal."

"That's good," said Teri automatically, though she didn't know why she cared about the health of two people who had tried to kill her. Even if they had failed miserably, they were still assassins.

"They mentioned something about Gorgax," said Phil.

"Gorgoz," corrected Watson. "According to our records this Gorgoz is a deity engaged in a holy war with your own registered god."

"But that's illegal," said Teri.

"Yes, miss. Rest assured that we take these violations of Divine Treaty very seriously."

"Are you currently engaged in polytheistic worship?" asked Watson.

"No," said Phil. "We just have the one."

"You do realize that it is deemed unlawful to follow a god without registering?"

Phil and Teri nodded.

"Are you sure you don't want to reconsider your previous statement?" asked Melody.

"We only have one god," said Phil.

"Can you explain the presence of an unregistered deity in your home then?"

They followed the agents' gaze to Quick, who was talking to another pair of agents.

"Oh, that's just Quick," said Teri. "He's not our god. He just sleeps on our couch."

"He's a friend of Lucky's," added Phil.

The agents exchanged an unreadable glance.

"It's not a crime to let a god crash at our place," said Teri, perhaps a bit too defensively. "We don't follow him. We don't offer him tribute."

"According to Article Seventy-one of the Divine Affairs Treaty, offers of lodging qualify as tribute."

"We didn't offer it," said Teri. "He just started doing it."

"I see," said Melody. "Would you like to file an official complaint then?"

Phil and Teri both had the same thought. They weren't sure how they felt about Quick in their home, but they'd come to like him over the past few weeks. They didn't want to get him into trouble, but they weren't feeling very charitable toward gods in general.

"Maybe," said Phil uneasily.

"Can we get back to this holy war thing?" asked Teri. "How does something like that still happen in this day and age? And why weren't we told about it before we registered with Lucky?"

Watson's cell phone rang. He walked away to answer it.

"It happens," said Melody. "Though at this stage the holy wars are more underground, less obvious. More like holy guerrilla wars. Most gods play by the rules. But some can't stomach having to live by rules at all. So they went underground, where they still find followers among the unscrupulous. As for your god... well... he has no legal obligation to inform you of this."

"What kind of system doesn't tell people they're getting in the middle of a holy war?"

"It's a complicated issue, miss," replied the agent, "but Divine Affairs is not just for the protection of mortals. The gods have rights, too."

"Including the right to lie?"

"Technically, it's nondisclosure, miss. Would you appreciate having your dirty laundry posted to the public record?"

"My dirty laundry doesn't get people killed."

"Correct me if I'm wrong, but you did agree to this, didn't you? No one forced you into it."

Teri fumed. "This is unbelievable. We're almost killed, and you're blaming us."

"We see a lot of this, Mrs. Robinson. Perhaps you should've considered your decision more carefully."

Teri shot her a glare, then looked to Phil to rise to her defense. But he didn't disagree with the agent. And he didn't see any benefit in arguing. This wasn't the time to point fingers.

She stormed away, grumbling. Phil considered going after her, but it was probably better to let her cool off.

"If you would like to sever your relationship with your god," said Melody, "we can start the paperwork. It can take a while, though, and there are penalties."

Phil's first reaction was to say yes to the offer. But the penalties part made him hesitate. The law didn't just protect mortals from the capricious nature of the gods. It protected the gods from the fickle nature of mortals. There had to be stability, a reliable exchange of tribute and favor. He got all that. It wasn't a perfect system, but it was the best they had. And even if it had its flaws, it had kept things in order. No longer did mortals have to fear seeing their city erupt in fire and brimstone just because a few of their mortals offended a powerful deity who didn't understand subtlety. Now if your house blew up, you'd earned it. Or at least put yourself in the line of wrath, even if indirectly.

"No, it's okay," he said. "Maybe later. How long has this holy war been going on?"

"I'm sorry, but that's—"

"Privileged information," he said. "I got it."

Watson returned. "Mr. Robinson, was there an incident in your office this Tuesday?"

"My boss had a heart attack." The realization dawned on him slowly, but the agents gave him time.

"Wait. Oh my . . . it wasn't an accident, was it?"

"We aren't allowed to discuss pending investigations in detail."

Phil shook his head. "Oh, come on. This isn't right. We must have some rights. It's bad enough our own god failed to mention we might get killed just for letting him sleep in our spare bedroom. Now you ask me about a mysterious death and don't want to give me any information. How is that fair?"

Agent Melody shrugged. "A forensic team turned up a death rune written on his coffee mug. It was written in invisible ink. We're lucky to have caught it."

"Somebody killed him?"

"In a manner of speaking," said Agent Melody. "We believe he was trying to kill you and that the attempt backfired. You were supposed to drink from the mug. He most likely planned to switch it out so that there would be no evidence, making it look like a coronary. Probably would have worked, too, if he hadn't mixed up the cups. Lucky break for you, Mr. Robinson."

"Yeah, lucky."

But it hadn't been blind luck. If Phil hadn't spilled his coffee, if he hadn't switched mugs to try and cover the mistake, he'd be dead right now. Lucky had neglected to mention Gorgoz, but Lucky's influence had also saved Phil's life. It was complicated.

"A search of Rosenquist's home turned up a secret altar and contraband paraphernalia," added Watson. "From the looks of things, we think he was giving tribute to Gorgoz."

"But he was a business executive," said Phil. "Why would he be following an illegal god?"

"Happens more than you might think," said the mortal. "Statistically, most unsanctioned tribute is committed by the middle class."

Phil didn't know what to think. Like most everyone, he was inclined to imagine the temple underground populated by lowlifes, thugs, and murderers. Those people who couldn't get ahead in this world and turned to the dark gods in desperation. But that really made no sense. Why wouldn't people who were willing to invoke unethical and dangerous powers get ahead? He'd met plenty of middle management and been impressed with their complete lack of practical job skills.

And what about all those other employees who were promoted, never to be seen again, despite promises to "keep in touch"? Were they inducted into a secret cabal, too busy engaging in ritual sacrifice and secret ceremonies to return phone calls or even just drop by and say hi? Or even more sinisterly, were their promotions just a ruse, an excuse for a convenient transfer to some obscure position in another city so that no one would question their disappearance, another sacrifice to dark gods to facilitate the sinister boardroom dealings?

It sure as hell would explain a lot.

"What are we supposed to do now?" asked Phil.

"I can understand your concerns, Mr. Robinson," said Agent Watson, "but you can rest assured that we're on top of this. These sort of incidents are the exception, not the norm. And Divine Affairs is very good at dealing with them."

"What's that mean?"

"It means we stand by our record," replied Agent Melody.

"And what record is that?" asked Phil.

The agents turned their backs and exchanged whispers.

Divine Affairs offered vague reassurances, but nothing tangible. There was a twisted god out there, somewhere, issuing death warrants for Phil and Teri. Their own god, meanwhile, didn't appear as trustworthy as they'd hoped. And he wasn't anywhere to be found. Maybe he'd heard about the incident and flown back to Wisconsin rather than stick around and face the wrath of Teri.

Phil waited for the agents to finish their conversation, though he was positive they wouldn't have any real help to offer. Just a vague promise to look into things and get back to him. They'd give him some phone number to call in case of trouble to make him feel better, but what good could it be?

"Cripes," he groaned as he looked to the heavens, which now appeared so indifferent to his problems, more than ever before. And he spotted his god floating overhead in his signature globe of light.

He had no idea how long Lucky had been hovering there. The god chewed on a piece of beef jerky, sipped on a Big Gulp, and surveyed the scene. He spotted Phil, shrugged, and descended to earth reluctantly. Before Phil could speak with him, the agents pulled Lucky aside.

Phil waited for his shot at his god. While he waited, Teri and Quick returned.

"Don't be too hard on him," said Quick. "He's not such a bad guy, really."

Phil and Teri were having none of it. They wouldn't have been surprised if, after finishing his conversation with the agents, Lucky had flown away rather than talk to them. But he didn't.

"Hey, buddy," he said with every ounce of carefree charm, "how's it going?"

"Not so good," replied Phil.

"So I gathered." Lucky's smile dropped. "I know this looks bad—"

"You're damn right it looks bad. It looks worse than bad. We were almost killed, sacrificed as tribute to some evil god with a grudge against you."

"I can explain—"

"You lied to us."

"I never said—"

"Lying by omission is still lying. And what about those red animals? When I specifically asked you about them, you said they were no big deal. But they are a big deal after all. They have something to do with Gorgoz, right?"

"They usually go away after a while," said Lucky. "So maybe I should've mentioned it. But I'm immortal. I bring a lot of baggage with me. I can't be expected to remember every little incident from the past that might be of consequence today. It's been a while since Gorgoz tried anything like this. I'd just assumed that he'd gotten over it by now. A few hundred years is usually enough for any god. Damn, when Ngai found out I slept with his wife he vowed eternal revenge, too. But now we play poker and laugh about it over beers. That's the way it works. Maybe in the old days we could nurse a grudge, but that old-way bullshit doesn't happen anymore. At least, it's not supposed to happen anymore."

"But it did happen," said Teri, "and it nearly happened to us."

"I'm on top of it," said Lucky.

"Stop lying." She thrust her finger at him. "You're full of crap."

"I know you're upset, Teri, so I'll overlook—"

"No. You're not going to turn this around and make it about us. We didn't do anything wrong. You're the wrong one. You're the one who let us down. We came into this straight. We did what we promised. And you promised to look after us, to help us out. And the last time I checked, keeping us from getting killed by some rogue god is your job."

He withered under her glare.

"Do your job, Lucky. Or get the hell out of my house."

She marched away, going inside, slamming the door.

"She's just upset," said Phil.

The door opened. Teri stuck her head out.

"And Phil, don't you dare apologize for me!"

She slammed the door shut again.

Phil paused, torn between placating his god and his wife.

"Go on, Phil," said Lucky. "She needs you."

"Please, don't smite her," said Phil hastily as he ran into the house.

Lucky sucked on the straw, even as the gurgling noise indicated that the cup was empty.

"She's right," said Quick.

"Yeah. Maybe." Lucky chewed on a piece of ice. "All I know is that if I confront Gorgoz, he's going to kick my ass all across the Milky Way. And I'd rather not have that."

"Maybe if you tried apologizing, he'd forget the whole thing."

"First of all," said Lucky, "I'm not apologizing. I didn't do anything wrong. Secondly, it wouldn't make any difference. You know that. We're way past the apology stage."

"You could move out."

"If I move out, they're as good as dead. Without all the good fortune that comes from my presence, they'll be fodder for Gorgoz's minions."

They sat on the porch and ran over the problem several times. They didn't know where Gorgoz was hiding. And even if they did find him, they couldn't fight him. Lucky could keep Gorgoz's followers in check for a while, perhaps even years. But even the most powerful god of good fortune couldn't prevent every assassination attempt. Eventually, by the law of averages, one would succeed.

The problem was bigger than two gods could handle. And Divine Affairs might be able to find Gorgoz one day and put an end to his reign of terror. But that day was a long way off.

"Too bad we can't question those two moronic assassins," said Lucky.

"They wouldn't know anything," said Quick.

"Worth a try at least."

"Divine Affairs would never allow it."

"Yeah. Too bad. But what they don't know can't hurt us."

"What's that mean?"

"Why bother talking to the mortal when you can go right to the source? Does Morpheus still owe you that favor?"

"Why?"

"Maybe it's time you cashed it in."

"What are you getting at?" asked Quick.

Lucky smiled.

"Oh no. He'd never go along with it," said Quick.

"Can't hurt to talk to him, can it? And you forget"— Lucky winked—"I can be very persuasive."

"Should we tell them?" asked Quick, nodding toward the house.

"No reason to get their hopes up just yet."

"You realize this is a long shot," said Quick.

"You're forgetting something, buddy."

Lucky winked as the gods shot off into the sky.

"Long shots are my specialty."

18

It was Worthington's job to keep Gorgoz happy. A steady diet of beer and snack cakes, a big-screen television with a complete cable package, a massage chair, a small river of blood. These were usually all it took. And as long as Gorgoz was happy, Worthington's world was fine.

Gauging Gorgoz's happiness was difficult based on the god's behavior. He never left the basement and he rarely smiled. And when he spoke, his voice was rough and dour. Even his laugh, the few times Worthington had heard it, was a joyless scraping thing. Worthington was forced to rely on other signs and portents.

Six of his stocks had taken a big hit. And over a dozen people had lost fingers to faulty paper clips coming out of his Korean factories. And one of his real estate developments had burned to the ground, killing just over a hundred people. The deaths and mutilations meant nothing to him outside of requiring some out-of-court settlements. The incidents would barely register as a hiccup on his financial reports. But left unchecked, these omens could herald his undoing.

Worthington grabbed a six-pack of Old Milwaukee and a bag of pretzels and headed to the basement sanctuary of his crabby god. The bright flicker of *Leave It to Beaver* illuminated his darkened lair. He didn't take his eyes off the television as Worthington descended the stairs. Worthington kept his head bowed as he approached with his offerings.

"O glorious master, who dwells in eternal darkness, from death you arose and death shall be your gift to this world. This humble servant—"

Gorgoz snatched the beer and pretzels. He stuck a can in his toothy jaws and sheared the top off of it, chugging it down. Despite the size of his mouth, he managed to spill most of the beverage down his shirt and bathrobe.

"Are they dead?" he asked.

"I'm afraid not, Master."

Gorgoz growled.

"Am I not a generous benefactor, Worthington?"

"Yes, Master."

"And haven't I provided you with the wealth and power you pathetic mortals covet so?"

"Yes, Master."

"And all I ask is complete obedience. Yet now you disobey me."

"I didn't disobey."

"You have failed me."

"No, Master. It wasn't I, but other disciples who—"

"I don't need excuses for a botched job. As most favored among my disciples, their failures are your failures as far as I'm concerned."

Gorgoz slit the bag with the long claw on his index finger. He grabbed a handful of pretzels and tossed them into his mouth. His oddly shaped mouth and teeth spewed crumbs and sticky drool as he decreed, "Bring the offending incompetent before me so that I might devour him for his ineptitude."

"I'm afraid he's already dead."

Gorgoz's bulbous eyes narrowed. "Disappointing. Was it a painful death?"

"Most assuredly, Master," Worthington quickly replied, though he didn't know the details. His position of First Disciple among Gorgoz's followers allowed him control over a network of unscrupulous individuals willing to do whatever it took to gain power. Even engage in illegal worship of forsaken gods. Yet even he wasn't certain how far his reach extended because the followers of Gorgoz were a secretive lot. He made it a point to know only as much as he needed to know.

He had direct communication with only a handful of others in the temple. And they, in turn, had the same. Decrees among Gorgoz's disciples were like living things, sent out into the world to complete themselves as disciples competed for his favor. It wasn't the most efficient system in the world and it could lead to backstabbing and infighting within the temple, but these were necessary evils when you were following a god of chaos.

"Seems like it might just be easier to get up and kill these mortals myself." Gorgoz smiled sinisterly. "Might be good for me to get out of this place, roll up my sleeves, and do some personal smiting. Been too long, really. I really should stay in practice."

Worthington didn't like the sound of that. He liked

Gorgoz lounging in the basement. The dark god was too chaotic for him to be allowed to run around unchecked. All sorts of problems could arise then.

Worthington fell to his knees and prostrated himself before Gorgoz. "I beg your forgiveness. Give me another chance. Allow me to slay these foolish mortals and prove my devotion. I am unworthy to bask in your horrid aura. How may I—"

"Quiet." The god nodded to the television. "I can't hear Wally and the Beaver with all your ass-kissing."

Worthington stood and took a seat. Gorgoz chuckled as Wally called Beaver "a goof," then muted the sound.

"If I could go back in time, I'd give that Barbara Billingsley a good bang," said Gorgoz. "And rip off Hugh Beaumont's head. Preachy son of a bitch."

He leaned forward and for a second, it appeared as if he might actually rise from his recliner. But, of course, he didn't. Worthington wondered if gods could get bedsores. Gorgoz's greenish-blackish-reddish-grayish skin, what Worthington could see of it, was already moist and oozing and his ass was probably much the same.

"I am displeased and demand a tribute of blood from all my followers as appeasement."

"Yes, Master."

"Quiet. I'm not finished."

"Yes, Master."

The god snorted. "Each of my disciples must steal a thousand dollars and then burn it in my name."

He tapped his long black nails together.

"Also, they must eat a raw gopher."

"A gopher?"

"Yes, a gopher!" growled Gorgoz. "The whole thing!"

"Even the bones?"

"Did I stutter?"

"It's just, well, you do realize that we mortals don't have the correct teeth or jaws to eat a gopher? It might be a little difficult."

"Of course it will be difficult," grumbled Gorgoz. "That's why it's penance. If it was easy, it wouldn't be penance, would it?"

"But—"

He sighed. "You can put the bones in a blender or something if you have to."

"Blenders can't break down bones."

"What about a rock tumbler?" suggested Gorgoz. "Something like that."

"That might work," agreed Worthington, "but it still seems impractical."

Gorgoz shook his head. "Fine, fine. You don't have to eat the bones. But everything else! So I decree!"

"Even the fur?"

"Everything!"

"As you command, glorious—"

"Will you shut up? I'm not done."

"You aren't? Forgive me for saying so, Master, but isn't this unusually harsh? Even by your rigid standards."

The basement quaked with Gorgoz's displeasure.

"What is it about these two specific people that has attracted your wrath?" asked Worthington. "If I may be so bold as to ask. How have they offended you? Does this have something to do with the raccoon god?"

"You presume too much."

"I only wish to serve you better."

"Your lot is to do as I say. Blind devotion is all that is required to serve me."

"As you decree." Worthington turned to leave, but he was interrupted by Gorgoz.

"Five thousand and forty-three," said Gorgoz softly.

"I most humbly beg your pardon."

"Five thousand and forty-three followers," explained Gorgoz. "That is how many the raccoon god has now. Do you know how many I have?"

"No."

"Five thousand and forty-three." The god snarled. "Make that 5,042. Do you see the problem now?"

Worthington knew of Gorgoz's rivalry with the raccoon god, though he didn't know the origin of it.

"If you would permit me, Master, to make a suggestion. If this bothers you, we could always send out an order to thin the ranks of this false god."

"No, it has to be these two."

Worthington had done some research on Phil and Teri Robinson. They seemed perfectly unremarkable.

"He lives with them," said Gorgoz. "In their home. They are his favored children, and for that sin, they must perish. And after they are dead, torn to pieces before his very eyes, he shall know that my power is greater than his and that he shall always dwell in my shadow."

He laughed, long and hard, and the walls began to bleed thick black syrup that smelled of old blood.

"Oookay," said Worthington. "If that's all you'll be needing then..."

"Wait. I didn't finish my demands of penance."

"There's more?"

"Yes. And as a final act of contrition I demand that . . . hey, what time is it?"

"Five till nine," replied Worthington.

"Oh, *Gunsmoke* is almost on."

Worthington took advantage of the distraction and slipped away as Gorgoz started flipping through channels.

19

The Somnambulist Café sat on the edge of the collective unconscious of humanity. It was smallish. Or biggish. Or any size in between depending on what mortals were asleep at the time and what they were dreaming. Right now it was on the biggish side of smallish. The exterior resembled a termite mound while the inside was filled with furniture made of chocolate, including the chairs Lucky, Quick, and Morpheus sat in.

The god of dreams sipped coffee from a cup in the shape of a life-size chicken. It was awkward to use. The handle on the side was small and inconveniently placed. Even if Morpheus had tried to hold it, it wouldn't have been much good. Two hands were required to keep the chicken from wandering away.

Morpheus yawned. "You can't be serious."

Lucky had ordered a tuna melt but the moose-headed waiter had brought a feather between two neatly folded tweed sweaters. He pretended to nibble at it anyway so that Quick could do the talking. But Quick just used his spoon to stir his pink lollipop soup.

"It's against the rules," replied Morpheus. "You know that."

"I know," said Quick.

Morpheus tried to give Quick a hard glare, but the god of dreams had trouble keeping his eyes wider than halfway open for more than a few seconds.

"It's unethical," said Morpheus. "I am charged with safeguarding the realm of the human subconscious, and it is not a duty I take lightly."

"I know, I know. Believe me, we wouldn't be asking if it wasn't important."

Morpheus set down his cup and stretched. The chicken hopped off the table and marched away, spilling coffee all over the cobblestone floor. A robotic waiter covered in jewels instantly delivered a fresh cup in the shape of a miniature television playing an episode of *The Honeymooners*.

"Is this decaf?" asked Morpheus.

The robot beeped in reply, and it seemed to satisfy the god.

"I don't want to be up all night," Morpheus explained to Quick. "The answer is no. We gods of dream and reverie live by a different code than you divinities of the physical realm. We take our responsibilities very seriously."

Lucky cleared his throat and elbowed Quick. Quick shrugged.

"Oh, for Ymir's sake," said Lucky. "Look, Morph. Can I call you Morph?"

Morpheus yawned. "Yeah, sure."

"Morph," said Lucky, "this is about responsibilities.

There are two very nice mortals who are depending on me to do the right thing and look out for them. That's my responsibility, and I take it seriously, too."

The god of sleep rubbed his eyes. "I could get in trouble."

"What? You're allowed to go in there, right? That's your province, isn't it?"

"It's not like it used to be," said Morpheus. "The unconscious is highly regulated now. We aren't allowed to muck about."

"Who said anything about mucking about? All I'm asking is for you to show me the way to one mortal's unconscious so I can have a brief Q and A with his unconscious. I'm not going to plant any suggestions or steal his dreams or rearrange his mental furniture in the slightest. In and out, gone before anyone even notices we were there."

"I'm still not sure of the ethical—"

"Screw it." Lucky pointed to Quick. "You owe him, and he's calling in the favor."

Morpheus said, "So that's it then? That's what it's all about, Quick?"

The golden serpent god's feathers ruffled. "They're really very nice mortals we're trying to help."

"Okay." Morpheus scowled, but it degenerated into a yawn. "But then we're even."

The entrance to the collective unconscious was behind the café. From the outside, the realm looked like a giant warehouse. Nothing fancy or terribly metaphorical about it. Although that was really the symbolism of it. The unconscious looked like nothing from the outside. It was only beneath the surface that anything interesting was happening.

There wasn't a guard. Just a velvet rope with a warning sign about venturing inside with great care. The collective unconscious of humanity was a twisting maze of hallways. Mortals thought their dreams were unique to them, but the collective unconscious had a central casting office. But one giant spider or Amazon space princess was just as good as any other. The assembled phantasms and phobias of humanity roamed the labyrinth.

"Hi, Morpheus," said a passing five-headed mother-in-law beast.

"Hi, Vera," replied the god of dreams.

Without a guide, it was difficult to navigate the labyrinth. Not dangerous but confusing. It could take hours to find the right soundstage. The doors were marked, but not in a reliable way. Some had initials. Others had faces. And some had cryptic symbols or pictograms. They passed a door with a cave painting of a man battling a gerbil in a top hat.

Morpheus led them down the halls. Lucky and Quick didn't even try to keep track of the route. It would've changed if they'd tried to backtrack. Even gods could get lost in the realm of dreams.

They stopped at a door inscribed with the name GERALD.

"This is it?" asked Lucky.

"This is it."

"But the guy we're looking for is named Rick."

Morpheus said, "Do I tell you how to find winning lottery tickets?"

"Fair enough," admitted Lucky as the god of dreams opened the door.

They entered the soundstage of Rick's dreams. Props

littered the set, which was in mid-construction. The cast
of characters sat around, waiting. Building dreams was a
complicated affair, and at least half of the cast would be
shuttled out before the mortal architect fell asleep. Whatever passed through the dreamer's mind, conscious and
unconscious, would shape the show. This was why mortal
dreams were so confusing. It wasn't because the unconscious was revealing transcendent mysteries or the dreaming mind was unable to maintain a coherent thought. No,
it was simply central casting and the prop department
being unable to keep up with last-minute rewrites.

"Hey, Rita," said Morpheus to a Vegas showgirl.

She nodded to him, sucking on a cigarette as a wardrobe assistant slipped her out of a pleather catsuit and into
a pair of long johns.

"Recognize this guy?" asked Quick, pointing to a lanky
cast member concealed in a voluminous brown robe. His
mottled arms were long and scaly. It was a dead-on like-
ness of Gorgoz except for the chubby face. A makeup
assistant was still painting the spots on there.

"This must be the place," said Lucky. "Cripes, do you
think he still looks like that?"

"He always was slow to change," said Quick.

"Yeah, it's no wonder he had to go underground."
Lucky chuckled. "That might've impressed the yokels at
the dawn of time, but you have to update every so often."

They found the director of this mortal dreamscape sitting in a darkened corner, watching a small TV set playing
out his waking life. He stared intently at the small black-
and-white screen and strained to hear the low sound.

"Excuse me," said Lucky.

The director looked up, put a finger to his lips.

"Sorry to bother you, but—"

The director repeated the gesture, this time following it with a loud shushing sound.

Lucky stepped between the director and his television. "This will only take a few minutes of your time."

"Are you supposed to be in here? Where's your authorization?"

Morpheus waved a badge. The director checked it twice, then shrugged. "Okay. Whatever. I can never follow that show anyway. I don't know what the hell that guy is doing half the time."

"We have some questions about Gorgoz," said Lucky.

The director shuddered. "Him? Did he send you? Are you here to punish me for my failure?"

"We're not with him," said Quick absently as he picked through the catering cart. He sniffed a pig in a blanket. "We're looking for him."

"Why?"

"Because he needs to be stopped," said Lucky.

The director laughed. "Gorgoz is more dangerous than you can imagine."

"He's old news," said Lucky, "a relic."

"Precisely," said the director. "He doesn't care about the new rules. He's still playing the game the old-fashioned way. It might limit his power, but he's a lot more willing to use the power he does have. He's a cornered beast. And he doesn't give two shits about civilization or you or me or even himself. He sees himself on the top and everyone, mortal and immortal, is beneath him. And he'll burn the world to a cinder rather than compromise that ruthless ideal."

The lighting on the soundstage dimmed as the director

spoke. The crew put tints over the spotlights to tinge the air red. The carpenters quickly tore down the set as a new set of walls was wheeled in to make a shadowy and darkened room.

Gorgoz's phantasm grew taller and more menacing. He flipped his hood into place, hiding his face except for his two huge bloodshot eyes.

"If you thought he was so damn dangerous," asked Lucky, "why would you choose to follow him?"

"Why wouldn't I?" replied the director. "I needed an edge, and why would I settle with a small boon from a castrated deity when I could have access to all the raw power of a true primordial force? No offense about the castration comment."

"None taken," said Quick.

"And now it's gone bad." The director said, "Well, I guess I can't complain. I made my decision. Nothing to do but watch it play out."

"You're awfully calm about this."

"Hey, it's his problem." The director pointed toward the television. "Not mine."

Lucky pondered how the subconscious could be so blithely oblivious to the perils of its physical aspect. But then again, why should anyone expect a mortal's subconscious to be any more logical than any other part of his mind?

"Would you mind telling us where to find Gorgoz?" asked Lucky.

"I wouldn't mind," said the director, "but I don't really know. I did meet him once, but it was a secret ritual in an undisclosed location."

"Can you remember anything? Anything at all?"

"It was a few years ago. The details are kind of fuzzy. It was a dark room. Dusty. Smelled like rotten fish."

Several stagehands rushed in, throwing sawdust into the air. Several others carried in buckets of carp, placing the buckets in out-of-the-way corners. The director walked over to the set.

"There was a bunch of neophytes there. We all had on robes to hide our faces." Phantasm players crowded the set behind him. A wardrobe assistant threw a robe on the director. "There was the traditional Dirge of Gorgoz." He knelt before the phantasm in Gorgoz's role. They started chanting.

"Excuse me," said Lucky, pointing to a robed figure standing beside Gorgoz. "Hate to interrupt, but who is that?"

The actors in the memory kept chanting, but the director raised his head.

"That's Gorgoz's First Disciple," he said.

"You didn't see his face, did you?" asked Lucky.

"Sorry."

They resumed their chant.

Lucky picked his way across the stage, avoiding disturbing the ritual. He circled the First Disciple.

"Morph," said Lucky, "I suppose that since this guy didn't see the face and this is just his memory we can't see his face either."

After a moment's hesitation, Morpheus said, "No. It doesn't work that way."

"Why did you pause?"

Morpheus half-paused. "No reason."

"Don't tell me you're holding out on me, buddy. You have to know a few extra tricks, right? Some kind of dream god cheat code."

"Maybe there is something I can do, but there are certain risks. Things can go wrong."

"What can go wrong? You're Morpheus, god of dreams, master of the realm nocturnal, the big kahuna. Quick and I will stand aside and leave it in your able hands."

"Okay. Fine."

Morpheus waved his hand at the hooded assembly and spoke in hushed, reverent tones. "Right now, this is only a memory, a dim recollection of past events seen through one set of mortal eyes. But all memories, no matter how distant, no matter how distorted, have the shadow of truth underneath. Even the most imperfect memory is a window—"

"That's terrific," interrupted Lucky. "Love the metaphysics. But we're a little pressed for time."

"Basically, I just reach back and use my powers to re-create elements of the memory that the director couldn't know." Morpheus cracked his knuckles and clapped his hands. The lights snapped on bright and clear as everything was illuminated with the absolute light of truth. The scene froze.

Lucky hopped back into the set and walked over to the First Disciple of Gorgoz. He pulled back the hood.

"I have no idea who this guy is," said Lucky.

"What did you expect?" asked Quick. "A major movie star?"

"Would've made things easier." Lucky searched the disciple's pockets, but he came up empty. "That was a waste of time."

Morpheus snapped his fingers. "Check his pockets again."

The second search turned up a wallet.

"How did you do that?"

"It's a dream. Who is to say that the guy didn't have his wallet on him?"

"Morph, I like your style." Lucky found a driver's license. "Can I keep this?"

"Sure. What do I care?"

The phantasmal player of Gorgoz chuckled coldly. "You are as ridiculous as ever, Luka."

"Easy, big guy," said Lucky. "Don't get lost in the part."

Gorgoz stood. He pulled back his hood. The actor's face was gone, replaced with the twisted true visage. It'd been a few centuries since Lucky had seen Gorgoz face-to-face. He hadn't gotten any prettier.

"Easy, Gorg, ol' buddy."

"Always with the endless obnoxious chatter," said Gorgoz. "You blather on like a sideshow barker rather than a true god. It's no wonder the mortals have lost their fear of us." He roared, spewing slime and spit into the air. "You dare violate my domain, in the soul of one of my followers!"

"I don't remember him being so eloquent," said Lucky.

"He's a manifestation of the director's unconscious," explained Morpheus. "Not an exact copy."

Gorgoz pounced, seizing Lucky by the throat.

"Gorg, Gorgie, Gorgster," choked the god of prosperity.

"Quiet, you babbling fool," hissed Gorgoz. "Prepare to suffer the consequences of your trespass."

"Uh-oh," said Morpheus.

"Uh-oh, what?" asked Quick. "What's gone wrong?"

"I warned you it would be dangerous. The simulation is out of control."

"Uh, guys," squeaked Lucky. "Could use a little help here."

Quetzalcoatl sprang across the soundstage. He was batted aside with an offhand slap from Gorgoz, who chuckled with a low rasp.

"Look at you, god of blood and death. Look at what they've made you into. Luka was always a fool. But you . . . you were worshipped by an empire."

Quick rubbed his jaw. Being immortal didn't make him immune to pain, and Gorgoz, even in this form, packed a mean backhand.

Lucky transformed into a hulking beast, forcing Gorgoz to release him. The set broke into chaos as the phantasmal players scattered in all directions.

"Okay, Gorg!" roared Lucky as he pounded his huge fists together. "You asked for this!"

He pounced on Gorgoz. The two gods tumbled through the set, smashing their way through the faux brick walls. The shudders and booms of their titanic struggle shook the soundstage.

Quick and Morpheus waited a few moments. Neither god was terribly concerned. Immortality made even the most savage combat between deities an exercise in idiocy.

"Should we intervene?" asked Quick.

"This is my set!" screamed the director. "I'm in charge here!"

Lucky flew through the air, colliding with the overhead scaffold lighting. It all came crashing down. Lucky, back in his shorter, Hawaiian-shirt form, crawled from the wreckage. Patches of fur were missing here and there, and half his tail had been sheared off.

"For a simulation, he packs a helluva punch."

Gorgoz tore his way through the set. He leveled a finger at the director. "This is your fault. Not only do you fail me, but your weak mortal mind reveals secrets unfit for these fools to know. Now you shall suffer the consequences of your failure."

"He's really into seeing people suffering consequences," observed Quick.

"Some things never change," said Lucky.

The director cowered behind the gods.

"There's nothing to worry about," said Morpheus. "He can't hurt you. He's just a phantasm playing a part. A bit too well, perhaps, but it's still just a part. But you're the director of this subconscious. You're still in charge. You just have to remember it."

"Yes, that's right. I am." The director pushed his way past the gods and confronted Gorgoz's enraged dream duplicate. "You're fired," he said smugly. "Okay, people. Strike the set. Let's take a quick lunch break, then we'll set up for sex dream number eight. Y'know, the one with the naughty librarian and the whipped cream. I think we've earned it."

Gorgoz decapitated the director with one swipe of his claws. The head rolled to Morpheus's feet and glared.

"Thanks for the advice, asshole," grumbled the director before fading into oblivion. In the waking world, his physical aspect fell over dead.

Lucky and Quick stepped away from Morpheus, as if to avoid any guilt by association.

"That shouldn't be possible," said Morpheus.

Gorgoz chuckled. "All things are possible to me. While all of you were belched forth from the primordial at the dawn of existence, I was already here. I am the ultimate embodiment of the chaos that birthed the universe, and when all this is dust, when every mortal life is snuffed, when every soul is crushed, when every lesser god is returned to the nothingness from which they were spawned, I shall remain. Only madness endures. Only entropy is endless." He narrowed his orange eyes and grinned. Not easy with his messy arrangement of teeth and tusks.

"So piss off, you little shits."

Gorgoz snapped his fingers. The soundstage exploded, consumed by a screaming blast of white fire.

The gods were blown out the door and into the hall.

Lucky shook the gray ash off his scorched flesh. "What the hell was that?"

Morpheus wiped soot from his face. "That is a problem. But it's not my problem. I'm done. I'm out."

The door opened and Gorgoz stepped out. Lucky and Quick braced themselves for another attack, but the phantom was back to his harmless original actor. He rubbed his temples and moaned, wandering off.

"I was never here. Messing with Gorgoz is bad news." Morpheus started walking. Lucky and Quick ran after him so as not to get lost.

"But I thought he wasn't even Gorgoz," said Lucky.

"He wasn't. He was just a phantasm. But Gorgoz must have left something behind, some seed of power. That was real fire-and-brimstone stuff, right out of the Age of Legends. And it was just a leftover. It wasn't even the real him."

Morpheus stopped and wheeled on Lucky.

"I know you and Gorgoz have a thing going on. We all know he's an asshole, and I feel for you. But if you're thinking about going head-to-head with him, I'd advise against it. Just keep on doing what you're doing. Keep your head down and wait for him to get bored."

"It's been over a thousand years."

"So give it another thousand. Lay low. Don't push your luck, Lucky. That's all I'm saying."

He transformed into a swarm of butterflies and flew away, disappearing into the bustling hallways. Lucky and Quick pressed against the walls to avoid the crowds of phantasms and props being wheeled past.

Lucky pulled out the driver's license and stared at it.

"Don't tell me you've changed your mind," said Quick.

"No, I guess I'm still in."

Lucky pocketed the license and glanced around the maze of corridors. "Do you know the way out of this place?"

"I was hoping you did."

Lucky pointed down a random hall. "That way then."

"Do you know that's the right way?" asked Quick.

"Hey, I'm a god of fortune. Odds have gotta be pretty good."

20

There was a line to Bonnie's apartment. When she tried to enter, a man grabbed her by the arm.

"Hey. No cuts."

"I live here," said Bonnie.

"Yeah, right."

"Yeah, right!" She pulled from his grasp and pushed her way inside.

"You just made the list!" He pulled out a notepad and pen. "What's your name?"

She pushed her way past the crowd, squeezing past the doorjamb. People threw her dirty looks, but she was in no mood to explain herself.

Her apartment was jammed. She had to fight every step of the way, but she was pissed off enough that she had no trouble throwing elbows. After she bit someone who got too grabby, no one else dared stand in her way.

The line ended in her kitchenette. Syph sat at the table,

drinking tea with a woman whose hair was too blond and skin too bronze, making her look like a middle-aged Barbie doll who had invested just enough in plastic surgery to almost look human but who was an operation away from crossing the point of no return.

"This is my turn!" said the woman.

"This is my kitchen," grunted Bonnie. "What the hell is going on here?"

"I'll explain in a moment," said Syph. "We're almost done."

The woman flashed a condescending smile as Syph continued.

"Mortal, your story has moved my heart. Your ex-husband and his new wife shall be smote with boils that shall exude a foul stench. In return, you shall offer tribute of animal sacrifice and self-flagellation."

"Yes, about that," said the woman. "I'm not really big on animal sacrifice."

"It doesn't have to be a cute animal. It can be a snake or a frog or some other loathsome thing."

"I like snakes."

"You like snakes?"

The woman nodded slightly as if admitting a crime.

"Who likes snakes?" Syph glanced at Bonnie and repeated the question. "Who likes snakes?"

"I can take 'em or leave 'em," replied Bonnie.

"I'd rather not kill any animals," said the woman softly, "if it's all the same to you."

Syph said, "Is self-flagellation acceptable then? Because I'm not doing this for fun. I have to expect some compensation. Boils aren't as easy as you might think."

"That involves a whip or something, right?"

"Is that going to be a problem?"

"I don't have a whip."

"Buy one," said Syph. "I'm sure they still sell them."

"You could probably make one out of a jump rope," suggested Bonnie as she searched through her fridge for something to drink.

"I was hoping I could just offer you some cash," said the woman, pulling a thick wad of bills from her purse. "How about a thousand dollars? Would that be enough?"

"Sold," said Bonnie, snatching the money.

"Hey, that's my tribute," said Syph.

"Well, if you're going to rent out my place as your temple, I think I should get something for it." Bonnie peeled five hundred dollars off, stuck it in her pocket, and gave the rest to the goddess.

"Very well. This tribute is acceptable. However, in addition to this, I shall require you to slam your hand in your car door. Do this, and I shall be pleased. But the boils will only last two weeks. I'm not running a charity."

"Yes, goddess. You are as wise and beautiful as you are—"

"Yes, yes." Syph waved her away. "Go on then before I change my mind."

The woman left. Bonnie stepped in front of the man next in line. "One second, please."

The man was about to protest when Syph said, "It's all right. She's the . . . head priestess."

"Yes," agreed Bonnie. "Private church business. So back off for a minute."

The man relented. Bonnie exercised her priestly authority and pushed the line back as far as the crowd would allow so she could talk to Syph in semi-privacy.

She had a seat at the table. "What's going on here?"

"I'm getting over it," said Syph. "Wasn't that your suggestion?"

"So you're ruining other people's lives now? That's your way of moving on?"

A perplexed expression crossed Syph's face. "I am the goddess of heartbreak and tragedy. This *is* my job. What else would you expect of me?"

Bonnie had to admit that she hadn't thought about it. She had noticed that the overwhelming dread and misery she'd felt the past several days had faded. Probably because the goddess was no longer focusing all her influence on a single mortal. Syph had plenty of targets to aim her misery at now.

It left Bonnie with a bit of a dilemma. If she discouraged Syph from exacting revenge in the name of wronged mortals, then Bonnie was bringing all that down upon her head. But if she didn't, she was allowing Syph to hurt people. And it was even more complicated than that. Bonnie wasn't certain this operation was even legal. She wasn't up on the latest smiting regulations.

"Does it have to be so high-profile?" asked Bonnie.

"Things got a little out of hand," admitted Syph, "but I'm trying to make up for lost time. I have a lot of wrath to dispense."

"You're not killing people." Bonnie leaned closer and whispered. "You're not, right?"

"Don't be silly. That's against the law. And it's far too light a punishment for those who transgress against the sacred gifts of love."

She laughed. It wasn't much, but it was the first genuine moment of joy Bonnie had seen from the goddess. Syph was still colorless, still radiated a noticeable chill, and charged the air with a hint of gloom. But the goddess's tepid tea wasn't frozen in a solid block of ice, and things weren't spontaneously breaking or bursting into flame in the kitchen. That had to be a good thing.

"How was your day?" asked Syph, interrupting Bonnie's train of thought.

"Not good. I went to talk to your raccoon god."

Syph rasped, "You did what?"

"Calm down. He wasn't there. So I talked to his followers. Nice people. Anyway, then a couple of idiots with guns barged in and tried to offer us up as a blood sacrifice to their god. Yada yada yada. They ended up shot. I got out of there after the cops showed up. By the way, you're on notice with Divine Affairs. Filed a complaint since they were there."

Bonnie realized the dangers of taunting a goddess, but she didn't care. Maybe it was because she felt so damn good all of a sudden with that terrible burden of the goddess of heartbreak taken off her shoulders. Not entirely removed, but a good portion off in other places, doing nasty things to people who weren't her. Now it wasn't despair that gripped her, but a cheery malaise. The term might have seemed like a paradox a few hours ago, but everything was relative.

Syph said, "So these two men...did they happen to mention the name of their god?"

"Gorgoz. Why? Ever heard of him?"

"No. Can't say the name rings a bell."

The impatient grumbling from the crowd had been growing steadily louder.

"We both know I can't throw you out of here," said

Bonnie. "So feel free to hold court here until Divine Affairs gets off their butts and takes care of this. I'm going to get something to eat, maybe see a movie. When I get back, it'd be nice if this was wrapped up for the night."

She half-expected to be blasted to dust by the wrathful goddess, but Syph merely nodded. "Of course."

"We'll work out the scheduling arrangements in more detail later," said Bonnie.

Syph gave another slight nod. But this one warned Bonnie against pushing her luck.

"I'll be home late. Have fun helping people fulfill their spiteful natures."

Syph raised her teacup. "I always do."

21

Teri wasn't any good at waiting. It had been one of the things Phil liked about her. While he had been trying to figure the best way to ask her out on their first date, she'd shown up at his dorm room with an order of Chinese food and a DVD of *Logan's Run*. He hadn't fallen in love with her at just that moment, but he had started down the path. Later, after he'd learned that she'd done some research to know that Chinese food and sci-fi were the key to his heart and that she didn't like Chinese food or Michael York, Phil knew he'd end up marrying her. That was the way she was. She wasn't the kind of person to wait around for someone else to do what she could do perfectly well on her own. Most of the time that worked in her favor.

Not today. They were marked for death by a mad god, and there wasn't a damn thing she could do about it except wait in their house and hope either Divine Affairs or Lucky solved the problem.

Teri read a book, watched some television, read another book, and did some light chores. She vacuumed. Twice. She washed the dishes by hand even though they had a dishwasher. And she dusted every nook and cranny. When she tried to go out in the backyard, Phil stopped her.

"Why? It should be part of the protective shrine, right? It's part of the house."

"I don't know," he admitted. "Maybe."

"What's going to happen? I'm going to get smote in my own backyard?"

"It could happen," he said. "Maybe."

She flopped down next to him on the couch.

"I hate this."

"I know."

"I really hate this."

He put his arm around her. "I know."

"We're almost out of toilet paper," she said.

"Maybe you could call Janet. She could bring us some."

"I can't do that. What if that puts her in danger?"

"It's probably not dangerous, honey."

"Then why didn't you suggest any of your friends do it?"

"Janet is dating Lucky. It stands to reason that she's already a bit of a target in this mess. And since she is dating a god of good fortune, I have to assume she's well protected."

"I hate it when you make sense when I'm pissed off."

"I know you do. That's why I try not to make it a habit."

She kissed him, tousled his hair. Then went and made the phone call.

Janet arrived two hours later with several bags of supplies. She had to unload them all from her car herself since Teri and Phil couldn't safely step beyond the threshold of their front door. Teri and Janet unpacked the groceries. Phil stayed in the living room, playing video games. He would've helped, but he knew Teri needed time to vent.

"Ta-da." Janet made a sweeping supermodel gesture at a brand-new twenty-four-pack of toilet paper.

"Damn," said Teri, "just how long do you think we're going to be stuck in here?"

"I just assumed better safe than sorry."

"Jeez, there has to be three cubic feet of Hot Pockets here."

"Sorry about that," said Janet. "But I wasn't really sure if you liked to cook or not. So how are you holding up?"

"How do you think I'm holding up? Your boyfriend totally screwed us over."

"He's not my boyfriend," said Janet.

"He's not? Then I suppose that necklace is just something you had laying around."

Janet ran her fingers over the raccoon-headed emblem. "Okay, so maybe he's more than just a fling. But I wouldn't go so far as to call him my boyfriend."

Teri smirked. "If that makes you feel better."

"What do you mean by that?"

"What do you think I mean by that?" Teri opened the freezer and began theorizing on the complex geometric principles necessary to fit all the frozen meals in the limited space available.

"Oh, no," said Janet. "You don't get away with that. Not when I risked life and limb to bring you the creature comforts."

Teri, wryly grinning, withdrew a jar of spaghetti sauce from a bag. It would've been nicer if Janet had remembered to bring some spaghetti to go with it.

"I'm a terrible bomb shelter shopper. I admit it. Happy?" said Janet. "But you've been against me dating your god from the start. So why are you acting all smug about it now?"

Teri extracted a tinfoil lump from the freezer. She couldn't remember what it was, though it didn't smell quite right. Like year-old meatloaf or halibut gone bad or maybe stale melted plastic. She pondered peeling back the foil and revealing the mystery, but decided her sanity wasn't in a state for any more surprises. She threw it in the garbage.

"Go ahead," said Janet.

The mystery foil had derailed Teri's train of thought. It took her a few seconds to catch up to the conversation.

"You're just dying to tell me I told you so," said Janet. "So do it already."

Teri laughed. "Damn, you really don't get it, do you?"

"Get what?"

"I was wrong," said Teri, "about you and Lucky."

"You're saying it's a good idea now?"

"Oh, hell, no. Terrible idea. Horrible idea. Gods and mortals should not date. That's just obvious."

Teri paused, holding up a six-pack of off-brand banana-and-chocolate soda pop.

"It's delicious," said Janet.

"Then you take it."

"Maybe I will." Janet grabbed the pack, peeled off a can, and popped it open. After taking a sip, she calmly walked over to the sink and spit it out. She stuck her tongue under the running faucet. "Well, it sounded good. But I just thought it was worth trying." She stuck out her tongue. "Got any crackers?"

"Uh-hmm." Teri smirked again.

"You don't wear smug well," said Janet.

"I think you wear everything well, honey," said Phil as he entered the kitchen.

"Thank you, baby. Here, have a Hot Pocket."

"You're too good to me," he said.

"I know."

Janet and Teri put the conversation on hold until Phil had zapped his snack in the microwave and returned to the living room.

"Lucky is banana-and-chocolate soda," explained Teri. "Or at least, he was supposed to be."

"I hate metaphors," said Janet.

"Too bad. Because you're going to have to listen to this one." Teri took the remaining five cans of soda and put them in front of Janet. "This is what you do. Pop open a banana-and-chocolate soda. Sure. Why not? Maybe you'll love it. Maybe not, but hey, let's give it a shot. What do you have to lose?"

"You're losing me."

"No interruptions, please." Teri pushed the cans forward. "But here's the thing. Maybe you kind of like the soda because it's new and different and at least you can say you had the experience. But, ultimately, you know that banana-and-chocolate soda isn't going to become your favorite soft drink. Even if you drink the entire six-pack, the odds you'll ever buy another six-pack are minuscule. And that's assuming that they'll even keep making the soda, which is highly unlikely also.

"Dating gods is just the same. It's a new experience, good for a story and a chuckle. But you don't plan on doing anything more. And if by some chance you do develop some feelings, you know the god will take off before it gets serious."

"Commitment issues? That's your deep metaphorical insight? Hell, I could've told you that."

"Ah, but here's the catch," said Teri. "Sometimes, even when you don't mean to, even when you do your best to avoid it, you end up liking the banana-and-chocolate soda. A lot. And the soda likes you back. A lot. And then, before you know it, even when you didn't want it, you find yourself looking forward to cracking open your favorite soda. And worrying about if they ever stop making it."

"Can we ditch the metaphor at this point?"

"Okay, but you know I'm right."

Janet glowered. "Okay, so maybe you're right. So what?"

"So... nothing. Just an observation. Just so you know, I think Lucky really does like you a lot. And not just in that divine-infatuation way."

"Really?"

"Yep."

Janet smiled, then frowned, then smiled. "Crap."

"Welcome to a relationship," said Teri. "Whether you like it or not."

"You don't have to be so happy about it."

"Sorry. I just think it's funny, that's all."

"So what am I supposed to do now? I've never really been in a... well, one of these things. Not even with a mortal."

"Play it by ear," said Teri. "That's how everybody else does it."

"And doesn't that usually screw everything up?"

"Usually."

Janet ran her fingers along her necklace and slouched. "Crap."

Someone cleared his throat. It was Lucky. He stood on the table. Actually, he hovered a few inches over it, in a transparent projected form.

"Help me, Obi-Wan. You're my only hope."

The hologram chuckled.

"Sorry, I just always wanted to do that. Just thought I'd check in. Quick and I are lost in the collective unconscious right now. But we've got it figured out. A singing taco drew us a map on the back of a napkin."

He cocked his head to one side and listened to a voice only he could hear.

"No, Quick, that's not a turn. That's just when the pen slipped. Remember?" He scratched his head and turned his attention back toward Teri and Janet. "So it might take a while longer than anticipated, but we'll get out eventually. Just hang in there, kids. We're on it. Quick says hi by the way."

He started to fade.

"How long were you standing there?" asked Janet.

"Technically, I'm not standing here," he replied. "I'm just projecting."

"How long?"

"Not long." He looked a little embarrassed, but that could've been her imagination.

The doorbell rang. Teri answered it.

"Hello," said the stooped, withered old man. "Have you considered the value of changing your religion?"

"About once every three minutes," she said.

"Close the door," said Lucky's projection. "Close it now, Teri."

The man stuck his foot in the doorjamb, to keep her from getting the door shut. His shoes sizzled and burned with a sulfurous, yellow smoke. He didn't seem to mind. With one thin arm, he threw the door open, knocking Teri into Phil's arms.

"You can't enter here," said Lucky. "This is my temple."

Gorgoz's mortal disguise cracked. He grinned, revealing crooked and misshapen teeth. He stepped across the threshold, and immediately burst into flames. He took three more steps before collapsing in a heap of blackened bones.

"You have to get out of here," said Lucky. "Right now."

The skeleton raised his skull. "Oh, but we were just getting acquainted. What's the rush?" He stood. By the time he was back on his feet, his flesh and suit had re-formed. His liver spots had doubled in size, and his skin had turned a mottled puke green. And his eyes were two bloodshot orbs. He still smoldered, but the rate of regeneration had equalized, evening things out. The smell of burning flesh, along with his natural rotten-fish odor, was nauseating.

"I'm warning you," said Lucky, "if you harm one hair on these mortals' heads—"

"You'll what? Hmmm. You'll what? You're not even here. And even if you were, you couldn't stop me. Your favor is as worthless as the rest of the pathetic gods, shackled by the rules and regulations you've surrendered to. So why don't you do us all a favor and shut up? I'm trying to have a civilized conversation here."

The mortals eyed all the possible exits. Gorgoz

snapped his fingers, and every door and window closed and locked. And for that extra touch, he materialized various venomous serpents to guard them. Except for the front door, where he placed a two-headed mutant beast, something between a bear and a shark. The malformed creature was awkward, more likely to roll over people trying to exit than actually bite them. But that would have been just as fatal.

A cloud of buzzing locusts covered every window of the house, allowing just enough sunlight to keep the interior in shadowy twilight.

"It'll be okay," said Lucky. "Everything will be okay."

Gorgoz rolled his eyes. Considering the size of them, it was quite a feat. He waved his hand at Lucky. The projection faded away.

"He won't be bothering us for a while." Gorgoz gestured toward the sofa. "Have a seat."

The mortals hesitated.

"If I wanted to kill you, you'd be dead by now. Well, probably not by now. But you'd be on your way to dead, and you'd know it." He tried to smile pleasantly, but it only came across as hungry and menacing, the best he could manage.

They sat. Gorgoz took a seat in the chair beside the sofa. His charred form blackened the upholstery. Claws had sprung from his fingertips and a touch of slime dripped from his pores.

"Never really was very good at the mortal-disguise business."

In a flash, he sat before them in his true form, a seven-foot-tall, lanky god wrapped in a tattered bathrobe.

"You're probably wondering why you're not dead yet."

They nodded.

"Oh, sure. I could kill you right now. Allow your use-less god to project and then slay you right in front of him. And yes, it would be worth a laugh."

He gazed dreamily into the distance and smiled wistfully.

"No, no. Everyone keeps insisting this is a more civilized age. And I can play along. Sure, I can. Rather than kill you, I've decided to show you that even I can be...reasonable."

He leaned forward and interlaced his fingers.

"How would you like to renounce your god and take me on as your new lord and master? Hmmm? Doesn't that sound like fun?"

An awkward moment of silence filled the room.

"Oh, don't all speak up all at once." Gorgoz heaved a sigh. "I get it. You are all"—he made air quotes—"*nice* people. You're not the kinds of mortals to normally sign up with a god of chaos and death. And normally, such as you are beneath my notice. But I'm adaptable. And I want you to join my team."

There was another quiet moment.

"Any questions?" asked Gorgoz. "Any questions at all? I promise I won't bite your heads off." He leaned back and studied his claws. "I usually like to start with the limbs."

Janet said, "Why us?"

"A fair question. And I'll give you an honest answer. I've killed or had killed a few hundred of Lucky's follow-ers over the centuries. And I could devour you all now, and it would amuse me. But I came upon an idea that would amuse me more. Why slay you when I can steal you away?

"I know what you're thinking. What's the catch? What do you have to do to convince me of your sincerity? And here's the best part." Gorgoz cleared his throat and smiled. "All I'm asking in return is absolutely nothing. That's right. Not a drop of spilled blood or a single dime. Not a prayer or an inconvenient, arbitrary behavioral inhibition. Not a single act of tribute. You won't have to do a thing different than how you're living your life now and in return, you shall have my favor. Your enemies shall perish. Wealth will fall into your laps. And every desire you could ever ask for will be yours until your weak mortal bodies finally succumb to their inevitable frailty. And all you have to do is renounce your god and proclaim me as your new lord."

Gorgoz spread his hands, palms out, in a wide, welcoming gesture. His toothy grin was anything but reassuring.

"Oh, I know what's going through your troubled mortal minds. How can you possibly trust me? To which I reply…"

He threw back his head and cackled.

"You can't. I could be lying. I most probably am. This could all be some twisted game I'm playing where I'm just trying to screw with Lucky by getting you to abandon him. Then I'll devour you anyway because… well, I'd be lying if I didn't say it sounded like it would be worth a giggle. But all of that is hardly relevant. What should allow you to make this decision, all you truly need to know, is that you don't really have a choice. It's the slim hope that I'll keep my word versus the absolute certainty that I will kill you if you refuse."

A clap of thunder rattled the house.

"Ah, excellent. My demonstration has arrived. Come along. You must see this. I think you'll find it enlightening."

The locusts flew away. The vipers disappeared. And

the shark/bear creature lumbered to one side as Gorgoz exited the front door. Several Divine Affairs automobiles had blocked off the street. The agents stood at the ready. One of them shouted into a megaphone.

"Gorgoz, you are instructed to surrender for disciplinary action."

"I was hoping they'd be watching," said Gorgoz with a smile.

Thick clouds roiled overhead. A bolt of lightning struck the front yard and a tall, broad-shouldered, redheaded god stood in its wake.

"Thor," remarked Gorgoz, "how long has it been?"

"Not nearly long enough," replied Thor.

The clouds churned, swirling into a funnel that touched down beside the god of thunder. A red-faced deity with the face of a leopard stepped from the howling winds. He carried a bag over his shoulder.

"I don't believe we've had the pleasure," said Gorgoz.

"Fujin!" When the deity spoke, a gale blasted from his lungs, stripping the leaves from a tree and then uprooting it. He covered his mouth and winced. "Sorry!"

Fujin's shadow stretched out from his feet and expanded to three dimensions. This god was a living darkness.

Gorgoz scowled. "Oh, Og, don't tell me they tamed you, too?"

"Times have changed," said Ogbunabali. "We've come to see that you finally change with them."

"This is what it's come to?" asked Gorgoz. "We're not only allowing mortals to skitter about unchallenged, we're even enforcing their rules?"

"It's not like that," said Thor, unbuttoning his double-breasted suit. He pulled out his hammer, a massive weapon that crackled with electricity. "We don't boss the mortals around, and they don't boss us. It's a partnership. It always has been."

"Some of us just figured it out sooner than others!" shouted Fujin, stripping half the grass off the lawn.

"It doesn't have to go down like this," said Ogbunabali.

"No, it doesn't," replied Gorgoz. "Join me. It's time for us to rise up and show these—"

"Enough talk." Thor hurled his hammer. It collided with Gorgoz, knocking him off his feet. The hammer swerved upward, carrying Gorgoz with it. It soared upward a mile, reversed, then came crashing to earth, all within the blink of an eye. Gorgoz was driven into the ground with a deafening thunderclap. The shock wave knocked several cars over. Underground pipes burst, spewing geysers into the air.

The gods advanced on the smoking crater in the front lawn.

"That was a little much, don't you think?" asked Og.

"He wanted to do it the hard way," said Thor.

The ground rumbled. Coughing, Gorgoz climbed up to the pit's edge. Half of his teeth were missing, and he spit up a glob of black slime.

"Not bad, not bad. Nice to see you have a little fight left in you."

"Do yourself a favor and stay down, Gorg. I don't relish beating the snot out of you." Thor raised his hammer. "Maybe I relish it a little."

He brought it down on Gorgoz's skull. Or tried to. But Gorgoz caught Thor's wrist. The gods struggled for a moment, and then, with a grin and a twist, Gorgoz forced Thor to his knees.

Gorgoz wrenched the hammer free, grabbed Thor by

the throat, and with a whirl like a discus thrower, hurled
the god of thunder into the atmosphere.

"I was aiming for Australia," said Gorgoz, "but I think
I overshot."

He released the hammer quivering in his grasp. It shot
into the sky, chasing after its owner.

Fujin opened his bag of winds. They swept Gorgoz in
a screaming vortex, shredding his robes and freezing his
flesh. The temperature dropped. Frost formed on everything, killing all the nearby plants. Gorgoz was pulled
into Fujin's bag. The lord of winds threw it down on the
ground and started kicking it.

He stopped mid-kick as Ogbunabali watched with
disapproval.

"It's not fancy!" said Fujin. "But it gets the job done!"

The shadowy death god joined Fujin in a fresh round
of kicks and punches. They kept at it until Gorgoz's shouts
died down. The bag still rustled and wriggled, but no more
than was expected with the winds trapped inside.

"That was easier than I expected," said Og.

"I knew he was all talk!" roared Fujin.

Gorgoz's claw tore through the sack. He shredded it,
freeing himself and the winds. They howled, slipping
from Fujin's efforts to recapture them. One picked up a
car and smashed it into a house across the street. Another
tore off the sidewalk and playfully set it down in a giant
stack that promptly fell over onto several Affairs agents.

Fujin ran after the rogue zephyrs. He bellowed orders
that the winds ignored as they worked their way down the
street, wreaking gleeful havoc.

"Go ahead, Og," said Gorgoz. "Take your shot."

Ogbunabali stepped back. "No, thanks. I'm good."

Gorgoz adjusted his robe and shook his head. "What's happened to you? Mortals used to shit their pants at your name. I remember when you slaughtered whole villages just because you were bored.

"These mortals have robbed you of all your power, Og. I, on the other hand, have been supping on a steady diet of greed, avarice, cruelty, and human sacrifice." Gorgoz chuckled. "I especially love the human sacrifice."

Ogbunabali said, "You know that this can't end well. You don't think you can stand against the hosts of the heavens."

"I did pretty well this time, didn't I?"

"We underestimated you. It won't happen again."

"No." Gorgoz chuckled. "It won't."

He walked back toward the house. When his back was to Ogbunabali, Og drew a scimitar of darkness from his own shadowy form.

Gorgoz didn't bother to turn around. "I wouldn't, if I were you."

Og rethought his course of action. He set aside his weapon and checked on the agents.

"I trust I've made my point," said Gorgoz to Teri, Phil, and Janet. "There is no one in this world or beyond who can stop me from destroying you. I'll give you some time to think about it. But when next we meet, I'll expect an answer." He threw off his robe, revealing himself as a giant, spotted, skeletal dragon. He spread his skeletal wings and rose in the air.

"Be seeing you."

With one powerful flap, he shot skyward. The air reverberated with a shrill scream. He was gone in an instant. His various beasts vanished in clouds of acrid smoke, leaving a stench behind.

Lucky's projection rematerialized.

"Oh thank me, you kids are still okay," he said. He took in the destruction around the neighborhood, the uprooted trees and mortals in disarray, the crater in the lawn and the broken street. A mischievous gust twirled an upended automobile like a top.

"Stop that right now and get back here!" shouted Fujin as he chased after it.

Teri, Phil, and Janet went back into the house and stood around the living room. No one said a word. They didn't even look at each other. Phil gave Teri a hug, but it was a fragile, uncertain gesture.

Teri and Phil didn't talk about it.

Janet left. They didn't ask where she was going. They spoke with several agents. They couldn't recall the details of the conversation other than some vague reassurances that Divine Affairs was "on top of the situation" and that everything "would be resolved shortly." Then the agents left, too.

And Teri and Phil, very deliberately, didn't talk about it. They didn't talk about Lucky, still lost somewhere in the collective unconscious. They didn't talk about the wreckage just outside their front door. They didn't talk about Gorgoz's offer. They exchanged maybe twenty words over the next few hours on no topic more uncomfortable than their favorite flavor of Hot Pockets. They were watching television when Phil finally dared to say something.

"We can't take the offer," he said.

"I know," she replied.

Another twenty minutes passed without another uttered

word. They even had the TV on mute. They watched the actors go about their business without really caring.

"We can't take it," Teri said.

"I know," he agreed. He paused. "We can't."

This was how it went for another two hours. One of them would remark that they couldn't take Gorgoz's offer, and the other would agree. But there would be a pause between the first observation and the second. And it would be longer every time.

"I'm sorry," he said. "This is all my fault."

"No, it isn't. It's mine."

"If I hadn't brought it up in the first place..."

"Yes, but if I hadn't changed my mind..."

"You're right," he said with a forced smile. "It is your fault."

She wanted to laugh, but snorted. "And they say chivalry is dead."

He kissed her forehead.

"We're screwed, baby."

"Yeah," she said. "We're screwed. We can't take the offer."

"No, we can't. We can't trust him to hold up his end of the deal. He even admitted it."

"Even if he did," said Teri, "I couldn't live with myself. Any favor we'd get from him would've been paid for by someone else's blood. Somewhere."

The favor of Gorgoz didn't come without a price. He was a god of death and chaos, and there had to be consequences to taking him on. Things they couldn't conceive of. Gods were a deceptive bunch. Lucky had lied by omission, but at least he hadn't been out to screw them. Not like Gorgoz most likely was.

Teri went to the bathroom.

Phil paced around the coffee table a few times.

"Damn."

He ran outside before he could think too much about this.

"I know you're out here!" he shouted. "I know you're watching! Show yourself!"

A red spotted pigeon with blue eyes settled on the uprooted tree on Phil's lawn.

"No need to shout," the bird said with Gorgoz's voice. "So have you come to a decision?"

"It's a deal," Phil said, "but only for me."

The pigeon cackled. "Lovely. Selling out your friends to spare yourself. How delightfully self-serving. You'll go far in my organization."

"No," said Phil. "You take me, but you leave them out of this. You leave them alone, never bother them again."

The pigeon cocked its head and fluffed up its breast. "You dare dictate terms to me?"

"None of this is their fault. This is all because of me. We wouldn't even know Lucky if I hadn't brought this up in the first place. I started this. I have to finish it."

"How noble." The pigeon took a moment to preen its wings. "You're an eager and shortsighted mortal, Mr. Robinson. I like that in a follower."

Phil glanced at the front door. He couldn't have much time left.

"Do we have a deal then?" asked Phil.

Teri opened the front door. "What are you doing out here?"

"Do we have a deal?"

The pigeon chuckled. "We have a deal."

A tremor shook the earth as the pigeon grew into a giant bat.

"Oh no," said Teri. "What did you do, Phil? What did you do, you idiot?"

The bat folded its wings around Phil.

"Everything will be okay now," said Phil.

"You son of a bitch," she said. "Don't you dare pull that noble sacrifice bullshit!"

The bat launched itself into the sky, leaving the cold chuckle of Gorgoz hanging over the backyard for a long time.

23

By the time Lucky and Quick managed to navigate their
way out of the collective unconscious, it was early morning. They floated in Lucky's globe of flying light and
landed on the front porch of Phil and Teri's house. Neither
god remarked on the destruction in the neighborhood or
the dirty looks the mortals threw their way.

"Hey, kids," said Lucky as he threw open the door.
"Great news! I think we finally have a handle on this
thing."

The living room was in disarray. Several boxes had
been brought in and torn open, their contents spilled
across the floor. Old photos and random scraps of paper,
stuffed animals, and other odds and ends occupied most
of the space around the couch and coffee table.

Teri was curled up on the couch, snoring.

"Has she been drinking?" asked Quick.

Lucky righted the bottle of scotch tipped over on the

coffee table. Half the scotch was spilled in a puddle on the carpet.

"Teri, Teri." Lucky shook her gently. "Wake up. It's okay now. I'm back."

She opened her eyes halfway and dimly focused on him.

"This is all your fault," she mumbled.

"I know, and I'm going to fix it."

She laughed uncontrollably. "Fix it? Fix it! You can't fix anything!" Her laughter turned desperate, almost delirious, as tears ran down her face. "You're the god of prosperity. How could you have screwed it all up so completely?"

"I know you're upset but there's no need to get personal."

"He's gone! Phil's gone! And it's all your fault!"

She pushed Lucky away and turned her back to him.

"Go away. You can't do anything else to us."

"I'm sure he'll come back," said Lucky. "Mortals can be rash, but I'm sure he'll realize how much he loves you."

Quick shoved Lucky aside. "Geez, you are an insensitive idiot sometimes."

"I was trying to be comforting."

"You really don't know these people at all. Phil isn't the kind of guy to run off like this. He's not that selfish. He's also not that stupid. He knows that wherever he runs, Gorgoz would still find him."

"He took the deal," said Teri, mumbling into the sofa cushions. "That goddamn moron took Gorgoz's deal. I should've known." She rolled over and stared at the ceiling. "He always was a sexist bastard, opening doors and paying for dates. That should've been my first clue. I bet he couldn't wait to do his alpha male protector bit when he finally had the chance. What does he think I am? A helpless princess who can't fend for herself? It's insulting."

"I'm sure he meant well," said Lucky.

"What an asshole," she grumbled.

"Who?" asked Lucky. "Me or Phil?"

"Maybe you should get something to eat," said Quick, "while Teri and I sort through the details."

"I'm not really hungry."

Quick made a sharp pointing gesture toward the kitchen.

"Fine. I guess I could eat a sandwich. Hey, Teri, we don't have any bologna, do we?"

Quick repeated the gesture.

"Never mind. I'm sure I'll find something," Lucky mumbled as he left the room. "Like not answering a simple bologna question will bring back Phil. I swear, these mortals are so egocentric."

"Want to talk about it?" asked Quick.

"What's left to talk about?" She sat up and made a feeble effort to fix her frazzled hair. "And why would I want to talk to you about it? You're just as bad as any of them."

"Maybe." He coiled beside her and put a wing around her shoulder. "I'm not perfect. None of us are. All we can do is try, right? And hope we don't screw things up too badly."

"Why bother? If it's all going to go wrong anyway, why even try?" She grabbed the scotch bottle and swirled the little bit that was left before drinking.

She leaned into Quick. He wrapped his feathers around her. "Where did you find that?"

"Cupboard. Didn't even know it was in there." She laughed bitterly. "Lucky break, huh?"

"Maybe we try because what's the point in not trying?

Just sitting around, thinking about ourselves all the time, it doesn't work out either. Trust me. I learned that the hard way. So if we're going to screw it up, we might as well screw it up with good intentions rather than bad."

She cried in the serpent god's embrace. Her tears glittered off his rainbow scales.

"Want some coffee?" he asked.

"I don't want anything."

"A little caffeine in the morning never hurt anybody. Maybe we'll get some eggs going, too." Quick called to the kitchen. "Lucky, could you make us some coffee?"

When there was no response, Quick excused himself to check on Lucky.

The kitchen was empty. The back door was open. Lucky was nowhere to be seen.

"Damn it, Lucky."

Quick closed the door, turned on the coffeemaker, and started making breakfast.

"Hey, baby," said Lucky with a smile on his face and a bouquet of flowers in his hands. "I'm back."

She took the flowers. They were the cheap kind, found in discount drugstores everywhere. But it was the thought that counted, she supposed.

"No hug?" he asked.

"Sorry."

They shared a brief embrace. He stood there a moment, waiting for her to invite him in.

"So . . ." he said.

She apologized again, stepping aside.

"Great news, babe. Gorgoz is handled, so no more worries there."

She perked up. "Really?"

"Yep. You're free and clear."

Janet scooped him up in her arms and squeezed him close. "Oh, Lucky, I'm so glad to hear that. You have no idea how worried we were."

"Why worry? I am the god of good fortune. Things always work out for me. And my special lady."

She hugged him tight. "This is wonderful news. Have you told Phil and Teri yet?"

"They already know."

"That's terrific." She whirled around in a dance across the room.

"I was thinking, babe," said Lucky. "We should take a vacation. Go somewhere nice. Ever been to Tahiti?"

"I have a job."

"We'll fly over for the afternoon. Be back by midnight. I promise."

"I'll pack my swimsuit." She rubbed his ears and ran into the bedroom. "So what did you do?"

"What?"

"How did you solve the problem?" asked Janet.

"Does it matter?" He sniffed the flowers. "It's solved."

She stuck her head out of the bedroom.

"Well, if you have to know, I didn't actually have to do anything. Good ol' Phil took care of it, the romantic lug. Seemed he went and made a deal to get you and Teri out from under Gorgoz's thumb. Very proactive. You know the old saying. He who helps himself . . . something like that."

Janet walked over and put her hands on her hips. "What about Phil?"

"Oh, he'll be fine. He's a survivor, rolls with the punches, makes the best of it—"

"Lucky..."

"I didn't stick around for the exact details. But I think you're losing sight of the big picture. The problem is solved. Who cares who solved it?"

"I care. And I'm willing to bet Teri cares, too."

"To make any deal with Gorgoz, Phil had to renounce me," said Lucky. "That means his fate isn't my problem."

"You're just going to abandon him?"

"I kind of have to."

Janet cupped his head in her hands, leaned in, and kissed his forehead. She unclasped her necklace and put it on the coffee table, then headed toward the front door.

"Where are you going?" he asked.

"I like you, Lucky. I like you a lot. You're romantic and sweet and able to fly me to Tahiti at a moment's notice. But if you can leave Phil to the mercy of some mad chaos god then you're not the guy I hoped you were."

"Babe, I want to help. I do."

She glanced over her shoulder at him. "Then help."

"It's against the rules."

"Gorgoz doesn't follow the rules. Screw the rules. If you're interested in doing the right thing, you know where to find me."

"You don't get this guy. He's bad news. He's dangerous. Just because I'm immortal that doesn't mean he can't do all sorts of nasty things to me."

"That's it then? It's all about you?"

"You, too. If you go up against Gorgoz, an ugly death is the best you can hope for."

"And you'll let me go to that ugly death."

"I am trying to stop you."

She opened the door.

"Wait up." Lucky hopped off the couch and fished around in his pockets. "You might want this. It could be important." He handed her the driver's license. "Took it out of the collective unconscious. Might be worth something."

"Thanks."

She reached for the license, but he pulled it away.

"This is it then?" he asked. "You're breaking up with me?"

"I don't know." She snatched the license away. "Am I?"

Lucky shrugged.

"Whatever, babe. You just blew a good thing. Have fun with the rest of your life. However brief it might be."

He jumped back on the sofa and turned on the television.

"Mind if I just kick back here for a few hours? There's a *Gilligan's Island* marathon on. Hate to miss that."

"Fine. Just remember to lock up when you leave."

After the door closed, Lucky turned off the television. Janet might have had a nice rack and great ass. She might have been fun and cool and the kind of mortal a god didn't run into every century. But she was just another mortal skirt. There were millions of them on this pitiful planet. It would be absurd to go up against Gorgoz for one insignificant woman.

Lucky wasn't heartless. He felt bad about Phil. But that was the way it went in this world. Mortals came and went. Civilizations rose and fell. There was no point in getting attached to any of it. His relationship with Janet had been doomed from the start. Better to have it end now before it got any more serious.

Janet's necklace stared at him from the coffee table. He made it disappear. Then made it reappear. Then made it disappear once again.

Grumbling, he made it appear again and stuck it in his shirt pocket. Then he turned on the television and tried, with only marginal success, to lose himself in the antics of zany castaways.

Bonnie and Syph sat in the car parked in Janet's apartment complex.

"I still don't see why I had to drive you here," said Bonnie. "Couldn't you just have teleported here or whatever the hell you gods do?"

"Because I'm conserving my energies," said Syph. "I've gathered just enough tribute for what I need."

Bonnie wasn't in a great mood. While her life wasn't in danger of being devoured by the goddess's influence, she still had to deal with the comings and goings of Syph's new influx of followers in and out of the apartment at all hours of the day. The long lines had died down, but it still wasn't unusual to have five or six strangers in her apartment at any moment. They'd left a few standing outside her front door when they'd gone off on this errand.

Syph had been taking on as many clients as she could and throwing in a few stinking boils and withered genitals to keep the clientele coming back for more revenge. She'd been stockpiling tribute. Bonnie hadn't asked why, but when she saw Janet come around a corner, she figured it out.

Syph jumped out of the car.

"Stay out of it," Bonnie mumbled to herself.

The sky darkened overhead. The three fluffy white clouds contorted into twisted, agonized faces.

"Stay out of it."

A cat in a tree let out a howl and fell off its perch. It was dead before it hit the ground.

"Oh, hell."

She exited the vehicle and caught up with Syph.

"You should stay in the car." The goddess never took her eyes off Janet. "This won't take a minute."

Cracks formed in the pavement with Syph's every step.

Janet, oblivious to the approaching wrath, fumbled with her car keys. Bonnie didn't have to do much detective work to figure that Janet was having a bad day and that it was probably about to get worse.

Syph bellowed, shaking the earth. "Mortal, prepare yourself to face the vengeance of a goddess spurned!"

Bonnie was nearly knocked off her feet, and Janet jumped, dropping her keys.

"For your arrogance, I shall see you thrown into the depths of agony and despair, the endless pits of suffering, the realm of waking nightmares and dreams of pain where only the most presumptuous of mortal transgressors shall shriek and thrash for eternity! There you shall suffer until the end of time, until only the sanctuary of madness shall—"

Janet held up her hands.

"I don't mean to interrupt, but is this about Lucky? Because if you want him, you can have him."

Syph hesitated. She'd rehearsed the speech and hadn't planned on any interruptions beyond some incidental begging and pleading. Janet was crying. Just a little. But it wasn't motivated by terror.

Syph kept on.

"It's too late for repentance, mortal! You have earned the ire of the heavens! The only mercy you shall be given is the sanctuary of madness—"

"You already said that," said Bonnie.

Syph glared. "You can wait in the car. I don't mind."

Bonnie said, "Sorry. Go right ahead."

Syph cleared her throat and threw her hands in the air. A gale-force wind whipped across the lot as she roared, "The ire of the heavens shall rain upon you until the end of time! Your suffering shall be legendary! Your agony, a cautionary tale told to children who dare trifle in godly affairs!"

She paused. She'd had it all worked out, but now it was all jumbled. She knew she should've written notes.

"Madness shall be your...uhm...your...oh, damn." She lowered her arms and the winds died down. "See what you made me do? You've completely thrown off my timing."

"Sorry," said Bonnie. "But I think *sanctuary* was the word you were looking for."

Janet, meanwhile, had found her keys, gotten into her car, and started it. She stuck her head out the window and asked Syph and Bonnie to step aside so she could be on her way.

Syph scowled. The engine died. Janet tried to start it again, but there was no response. Not so much as a sputter.

Janet got out and walked up to Syph. "Why the hell did you do that?"

"There is no escape from the righteous fury of divine..." Syph took another awkward pause.

"Furiousness," suggested Bonnie.

"Oh, yes. That's terrifically poetic," replied Syph.

"I already told you. He's all yours," said Janet. "You two deserve each other." She wiped a tear from her eye.

"Well, this is no good," said Syph in a huff. "This is just no good at all."

"Why not? You want him. Now you can have him."

"You don't understand. I'm here for revenge, the smiting and the terror and the righteous furiousness. Not this. This is just sad."

"Sorry to disappoint you," said Janet.

"He dumped you then, I take it," said Syph.

"No, I dumped him."

"You dumped him?"

"Yes."

"You." Syph pointed very deliberately at Janet. "Dumped him."

"Yes. Still hurts like hell though."

"But why?" asked Syph. "You dumped him! You win!"

Janet and Bonnie cast curious looks at Syph.

"If he dumps you, then you lose," explained Syph, "but if you dump him, then you win."

Janet laughed bitterly. "Yeah, I win."

"Clearly, if you dumped him then you must have been unhappy in the relationship, right?" asked Syph.

"Wrong. I was having a great time."

"Oh." Syph mulled this over. "I get it. You knew he was just about to dump you, and you beat him to the punch."

Bonnie pulled Syph aside. "Didn't you tell me you were the goddess of love at some point? Don't you get it?"

Though Syph kept it to herself, she had to admit she didn't.

Janet leaned against her car and held back tears. Not a great flood, but a few embarrassing drops. As goddess of heartbreak, Syph could sense Janet's pain. It irked Syph to see the object of her vengeance like this. It was hard to enjoy revenge when Janet was down in the dumps. It was like kicking a puppy.

"Well, this just ruins my day," said Syph as she strolled away. "I'll be in the car."

Bonnie stood there, uncertain of what to do. She didn't know Janet. But Bonnie's experiences with the goddess of heartbreak and tragedy, along with a few failed relationships along the way, had left an impression. She knew that there really wasn't anything to say to make it better. But she also knew she had to try.

"Gods, huh? What a bunch of dumbasses."

Janet half-smiled. She sniffled, wiping her nose on the back of her sleeve. "Why do we bother?"

"Can't live with 'em," said Bonnie. "Can't kill 'em."

She leaned next to Janet.

"See, that was a joke. They're immortal. You can't kill them. Get it?"

"Yeah, it was funny." Janet made a halfhearted attempt to laugh that just came out as a whimper. "This is so damn stupid. It's not like we were going out a long time. Just a little over two weeks. And it's not like it was serious. Just fun, y'know."

"I know."

"But you really want to know what pisses me off?" said Janet. "In a hundred years, he'll be off gallivanting about, having a grand old time. Y'know that *the best revenge is living well* bullshit? He'll be living well, all right. And I'll be dead while he's whooping it up with some bimbo who isn't even born yet."

"Look at it this way," said Bonnie. "At least it's over."

Janet perked up. "Damn it. It's not over. I'm mooning over some worthless god while Phil's about to throw himself into the jaws of a dark god to protect his wife." She jumped in the car. It still wouldn't start.

"Something's happened to Phil?" asked Bonnie.

"You know Phil?"

"I know him. What's wrong with him? Is this about Gorgoz?"

"You know about Gorgoz?"

"I should. I was nearly sacrificed to him," said Bonnie.

Janet twisted the car keys with the same result every time.

"Come on," said Bonnie. "We can take my car."

Five minutes later, as they drove down the freeway, Syph kept glaring at Janet in the backseat.

She leaned close to Bonnie and whispered, "Why are we giving her a ride again?"

"Because you wouldn't start her car."

"I'm not wasting my favor making her life easier," said Syph with a snort.

"Then sit back and be quiet."

"Careful. You overstep your bounds, High Priestess."

"Guess that's a chance I'll have to take," replied Bonnie.

Syph folded her arms and sulked for the rest of the ride. Ice formed on the windows, but Bonnie steadfastly ignored it.

Worthington, drinking a glass of wine, sat by his swimming pool. He checked his watch.

His cell phone rang out with "Don't Fear the Reaper."

"Yes?"

Gorgoz's voice asked, "Worthington? Is that you?"

"This is my phone, my dark lord." Worthington struggled to suppress his annoyance. "You don't need to ask that every time."

Gorgoz had a bad habit of shouting into his phone. "When our guest arrives, see that he is brought to me immediately."

Worthington moved his cell away from his ear. "As you wish, Master."

The phone went silent for a moment.

"Wretched mortal," grumbled Gorgoz. "One day, he will burn in eternal agony for his attitude." An evil laugh rumbled from the speaker. "We'll see how smug he is when his intestines are pulled out through his—"

Worthington cleared his throat. Loudly.

"Lord, you have to either close the phone or push the button to end the conversation."

"Oh, bloody hell." Several bangs and clunks echoed from the phone. "Thinks he's so clever just because he can operate a fucking phone. I'm the damned lord of chaos. I'm sure that skill will be very helpful when he's impaled—"

Worthington performed a stage cough.

"Son of a Babylonian whore," hissed Gorgoz. "Which damn button is it?"

"The END button," said Worthington. "To *end* the phone call."

His phone beeped several times as Gorgoz stabbed at random buttons.

"Worthington?" he asked quietly. "Worthington, are you still there?"

Worthington snapped his phone shut. If previous experience was any guide, Gorgoz would eye his own phone for several minutes until he just ate it to solve the problem.

A shadowy creature swooped down from the sky. It dropped a screaming figure into the pool, then landed on the patio. The monster gnawed on something. Possibly the carcass of a small dog or a large cat. Worthington didn't check.

Phil pulled himself out of the water. Worthington tossed him a towel.

"Take off your clothes. You're not dripping on my carpets."

Phil shivered in the cool night air, but he didn't argue, much to Worthington's pleasure. He led the naked convert through his house. They didn't make it to the basement, though, because Gorgoz met them halfway.

Worthington didn't like this turn. Gorgoz wasn't supposed to leave the basement. Of course, he could, but it was a habit Worthington wanted to discourage. He preferred his god sitting on his divine ass, sucking up tribute and spitting out favor while watching television and drinking beer.

"Phil, you made it." Gorgoz smiled with menace. "Welcome to the cult. I know you'll love it. Isn't that right, Worthington?"

Worthington would also have preferred it if Gorgoz had refrained from using his name. He forced a smile. "Yes, Lord."

Gorgoz took Phil by the shoulders. "Presenting yourself naked, eh? That's classic, real humility. You could learn a thing or two from this guy, Roger."

"Yes, Master."

He put his arm around Phil. "You're shivering. Worthington, get him something to wear. One of those expensive robes you own should do."

"Yes, Master. Shall I bring it to the basement?"

"I don't know if you noticed it or not, but it kind of smells in there. Why don't you do your lord and master a favor and spray some air freshener down there while Phil and I discuss things in the sitting room? We do have a sitting room, don't we?"

"I assume."

"We'll find it." Gorgoz led Phil away.

"Don't mind Roger," said Gorgoz. "He's a bit of a douche bag. Like most of my followers. That's why I'm so excited to have you on board. I was just going to eat you once you got here. Then I thought that would be too easy. Maybe I could abduct your lovely wife and devour her while you watched."

"But you said—"

"I lie. I do it all the time. But at least I'm honest about it. It's amazing that mortals still follow me. Shows just how idiotic they are. They only live a few measly decades, if they're lucky, and yet most of them even screw up that meager portion of time."

Gorgoz chuckled.

"This is what I like about you, Phil. I can be honest with you. It's refreshing, really."

They walked down several hallways. Gorgoz paused at each door, opening as they went.

"Do you know what a sitting room looks like?" he asked. "Do you think this is what it would look like?"

Phil shrugged, having never seen one either.

They walked a few minutes more before Gorgoz settled on a room. "I guess this is close enough." The room was decorated with expensive furnishings. But every room had been so far. Several stuffed animal heads and an entire stuffed tiger, caught in mid-leap, were the only noticeable difference.

Phil had a seat at Gorgoz's urging. The god fumbled around in his robe, producing a cell phone. He pushed a few buttons. He shouted into the cell.

"Worthington. We may or may not be in the sitting room. There's a big stuffed moose head. Or is that a caribou? Phil, does that look like a caribou to you?"

"Moose."

"We're in the moose room," replied Gorgoz. "Bring the clothing here and a beer. Are you hungry, Phil? Can I get you anything?"

"No."

"Are you sure? Roger can make you a sandwich. He

has this Dijon mustard that is just fabulous." He pursed his lips and made a sucking sound. "Goes great on salami."

"Thank you, I'm good."

"I'll take one," said Gorgoz. "Y'know what? I think I'll have him make two. Just in case."

He placed his order with Worthington, then set the phone down, and sat across from Phil. Neither god nor mortal said anything for about a minute. Phil sat slouched in a large chair, covering his groin with his hands, and avoiding looking at Gorgoz.

"I don't think you ended the call," said Phil.

"I'm pretty sure I did," replied Gorgoz.

"Did you press the END button?" asked Phil in an apologetic tone.

"Which one is that?"

"The one that has END printed on it."

Gorgoz picked up the phone and snarled at it. "Worthington, are you still there?"

He put the phone to his ear, then glared at it.

"Yes, Lord, I'm here," replied Worthington.

Philip tried to help, even miming the gesture. "You just have to flip it—"

"Piece of crap." Gorgoz chucked the phone into his mouth, chewed it with a victorious grin, and swallowed. "I prefer the good ol' days of scroll-bearing messengers. They were tastier."

He chuckled, and his chuckle triggered some light nervous laughter from Phil.

"So what am I going to do with you?" asked Gorgoz.

Phil hesitated.

"I suppose I could corrupt you," said the god. "That might be fun. I've never actually done that. My followers are usually corrupt by the time they come to me. So tell me, Phil, what would it take to turn you to the dark side?"

Phil pretended to contemplate the question.

"Every mortal has their price," said Gorgoz. "I can give you anything. Pleasures beyond your wildest imagination."

A pair of femalelike creatures rose up behind Gorgoz's chair and slunk toward Phil. They were red with black spots and large blue eyes. One sat on his armrest and cupped his chin while the second walked behind Phil and massaged his shoulders. Though the women were scantily clad and well-proportioned, they weren't really human enough to instill thoughts of lust in Phil. Their claws and hungry eyes didn't help. And Gorgoz, leering like a twisted old man at a peep show, really killed the mood.

Gorgoz frowned. "What's wrong, Phil? Don't tell me you don't like girls?" He leaned forward. "You're not... like we used to say in the... of a Spartan persuasion?"

Phil shook his head as much as he dared. He feared if he moved too suddenly one of the demon concubines would slit his throat by instinct.

"Well, you must want something," said Gorgoz. "Some twisted delight that you've never dared speak about."

"Not really," said Phil.

"There must be some enemy you want dead. Or some possession you covet."

Phil thought about it. The only enemy he could think of was the god sitting right across from him. And the only possession he wanted was his old god-free life.

Gorgoz sighed. The women transformed into a pair of speckled boa constrictors. They slithered across Phil's shoulders and lap.

"You think you're a good person, don't you, Phil?"

"I don't know." Phil hadn't given it much thought up to this point.

"You aren't. You're simply unimaginative and frightened. Too stupid to know what you really want and too weak to take it even if you did know."

One of the snakes curled around Phil's neck. Gorgoz narrowed his bulbous eyes and spoke through clenched teeth.

"You disgust me. You and every mortal like you."

Phil gasped as the serpent coiled tighter. He could breathe, but just barely. Gorgoz, his hideous face a blank, watched in silence as Phil choked for air as the snake slowly constricted.

The door opened, and Worthington entered with a robe and a tray of food. Gorgoz jumped to his feet and grabbed a sandwich. "About time, Roger. What kept you?"

"I couldn't remember which was the moose room, Master."

Gorgoz popped open a beer and took a bite of his sandwich. "Phil, you gotta try this mustard. It's fantastic!"

He glanced over at Phil, who was just starting to turn blue.

"Whoops."

The snakes transformed into spotted tarantulas and skittered away.

"How embarrassing," said Gorgoz. "Hate to kill him before I've had more fun with him."

"Indeed," said Worthington.

Gorgoz threw a robe to the wheezing Phil.

"Are you a betting man?" asked the chaos god.

Phil shook his head. "Not really."

"Well, dammit, Phil. What vices do you have? You're not giving me much to work with. How about a small wager anyway? If I win, then someone dies. Not you, but someone precious to you. Your wife perhaps?"

"But—"

"Did I mention I'm a liar? But if you're going to be such a prissy little spoilsport, I guess we could wager on your right arm. If you win, you keep it. If I win..."

He snapped his fingers at Worthington.

"Fetch our game of Mouse Trap and be quick about it. And bring some of that spicy mustard back with you."

Gorgoz licked his lips.

"Just in case."

25

The first thing Janet did was give Teri a hug.

"I'm so sorry, hon."

"Why are we still here?" Syph asked Bonnie. "I thought we were just going to drop her off."

"We'll find a way to fix this," said Janet.

"He's probably already dead," remarked Syph. "Or worse."

The mortals glared.

"What? I'm just saying what everyone is already thinking."

"Being the goddess of heartbreak doesn't give you the right to be an insensitive bitch," said Bonnie.

"What about my sympathy? My revenge was ruined today. And I was really looking forward to it."

The mortals went inside and shut the door on her.

Syph huffed, transformed into a rain cloud, and slipped

under the door to follow. In cloud form, she hovered before Quetzalcoatl.

"Hello, Syph," he said icily.

"Hello, Quick," she replied. "Still bumming off Lucky's followers, I see."

"Still obsessing over Lucky's girlfriends, I see."

She darkened and rumbled.

"Would you mind changing into something less rainy?" he asked. "You're ruining the carpet."

Syph transformed into her human form. She joined everyone in the living room.

"I should never have agreed to it," said Teri. "If I hadn't agreed..."

"Shush, hon," said Janet. "There'll be plenty of time for blame later. After we get Phil back."

Syph laughed.

"Who is she?" asked Teri.

"She's just another stupid goddess," said Bonnie.

"Wrong," said Quick.

Everyone looked to him, surprised to see him defending her.

"She's not just another stupid goddess," he explained. "She's exactly the stupid goddess we need."

Smiling, he slithered beside Syph. "Do you want to know why Lucky and Gorgoz had their falling-out?"

He put a wing around her.

Syph said, "Oh, this can't still be about that. Who could hold a grudge this long over a silly little thing a few thousand years ago?"

"Why don't you tell them all about that silly little thing?"

"I really don't see how it's any of their business."

"Syph…"

"Oh, all right. But it was a very long time ago. I hardly remember it at all. I had so many suitors back then. I can't be expected to place significance on all of them." She lowered her voice, as if admitting something she'd rather not. "Gorgoz and I used to date."

"You went out with that guy?" asked Janet.

"I dated chaos and death gods almost exclusively for a few centuries. Hades, Ahzuulrah, Frush'ee'aghov the Lesser, Shalim, Tezcatlipoca, Nyx."

Quick raised an eye ridge with the last one.

"Hey, it was the dawn of time," said Syph. "Everybody was experimenting a little. So I went through a bad-boy phase. Gorgoz came near the end of it. We only went on a few dates. Nothing special."

"But…" said Quick, encouraging her to continue.

"But…he didn't want to end things. The sap wouldn't take no for an answer. Kept on pestering me. What a loser, right?"

Everyone replied with silence, and Syph continued, oblivious to the irony.

"Eventually, I'd had enough. So I told him that I was in love with someone else and that he would just have to accept that. Poor guy took it hard, I guess. Who could blame him? I was the most desirable goddess in all of creation. He vowed revenge on my love, swearing to destroy all of the god's followers, then the god himself, then all of the universe if that was what it took to convince me of his devotion."

She sighed.

"Kind of sweet, actually. In a mad-lord-of-oblivion sort of way."

Bonnie said, "All of this is because this Gorgoz wants you and you don't want him. And you want Lucky, but he doesn't want you…"

Syph glowered.

"This is all because of a divine love triangle?" asked Teri.

"I'm not sure it's a true love triangle," said Janet. "More like a love one-way street."

"It's like an episode of a bad teen drama. It might even be funny if my husband, my stupid, noble, self-sacrificing son-of-a-bitch husband, wasn't going to die because you all can't just sit down and talk about this. What's the point of being immortal if you waste eternity worrying about stupid shit like this?"

"It's complicated."

"No, it's not," said Teri. "You have to go talk to Gorgoz, explain things to him so that he'll stop this ridiculous vendetta and give me back my husband."

"Oh, no. I couldn't do that."

"I wasn't asking you. I was telling you."

"You're giving me orders?" Syph chuckled. "You're fortunate I find that so amusing. Otherwise, I'd kill you where you stood."

"Go ahead," said Teri. "Smite me."

"Excuse me?"

"I'm inviting you to smite me. They all heard me. So go ahead and smite me."

"I will not be taunted."

"I'm waiting."

"Hold on," said Bonnie. "Let's not get crazy. Teri, you're distraught." She interposed herself between Syph and Teri. "She's upset."

"You're damn right I'm upset."

Teri pushed Bonnie aside and advanced on Syph.

"You better smite me. Because if you don't, I'm going to chase you to the ends of the Earth. I'll come after you. I'll make deals with any gods I have to and do whatever is necessary to bring you down. If you think your endless life is miserable now, just give me some time."

Syph raised her hand. Dark power danced on her fingertips. Teri stood defiant before the goddess, who reached for her.

Quick grabbed Syph's wrist.

"Time out on the pissing contest, ladies."

"Stay out of this," they replied in unison.

"Love to, but I can't. I think we're losing sight of the big picture here. Syph, Teri might be asking for a smiting, but she's also right that this thing with Lucky and Gorgoz has gone on way too long. And, Teri, railing against the heavens in noble defiance might satisfy some self-destructive mortal impulse you're struggling with, but it never ends well.

"So here's what we're going to do. Syph and I are going to have a talk with Gorgoz, straighten things out like reasonable deities, put a stop to this absurd cycle, and, most importantly, get Phil back."

"I'm not agreeing to this," said Syph.

"Yes, you are. Because you know it's the right thing to do. For Phil, and you, and Gorgoz, and Lucky. It's the right thing to do for everybody when it comes right down to it."

"Fine, but in return I demand the following tribute from everyone present."

Quick said, "No tribute. See, when something's the right thing to do, you don't do it for a reward."

It was clear to everyone that Syph didn't understand that concept. But Quick assured them that he'd explain it more thoroughly on the way.

"Great. I'll get my keys," said Teri. "I'm driving."

"Oh, no," replied Quick. "Putting you two into a car right now would probably be a very bad idea. Wrathful goddess and defiant mortal do not mix. And, to be perfectly honest, you'll only get in the way."

"I can't just sit here."

"Yes, you can." He slithered over, took her by the shoulders, and very deliberately pushed her down into the sofa. "Don't make me swallow you whole to make you behave."

"If you swallowed her whole, wouldn't she end up going with us?" asked Syph.

Everyone ignored the goddess.

"Just making an observation."

"Teri, I want you to wait an hour. If you don't hear from us by then, call Divine Affairs and let them know where to find us."

"I don't see why we can't just call them now," said Syph.

"Because so far Gorgoz has outmatched all of us," said Quick. "Our best chance is to reason with him."

"Because he's so reasonable," said Syph.

"It's worth a shot."

"Oh, all right," said Syph as Quick guided her toward the door. "But I don't see why one insignificant mortal life is worth getting this worked up over."

"One hour," said Quick to Teri just before the gods took to the sky and flew away.

Teri grabbed her keys.

"Where are you going?" asked Janet.

"Where do you think I'm going?" replied Teri.

"But Quick said—"

"I know what he said. And I don't care. The gods got me into this mess. I'll be damned if I'll just stand aside and let them try to get me out of it."

"Aren't we at least going to call Divine Affairs?" asked Janet.

"So they can blow up Gorgoz and any unfortunate mortals who happen to be standing beside him?"

Janet and Bonnie stepped between Teri and the garage.

"You're not thinking this through," said Bonnie.

"No, I'm not. I'm being foolish and impetuous and headstrong. Because that's the only way to deal with gods. You don't negotiate. You just charge right in and tell them you're not going to put up with their crap anymore."

"And then you end up turned into a spider," observed Bonnie.

"Not always. Sometimes you earn their respect."

Janet and Bonnie tried to remember any historical precedent. There were a few here and there, but for the most part, mortals who challenged the gods ended up squashed beneath their feet.

"I have to do this," said Teri. "And if I'm not going to let gods stop me, what makes you think I'll let you?"

There was an edge in her voice that let Janet and Bonnie know that Teri was deadly serious. Janet was a few inches taller than Teri, and Bonnie outweighed her by perhaps ten pounds. But both women knew that standing in her way was probably the worst place for mortal or god to be right now. Teri was charged with righteous indignation. It was indeed the kind of determination that could even get the heavens to stand up and take notice. Whether those same heavens parted the seas or razed a civilization in response was always up in the air, though.

"I'm going with you," said Janet.

"Me, too," said Bonnie.

"Fine. I don't have time to argue."

Teri jumped in her car, but locked the doors before the others could get in.

Janet pounded on the window. "Teri, don't you dare do this."

Teri slammed on the accelerator, not even bothering to open the garage door. The indestructible car smashed its way through. Teri barreled down the street without looking back.

"Do you remember the address?" asked Bonnie.

"No, damn it," replied Janet.

"She's going to get herself killed," said Bonnie.

"If she's lucky."

26

There was a time, centuries ago, when Lucky had loved blowing off the day to watch the latest round of good, clean carnage Valhalla had to offer. But that was before Odin put in the stadium seating and the concession stands and started selling tickets to the show. Back before the warriors were all divided into teams and the play-off system was instituted. Back when warriors battled for the love of slaughter and the promise of a resurrection and feast at the end of the day.

Things had changed. Things always did. But not every change was for the better. Lucky couldn't blame Odin for selling out. He had to pay the bills somehow. It wasn't enough to get by on tribute anymore. Any god with a real operation had to have some cold hard cash in the bank, too.

But Lucky did miss the days when the fields of Valhalla were a little more exclusive, before any mortal with a few hundred bucks to spare could buy a season ticket, paint his body red, and scream at the top of his lungs like a moron while blocking Lucky's view.

It was battle-ax giveaway day, and Lucky considered planting the weapon right in the mortal's back. But this was frowned upon, and it was bound to get him kicked out.

He glanced around the shrieking mortal, but the battle raging below was a distant chaos of tiny combatants. Balder had promised to hook Lucky up. The short notice wasn't supposed to be a problem. Apparently that meant the cheap seats in the nosebleed section, seated among a throng of mortals. Lucky hadn't expected a skybox, but something behind fort hill wouldn't have been too much to ask. He couldn't even hear the cheerleaders as they banged their shields and swords together to work up the crowd.

A Valkyrie vending refreshments walked up the aisle. Lucky tried to catch her attention, but her back always seemed to be turned. He struggled to get comfortable in the cheap plastic seats, but if there was a trick to it, he hadn't figured it out.

The guy next to Lucky said something. Rather than admit that he hadn't caught it, Lucky nodded, forced a polite smile, and hoped the man would take the hint.

"I'm Bob," he shouted above the din. "Bob Saget. Not the actor and comedian, though I have been told I look like him."

"Uh-hmm," said Lucky, intently watching the Valkyrie to avoid missing his chance.

"It's why I grew the beard," said Bob. "The wife isn't crazy about it, but I told her that it was her own fault for marrying a man named Bob Saget who resembles Bob Saget."

The Valkyrie turned. Lucky raised his hand.

"Guess what she said?" asked Bob.

Lucky glanced over his shoulder. "What?"

"Guess what she said? My wife."

"I don't know." Lucky looked back, but the Valkyrie had wandered in another direction.

"She said that was why she married me. Because I looked like Bob Saget. Someone actually married me because of my resemblance to Bob Saget? Can you imagine that?"

"Can't say that I can." Lucky slid back into his seat with a sigh.

"You gotta like the Barbarians this season," said Bob. "They'll never make the Battle Royale, of course. Not until they get a few guns in the lineup. Swords and axes will only get you so far these days."

Catapults launched several flaming projectiles that sailed across the field and exploded. A dragon roared its hideous death rattle as soldiers riddled it with semiautomatic machine gun fire. The Legionnaires pushed closer to the Barbarians' fortress, but it was still anyone's battle. The crowd cheered.

And Lucky couldn't care less.

This was supposed to help get his mind off of his problems. But fate was conspiring against him. Fate, cheap seats, Valkyries that were deliberately ignoring him (he was pretty sure). And Bob. He couldn't forget about Bob.

"I've heard rumors they're considering letting the Joes field a Sherman tank next year."

Lucky jumped out of his seat without excusing himself. Bob was probably still talking. Lucky didn't look back to check. He approached the Valkyrie.

"One mead lite, please."

She glared at him with stern judgment, but that was a standard expression among Valkyries. Especially Valkyries in miniskirts, stuck selling hot dogs and turkey legs.

"Sorry, sir. We're all out."

"One regular mead then."

"All out of that, too."

"Fine. I'll take that." He pointed to the last mug on her tray. "Whatever it is."

"Oh, I'm afraid I just sold it."

"Sold it? To who?"

"This gentleman." She handed the mug to a customer sitting within arm's reach.

He said, "Excuse me, but I didn't ask for—"

"Yes, you did."

"But—"

"On the house. Enjoy with our compliments, sir." She turned and walked away.

He shrugged, then took a drink.

Lucky ran after the Valkyrie.

"What was that about, lady? Do you know who I am? I'm close friends with ol' One-Eye himself. I could have you fired—"

"You don't remember me, do you?" she asked.

He swore under his breath. "Sure I do."

She covered her name tag. "What's my name?"

"Brunhilde."

The Valkyrie snarled. "Lucky guess."

She was right, and he felt guilty getting caught.

"Does the Hundred Years' War mean anything to you?" asked Brunhilde.

"Can you be more specific?"

"Rainy night. Hayloft."

"Can't say it rings a bell," he said.

"You said you'd keep in touch."

"Yeah, well, I meant to, but..."

He stopped.

"You know what? I'm not doing this. I really don't care about whatever wrong you think I've done to you. It was one night. I was just being polite. And that's that. So get over it, baby."

"Ass."

She walked away. Lucky visited the concession stand and tried to forget the encounter. If some leggy blonde couldn't let it go, it wasn't his problem. But he couldn't stop thinking of her withering scowl. Even after he bought his mead and turkey leg and returned to his seat, he couldn't enjoy them. And it wasn't because of Bob or the uncomfortable plastic seat or the dirty looks all the vendors were giving him now. Maybe driven by Valkyrie solidarity. Maybe because he'd shared a barn with several of them. He couldn't remember. They all looked alike, so it really wasn't his fault.

But they really weren't the problem. It was the combination of disgust and disappointment that got to him. And though they were blond and muscular and looked nothing like Janet, he kept seeing her face.

And Janet's face led to Teri's face led to Phil's face led to Gorgoz and Syph and Quick and the whole tangled mess.

He'd gotten involved. Standard protocol was to keep your distance when it came to mortals. It'd been so easy a thousand years ago. Gods above, mortals below. It'd been so simple. When the hell did it all get so complicated?

Lucky handed off his snacks to Bob and found Brunhilde.

"I just wanted to apologize. I don't know if it counts for anything, but that's all I wanted to say, Brunhilde."

"My name is Sonja."

"Oh, well, could you do me a favor and pass the message along? I'd do it myself, but I've got some mortals to save."

27

Quick pushed the button on the gate intercom. It took a few minutes and a few more button presses to finally get an answer.

"Yes?"

"We're here to see Gorgoz."

The security cameras above the gate swiveled in their direction.

"There's no Gorgoz here," replied the voice.

"Tell him it's Syph," said Quick.

The goddess performed a halfhearted wave for the cameras.

"There's no Gorgoz here," said the voice again.

"I told you this was a waste of time," said Syph.

"He's here," said Quick. He turned back to the cameras. "We're trying to be polite about this, but if you don't invite us in now, we'll call Divine Affairs and let them handle this. And I don't think any of us wants that, now do we?"

The gate buzzed and swung open.

"Thank you."

Gorgoz rolled the dice, then moved his race car to the B&O Railroad.

"Oh, drat," he said. "How much do I owe you, Phil?"

Phil collected his fee, and eyed the pile of colorful cash sitting before Gorgoz. It was a meager sum compared to Phil's own. He was winning, and Gorgoz had promised to devour some unspecified extremity should the god win.

So far, Phil had scored a slim victory in Sorry! to avoid having his knees broken and followed that up with a miraculous win in Candy Land that kept him from losing a thumb.

"I gotta say you're one lucky son of a bitch," remarked Gorgoz with a grin, though his tone was not amused. "Are you sure you renounced your old god? You wouldn't be trying to pull a fast one, would you?"

"No," said Phil. "Never."

Gorgoz's grin dropped.

"I would never do anything like that," said Phil through a tightening throat. Whether that was Gorgoz's doing or just Phil's own nerves, he couldn't tell.

"I'm just messing with you, buddy." Gorgoz picked up the dice, but stopped short of dropping them into Phil's hand.

"Now, I don't suppose you want to reconsider my offer? Just say the word, and I'll go consume your lovely wife and get you completely off the hook with our little wager."

"No, thank you."

"You're a good man, Phil. Boring, but good."

Phil wasn't sure how much longer he could keep this up. Or when Gorgoz would grow bored and discard this pretense. But he wasn't tempted to take the offer. It had less to do with being a good person, and everything to do with his complete distrust of Gorgoz, who had already admitted to lying all the time. Any deals weren't worth much, but Phil figured anything to keep the mad god occupied was all he could do. He didn't have a better plan than that. He was a pawn of the gods, but he wasn't a hero of legend. He was just a mortal in way over his head, and his only chance of getting out of this was a miracle.

But, given that his old god wasn't that reliable in the miracle department and his new god was why he needed a miracle at all, Phil just hoped to end up dying as quickly and painlessly as possible while ensuring Teri stayed alive.

"Are you going to roll those dice anytime soon?" asked Gorgoz. "Or do I have to break out the sand timer again?"

Worthington entered the room. He offered Gorgoz a whole roasted turkey.

"Excuse the interruption, Master, but you have visitors. I think they're here about...him."

"Then by all means, Roger, let's show them in." Gorgoz rose, grabbed the turkey, and exited with Worthington. "We'll be right back, Phil." He smiled and winked. "Don't cheat now."

Gorgoz greeted Quick and Syph at the front door. He had swapped out his crusty bathrobe for a clean smoking jacket. The sweatpants ruined the look. And the whole roasted turkey in his right hand didn't add anything.

He took a bite of the bird. It hadn't been deboned, and that was made obvious by the crunch of bones and his open-mouthed manner of chewing. Bits of flesh fell out of his jaws.

"Welcome to my temple." He wiped his hand on his jacket, leaving a stain of grease. "It's been a long time since we've had visitors. Isn't that right, Roger?"

He glanced around.

"I seem to have misplaced my First Disciple. Oh, well, I'm sure he'll turn up. In the meantime, let me show you around."

When Quick and Syph crossed the threshold, a wave of nausea hit them. This was the temple of Gorgoz. It'd been a while since either had encountered such pure, malevolent will.

Quick was reminded of his younger days, when human civilization consisted of tiny tribes hiding in caves offering blood sacrifices and scraps of food to appease the unknowable powers. Quick had been a part of that. It was the way it was done back then. Looking back on it now, it just felt so immature and crude, a childish phase he'd grown out of.

Not every god had done the same. There were those who still yearned for the good old days, for the absolute fear and devotion of terrified mortals. He wasn't surprised to find Gorgoz was one of those types.

Gorgoz led them down halls, pointing out rooms. More accurately, he pointed to closed doors and the rooms that might be behind them. "I think that's the den. And I think this one is the bowling alley. I'm pretty sure we have a bowling alley anyway."

He took another bite of turkey. "Syph, you look lovely by the way. What a pleasant surprise to see you again." Gorgoz pointed to another closed door. "Phil's in there. All in one piece. For now. If you'll excuse me, I have to go find my First Disciple. He's around here somewhere."

Quick and Syph found Phil pacing the room. Quick performed a fast introduction.

"Where's Lucky?" asked Phil.

"He's not here," said Quick.

"But he's supposed to rescue me."

Syph laughed.

"He's not coming, is he?" said Phil.

"No, he's not," admitted Quick.

"That son of a—" Acceptance quelled his rage. "I don't know why I'm surprised. He's been lying to us from the beginning, covering his own ass."

"You renounced him," said Syph.

"Only because he left me no other choice."

Syph laughed again.

"You find this amusing?" he asked.

"Not particularly," she replied.

"Yes, yes," interrupted Quick. "We all have our issues. But right now, we don't have long to come up with a game plan. So why don't we put aside our emotional baggage and try to figure a way to get you out of this situation.

"As I see it, you're just one insignificant mortal. Gorgoz only cares about you because of this vendetta he has going with Lucky. So, in a way, having Lucky abandon you is just about the only chance you have."

"Wasn't that considerate of him?" Phil sighed. "Do you really think you can talk him into letting me go?"

"Stranger things have happened," replied Quick.

"But I wouldn't count on it," added Syph.

The door swung open, and Gorgoz and Worthington entered.

"Roger, this is Quetzalcoatl and Syph. Just a couple of used-up gods that don't know when to call it quits. This is Roger, my First Disciple. Say hello, Roger."

"Hello."

Gorgoz thrust his uneaten half-turkey into Worthington's arms. "Hold that for a moment."

"Yes, Lord." Worthington stifled his annoyance at the stains of grease forming on his five-hundred-dollar shirt.

Gorgoz wiped his hand on his sweatpants. He threw an arm around Phil's neck, squeezing a bit too tightly. Phil choked as Gorgoz gave him a noogie with sharp knuckles, drawing a little blood. "Phil and I have been having a wonderful time."

Just when Phil was starting to turn blue, Gorgoz released him.

Gorgoz said, "Well, well, well. I have to wonder what is so special about our friend Phil here? When Lucky gave him up so easily I was beginning to think I'd overestimated this scrap of mortal flesh. Even thought about just letting him go. Never actually tried being merciful before. Thought it might be worth a chuckle."

A low laugh rolled out of his throat.

"But now you two show up, and I'm thinking perhaps I have something more valuable than I first realized. What's your investment in this, Quick? Seeking redemption? Do you think that intervening in the life of one worthless mortal can wash away the stain of a fallen empire?"

Quick's plumage wilted.

"And what about you, Syph? Why are you here?"

"I don't honestly know," she said.

"So you wouldn't mind if I devoured our mortal friend right now?"

"Be my guest," she said.

Gorgoz licked his lips. Phil stepped behind Quick.

"He's just one mortal," said Quetzalcoatl. "You've proven your point. You've won. Your power is greater than Lucky's. What would killing this poor speck accomplish?"

"What does letting him live accomplish? He's just a speck. Why should his life or death matter to any of us? He's not a king or a president or a dragon-slaying hero. I might understand if this was Perseus or Gilgamesh. But this is Phil Robinson. Even the name is unremarkable." He pointed to Worthington. "Roger, go find a phone book. Tell me how many Phil Robinsons are listed in it."

"Yes, Master."

Gorgoz stopped him from leaving.

"I was just kidding, Roger."

"Very amusing, Master."

"Get a load of this guy. And I thought Attila the Hun was a wet blanket." Gorgoz slapped Worthington on the shoulder. "You know I love you, buddy. Well, as much as I love any crumb of flesh that keeps me in tribute and chicken fingers."

Gorgoz took back his turkey and sheared off another bite.

"Phil stays with me. Until I get bored with him. Or I'm looking for a change of pace from chicken fingers."

Syph sighed. "All right, I'm still not really clear why I'm here, but I guess it has something to do with this mortal. Gorgie, are you sure you wouldn't change your mind? As a personal favor to me?"

She tried to smile coyly. But she was out of practice and failed miserably.

"I'd be very grateful."

Gorgoz stifled a chortle.

"What?" she asked.

He burst out laughing.

"Oh, Quick. Please don't tell me you brought her here to *persuade* me. That is priceless."

"But you love me," said Syph.

Gorgoz chuckled, wiping a tear from his eye. "Love is a bit of an overstatement. You were hot. I was horny."

"But what about Lucky?" asked Quick. "I thought you hated him."

"I do."

Gorgoz's huge eyes opened even wider.

"You don't mean to tell me that Lucky thought that I was angry with him because of her?" He pointed to Syph. "Her?"

Syph smoldered.

"That's absurd," said Gorgoz. "I may be petty and vindictive, but even I know a fling is just a fling."

Quick said, "Then why the hell do you hate Lucky?"

Gorgoz hesitated.

"Y'know, I can't quite remember." He laughed. "Isn't that funny? I'm sure it was for a very good reason."

Syph rose from her chair. "But you said you would fill the oceans with blood and cover the continents with bones. You promised you'd destroy universes for me."

"That was just pillow talk, baby."

Phil sized up Gorgoz in all his physical and spiritual repulsiveness. Gods were more flexible when it came to sleeping around, and Syph was no prize herself. But he still thought she could do better.

Gorgoz yawned. "I'm bored now. Roger, show our guests the door while Phil and I break out the checkers. I call red."

Syph pounced on the god. She roared.

"You son of a bitch! I'll see you chained to Atlas's armpit and reduced to a pile of bleached, wasted flesh!"

Gorgoz blinked. "Wow. Now that's the kind of goddess I can respect."

She hurled him into the fireplace. Flame exploded. Brick crumbled. The moose head mounted above the mantel fell onto the pile of rubble. She cracked her knuckles and narrowed her eyes.

"This could be bad," said Quick.

The moose head rose with Gorgoz underneath it.

"Okay, okay. I guess I can throw you a mercy screw if it'll cool you down."

Syph, abandoning any divine subtlety, hurled herself into Gorgoz. They crashed through the wall and out of the room.

"Hell hath no fury..." observed Quick.

This wasn't what he'd had in mind when bringing Syph, but a distraction was a distraction. The manor rattled with Syph and Gorgoz's howls. Worthington took advantage of the situation to bolt from the room.

"You better get out of here, Phil."

"But what about you?"

"Don't worry about me. I'm not sure how long Syph and I can keep him occupied."

"But—"

"Damn it, go!" Quick transformed into a ten-foot-tall

golden warrior with blazing eyes and bloody tattoos. "I can take care of myself."

"Be careful."

Quick nodded. "You, too."

He walked toward the sounds of battle.

Gorgoz had transformed into his hideous primal form, that of a dark green giant with three heads and four legs. Syph, a burning, pale goddess of rage, wrestled with the giant. She tore pieces of his flesh with her bare hands.

It was all so ridiculous, thought Quick. Direct conflict between immortals was little more than a cosmic pissing contest. It was possible to win, to hurt a god so badly that it took him a few minutes to recover. But that was about it.

A few minutes might help Phil get away, though, so Quick tightened his grip on his onyx spear and waded into the fray.

The house shook with the fury of the gods. The structure wasn't zoned for divine brawling. When Quick's spear pierced Gorgoz's thigh, the dark god's shriek burst the pipes, spewing scalding steam into the air. When Gorgoz snapped off the spear and smashed Quick with the broken handle, a load-bearing wall cracked and a section of the roof collapsed. And when Syph bit Gorgoz in a very sensitive place, the windows blew out. In the matter of a few seconds, the house was a death trap.

Phil navigated the deadly maze. He was nearly buried under a collapsing hallway, he almost fell into a bottomless pit, and he dodged a miniature tornado as it tore its way across his path.

Phil didn't know where he was going. He didn't know

the mansion's layout and the chaos didn't help any. He was just trying to find a way out without getting killed.

He pushed through a cloud of smoke and collided with someone.

"Watch it, you idiot!" growled Worthington.

Each man waited for the other to make the first move. Phil put his hands up, closed them into fists, and then flinched when he thought Worthington was going to attack. But he realized that Worthington was doing the exact same series of gestures.

A grand piano came crashing through a wall and nearly hit both men. They both decided, without saying a word, that they were just a pair of mere mortals trying to survive. Worthington ran, and Phil, trusting Worthington knew the way around his own crumbling house, followed.

They found the garage. The roof had collapsed, crushing the Mercedes and the Hummer. Worthington jumped into the Jag, and Phil climbed into the passenger seat. The car started up, and Worthington peeled out of the garage just as it collapsed into a pile of rubble.

There was a blinding flash and a sonic boom. A giant piece of flaming debris fell from the sky, landing directly in the Jag's path. Worthington jerked the wheel, losing control. The vehicle tore up his manicured lawn, flattening several bushes. He slammed on the brakes. The Jag spun out, sideswiping a tree. He hit his head on the steering wheel, which rattled him.

Phil's seat belt had prevented any serious injury. He had a few bruises, and his side hurt whenever he took a deep breath. He climbed out of the vehicle on unsteady legs.

The flaming mound of debris thrashed about in a

painful twitch. It was Quick, back in his rainbow serpent shape. He shrank, writhing and groaning as the flames went out. Phil knelt beside the charred, withered god. He didn't dare touch Quick, who looked as if he might crumble into ash at any moment.

Quick raised his head and smiled painfully. "I'll be fine."

"Oh, yes, he'll be fine," said Gorgoz from behind Phil.

The god strode toward Phil. Gorgoz dragged Syph, bloody and battered, by the hair. The goddess had been beaten to a pulp. Bruises and cuts covered every inch of her pale skin. Gorgoz wasn't without his own wounds. Lacerations oozed putrid bile and half his face had been torn away. Still, he was the only god walking at the moment.

"Sad, really. Are there no real powers left?" He tossed Syph away like a piece of refuse.

Quick rose. One of his wings broke off, and he winced. He slithered between Gorgoz and Phil.

"Do we really have to keep doing this?" asked Gorgoz. "Take a look at yourself. You're no match for me. Maybe in your prime." He laughed. "No, let's be honest. Not even then.

"Don't you see? Quick, you're a shadow of everything you once stood for. Oblivion and chaos are the only constant. The mortals may deny it, but you should know better. We all should know better. And if I have to destroy every single man, woman, and child on Earth to free us of their weakness, then so be it." He leered at Phil. "And this one is just as good a start as any."

Teri's coupe, horn blasting, came crashing through the front gate. The indestructible car zoomed toward Gorgoz.

It collided with him. Under normal circumstances, it would've bounced harmlessly off the god, but he was still weakened from his recent battle. The power of a Hephaestus-driven motor carried him forward. The coupe smashed into Worthington's Jag, pinning the god between the two vehicles.

Gorgoz strained to free himself. The car's wheels spun in the lawn, pushing back.

Teri jumped out of her car. The vehicle's navigation charm kept the wheels turning.

"I thought I told you to stay home," said Quick.

"You're not my god."

Phil and Teri hugged. He winced as she squeezed a bit too tight.

"You are such an idiot," she said.

"I missed you, too."

Syph had recovered enough to stand. She studied the two embracing mortals from a distance, both physical and metaphorical. It'd been a long time since she'd seen anything of the sort. It wasn't that mortal affection was difficult to find, but her own influence made it a rarity for her.

Quick peeled away his ashen skin to reveal fresh scales. "See? Not all romance is doomed."

She shrugged. "Eh, give it a few years."

Gorgoz flipped the coupe into the air. The vehicle bounced several times, landing on its side.

Roaring, he hefted the Jag with Worthington still inside and hurled it. Quick and Syph deflected the vehicle.

"Oh, shit," said Worthington, just before crashing into his crumbling mansion. The entire building collapsed, burying him and his ambitions in one unceremonious instant.

"Whoops," said Gorgoz. He hadn't meant to kill

Worthington. While he wasn't the kind of god to regret the loss of one insignificant mortal life, he also preferred to kill his disciples on purpose. Otherwise, it just didn't seem as enjoyable. Like eating a particularly tasty potato chip and only realizing afterward.

Quick and Syph braced themselves for Gorgoz's charge. He batted them aside like paper dolls. Phil and Teri cowered before the furious god.

A globe of light shot from the sky, engulfed the mortals, and swept them out of the way. Lucky and his globe of light soared over the raging Gorgoz.

"You came back," said Teri.

"Did you ever doubt I would?" asked Lucky. He followed that up with a hasty, "Don't answer that."

Gorgoz expanded. He fired a few blasts of shadow at the globe, which Lucky dodged.

"Face me like a true god, you coward," said Gorgoz.

Lucky touched down in front of the enormous deity. He stood between Phil and Teri and the furious Gorgoz.

"Okay," said Lucky. "This ends now."

"You're braver than I gave you credit for. Now watch, foolish mortals, as I rend your pathetic god limb from limb and set his bones to bleach in immortal agony until the end of time itself. Steal my girlfriend, will you?"

"I knew it!" said Syph. "You did start this vendetta because of me!"

"You? No, it was never about you. It was about me. No one takes what is rightfully mine. No one." Gorgoz growled. "And now you will finally pay."

"Ain't gonna happen," said Lucky.

"Your arrogance is only matched by your—"

Lucky pointed his finger at Gorgoz and winked.

"Bang."

Gorgoz exploded in a small mushroom cloud. Lucky's power kept Teri and Phil from being disintegrated, but the rest of the area was engulfed in righteous atomic fire. The blast shook the ground and scorched the earth bare. It took thirty seconds for the sound of the explosion to fade and a full minute for Teri and Phil's vision to clear enough for them to see Gorgoz standing there, seared but otherwise unharmed.

Gorgoz chuckled.

"Nice try."

Lucky shrugged. "Worth a shot."

"Anything else?" asked Gorgoz. "Anything at all?"

"No, that's it from me. Almost every ounce of saved power I had in me." He turned to Phil and Teri and lowered his sunglasses. "Don't worry, kids. I have enough left over to protect you from what's coming."

"You couldn't be more wrong," said Gorgoz.

"I hate to break it to you, buddy, but this isn't going to play out the way you expect. I know you were looking forward to beating the ever-living crap out of me in front of these two lovely mortals. But did you take a moment to ask yourself what that will really accomplish? Other than giving you a sick thrill?"

"Isn't that enough?"

Lucky sighed.

"You really are an asshole."

Gorgoz shrugged. "It's my nature."

The skies rumbled. The startled Gorgoz raised his eyes heavenward as a thunderbolt struck beside Lucky. Zeus, towering King of Olympus in all his golden-tracksuit, tanned, silver-bearded glory, materialized.

Mut, in the form of a white vulture, settled on the other side of Lucky. The bird transformed into the striking goddess, wearing a red dress, carrying a staff topped with a golden ankh.

She was followed by Marduk, a twenty-foot deity who just fell from the sky without any show other than the tremendous, earth-shaking thud of his landing.

"See?" said Lucky. "Unlike everyone else involved in this little fiasco, I had the good sense to call in a little backup. You've overextended yourself. Even the big guns of the heavens can't ignore it any longer."

"This is all you have?" Gorgoz laughed as he crackled with cosmic darkness. "It will take more than these three to stop me."

"We know," said Lucky with a smile.

The sky spit out several more deities. Chernobog, horned god of darkness, and Yongwang, dragon of the sea (wearing his seldom-used dragon form) floated downward. Lacambui, in all his divine plumpness, with a bucket of chicken in one hand and a blazing sword in the other, descended beside Nanook, astride an elephant-size polar bear. Jurupari, Pele, Izanami, Bobbi-Bobbi, and Kunapipi were right behind them.

"Am I supposed to be impressed? Frightened?" Gorgoz roared at the gods. "I will crush you all and cast you into—"

Lucky cleared his throat.

"We're not done yet."

The skies opened again, and a barrage of lesser deities spilled forth. Vesta, Fabulinus, and Ogma were among the most prominent of the obscure. But there were a dozen others among them. Gods of accounting, ichthyology, baking, bricklaying, and footwear. Goddesses of gambling, dreaming, agriculture, dowsing, and writing. Nearly every sphere of human endeavor was represented among the divine gathering. Except for the god of overkill. But his presence was hardly necessary.

Gorgoz's eyes widened.

"Congrats, buddy," said Lucky. "You've managed to do what no other force in all the universe has accomplished. You've united the heavens themselves. No squabbling, no bickering, no grabs for glory. We all agree on this one."

Divine power surged in the assembled gods. The sky turned red, and the earth quaked.

Lucky lowered his sunglasses to the tip of his nose.

"You've got to go."

The explosion of divine force was beyond any earthly measure. It could've easily split the planet in two and caused the sun to blink out of sheer embarrassment for its meager output. The destruction was only a portion of the power unleashed. Half the gods were there simply to contain the force and keep it from wreaking irreparable damage to the mortal sphere. It was mostly successful, though the city's water did transmute to grape soda and every pregnant dog on Earth gave spontaneous birth to a litter of winged puppies. Jormungandr, the world serpent, stirred in the ocean's depths, but a glance at his calendar informed him that Ragnarok wasn't due for at least another two millennia, so he rolled over and went back to sleep.

Phil and Teri, encased in Lucky's protective globe, shielded their eyes from the dazzling white light. The blast was completely silent, except for the far, far cry of Gorgoz.

It was over quickly.

Lucky dropped his shield. A crater was all that was left of Worthington's estate. And Gorgoz sat at the very bottom, looking very, very small.

"Be right back, kids."

Lucky floated to the bottom of the crater. Gorgoz, being only two inches tall, stripped of every ounce of power, glared.

"You cheated," said Gorgoz in a squeaky voice.

Lucky plucked Gorgoz up by the scruff of the neck. "My mistake. I didn't know there were rules."

One of Hephaestus's golden executives presented an adamantite cat carrier. Lucky chucked Gorgoz into it.

"Catch you later, Gorg."

The golden woman and most of the gods ascended into the heavens without saying a word.

Lucky returned to Phil and Teri's side. He winked at Zeus and Mut, the last two remaining divinities.

"Thanks for the help, guys."

Zeus and Mut looked down on the mortals and their god.

"Yes, thank you," said Phil.

Teri stepped forward. "Could I possibly trouble you for an autograph? It's not for me. It's for a friend of mine. She's a big fan."

Grinning, Zeus and Mut disappeared in a burst of light and a clap of thunder. Two autographed photos were left in their place.

"Wow," said Teri. "She'll love these."

"Yeah, the big guys are always class acts," said Lucky.

"Is that it?" asked Teri. "He's gone? Gorgoz is gone?"

"There's a place where they stick the troublemakers.

Less said about it, the better. He might get time off for good behavior, but I wouldn't count on it. Either way, he won't be seeing the light of day for a few thousand years."

"All you had to do this whole time was call in the gods?" asked Phil.

"You make it sound so easy. Have you ever tried to get two gods to agree on anything, much less a hundred?"

"So you just called in the cavalry?"

"It's a little deus ex machina, I'll grant you. But hey, who do you think invented that kind of thing?" Lucky made a show of wiping his hands. "Problem solved. Now, we can stand around and continue to debate the merits of my victory or we can get you guys home."

Teri's coupe rolled up. The windshield was cracked, the tires were melted, and the tailpipe spit out clouds of black smoke.

"Gotta hand it to Hephaestus," said Lucky. "He sure makes a great car."

The earth split open and a new god, one apparently pieced together from carpet scraps, emerged.

"Sorry, Kutkh," said Lucky. "You missed all the action."

"Ah, damn. He owed me money."

Grumbling, Kutkh descended into the earth.

28

Though she was technically not among Syph's followers,
it took Bonnie several months to get rid of the goddess.
The goddess herself didn't bother Bonnie so much. It was
the constant visits by heartbroken mortals that proved
more annoying. She was sick of hearing them whine about
their failed relationships. She realized that Syph would
never be out of a job as long as she trafficked in emotional
baggage and bad breakups. Syph realized that, too, and it
was why the goddess was never going back to love. It was
easier to exact vengeance, and Syph was a lazy, lazy goddess. She'd rather lounge around the apartment and exact
vengeance than find a new temple and try to bring people
together. It was a step up, though. At least now she wasn't
sitting around feeling sorry for herself. She was still ruining lives, but it was with a wider distribution and less
damage on a per-mortal basis. It wasn't strictly legal, but,
unlike Gorgoz's operation, it wasn't likely to draw more

than a written reprimand and a slap on the wrist from the heavens.

And it wasn't Bonnie's problem anymore. Even Syph couldn't ignore an official order from the Court of Divine Affairs, one that Bonnie happily presented to the goddess in the middle of one of her consultations.

Syph read the order quietly. She cut short her session, promising to fill some poor schmuck's car with toads, and showed the client the door.

"Bonnie, can't we work something out?" asked Syph.

"Nope. You don't have to go home, but you can't stay here."

Syph reread the order, then crumpled it.

Bonnie showed the goddess the door.

"You'll miss me when I'm gone," said Syph.

"I'll get over it," replied Bonnie as she slammed the door shut.

The ever-present chill in her apartment vanished. She'd been living with it so long, she'd stopped noticing. But now that it was gone, she felt cozy and warm and safe. Right now, the forces of the cosmos couldn't give a damn about her happiness or misery. She was just a speck of dust in charge of her own life again. And that wasn't such a bad place to be.

The phone rang. It was Walter. He apologized for breaking up with her and asked if she wanted to get together for dinner.

She told him no.

With Syph gone, Bonnie realized that she hadn't ever really liked Walter. She'd just stayed with him because it'd been easier than breaking up. But now the breaking up was done, and she might as well take advantage of it.

She went to the window, opened the curtains. The sky was gray, a combination of smog and clouds. But it was just the weather. It had nothing to do with her.

She smiled.

Everything was going to be just fine.

Teri opened the second can of banana-and-chocolate soda of the day. She sniffed it, scrunching her nose.

"I can't believe he likes this stuff." She poured the soda into the bowl held by the ceramic raccoon. The altar accepted the offering, drinking down the beverage with a loud slurp.

"I guess there's no accounting for taste," said Phil. "We're almost out. I checked the supermarkets, but they say it's no longer being made. Guess we'll have to figure out something else once we open the last case."

"I wouldn't worry too much," said Teri. "He'll probably let us slide for a while." She crushed the can. "He better."

Phil took her in his arms. "You're not still mad, are you?"

"I'm over it."

He squeezed her shoulders and raised an eyebrow.

"I'm not *completely* over it," she said. "He did nearly get us killed. That's a lot to forgive." She shrugged. "But nobody's perfect, and he is our god. He did come through for us in the end. And it doesn't hurt that we've recovered enough loose change this month to pay our mortgage, all for the price of a few cans of soda."

Lucky had offered to release them, free and clear, from any obligation. They'd considered it. Said they'd let him know in a few days. Lucky gave them their space, didn't rush anything. Days became weeks. And weeks became three months. They still hadn't made up their minds when a package arrived, along with a note.

A little pizza goes a long way, it read. *Your friend, Lucky.*

The small, easily-ignored altar now sat in the corner of the kitchen. Every day they'd put an offering of food in the bowl, watch it disappear, and collect the good fortune that came their way. It wasn't much. Nothing as dramatic or noticeable as having Lucky living in their home. But it made things easier.

"By the way, my sister called. She's coming for a visit," said Teri. "You might want to throw something extra-special in the bowl."

"I don't think that warrants divine intervention," he replied.

"Did I mention she's bringing the kids?" She paused dramatically. "All the kids."

Phil searched through the cabinets, looking for something special to offer to their god.

"We still have soda left," she said.

"I think this calls for more than that. Last time, the youngest one almost burned down the house."

"You're exaggerating. He was going through his pyromania phase. It's perfectly natural."

"Maybe so," said Phil, "but I still don't see why your sister gave him matches."

"She didn't want to stifle him."

He kept searching.

"Anchovies are on the top shelf," she said.

"Thanks." He found the tin and put it next to the altar so he wouldn't forget.

"We're going to be late."

They jumped into their car and gave the charm instructions to take them to the party. The gathering was small, a mix of mortals and fantastic creatures with a couple of gods as well. Quick greeted them at the door.

"Hola, guys. You made it!" Quick peeked behind Phil's back. "Is that for me? I told you not to bring anything."

"Just a housewarming gift," said Teri.

"Nice place, by the way," said Phil as he handed over the box. "Sorry we didn't have time to wrap it."

"Pictionary. Just what I wanted."

"Hope you like it," said Teri.

"Like it? I love it. It's not a party without Pictionary." Quick handed off the box to a passing shadow.

"Oooh," said Ogbunabali, god of death, "Pictionary."

Quick threw his wings around them. "I'm really glad you guys could make it."

"Thanks for inviting us," said Teri.

"Ah, I love you guys. You know that. Oh, and I wanted to thank you for referring me to that agency."

"So it's working out?"

"So far, so good. It's a smaller outfit, not-for-profit. They offer favor for needy families. The tribute isn't all that great, but it's good work. And just what I needed to get into the game again."

He showed them to a table spread with food and slithered away.

Teri nibbled on a crab puff. "It's funny."

"No good?" asked Phil.

She chuckled. "Wasn't talking about the puff. It's just... well, I never thought we'd be hobnobbing with gods. And liking it."

"Still feel like you're selling out?" he asked.

"A little bit." Teri leaned over to give him a kiss. "But I'll get over it."

A god of smoke roiled up to them. "Are you Teri and Phil?"

They nodded.

"We're trying to get a game of Trivial Pursuit going. But Quick says he'll only play if you two are on his team."

The smoke deity pointed to Quick. The rainbow serpent waved them over.

"Wow. Trivial Pursuit," whispered Teri into Phil's ear. "These guys really know how to party."

"Could be worse," he whispered back. "It could be charades."

"Thank Heaven for small miracles."

Smiling, she looped her arm in his and joined the gods around the coffee table.

Lucky, in Bermuda shorts, lounged on the ethereal beach. The silver sand reflected the three moons hanging overhead.

The waiter brought Lucky the drinks just as Janet, clad in a bikini, emerged from the ocean. Lucky tossed her a towel.

"Right on time," he said. "Hope you like nectar daiquiris."

He put the glass to her lips, and she took a sip.

"Not bad. Though I think I prefer strawberries." She pushed him over and sat on his beach chair. "I think that satyr was checking out my ass."

"Why shouldn't he?" replied Lucky. "It's the finest ass, mortal or immortal, on the beach. Except for maybe the nymph bartender over there."

She chuckled. "You do know how to flatter a woman."

They clinked their glasses together.

"Next time, I think I'd prefer Tahiti," she said, shaking the glittering points of light out of her hair.

He nodded. The Beaches of Eternity had become a little too rowdy. Gods and demigods pranced across the sands in drunken partying. Dionysus noisily ralphed into a trash can less than twenty feet away. And the hotel didn't even have cable.

"Do you think she'll ever get over it?" asked Janet.

"Who?" he asked innocently.

Janet smiled.

Syph hid just down the beach, lurking behind an umbrella. She'd been less insistent lately, less obvious. Perhaps it was her continuing inability to inflict any harm on Janet. Or perhaps it was the demands of her new temple. Either way, she was still a semi-regular presence lurking in the background of their lives. Never interfering. Never getting too close. Just watching.

"Kind of creepy, isn't it?" asked Janet.

"Less creepy than it used to be," he replied. "Give her some time. She'll figure it out."

"Figure what out?"

Lucky leaned back in his chair. "Aw, c'mon, babe. Don't make me say it."

"Well, one of us should say it."

"Be my guest."

"I can't believe that you're having commitment issues," she said. "It's like me having trouble committing to a fruit fly."

"A guy likes to keep his options open."

She leaned in and ran her finger along his ears. "Oh, come on. Say it. You know I *love* it when you say it."

"Relationship. Once Syph figures out that this is a real

relationship, she'll move on." He grinned. "Although who can really blame her? I am hard to get over."

Janet laughed. She grabbed his hand.

"Care for a swim?"

"You just got out."

"I feel refreshed. Must be the golden apple pancakes I had for breakfast. Just one more lap around the center of infinity. You know you want to."

"Oh, okay."

Lucky and Janet dove into the ocean of stars.

"Last one to the edge of the universe is a rotten egg," he said.

Together, they swam the backstroke across the heavens.

extras

orbit

extras

meet the author

A. LEE MARTINEZ was born in El Paso, Texas. At the age of eighteen, for no apparent reason, he started writing novels. Thirteen short years (and a little over a dozen manuscripts) later, his first novel, *Gil's All Fright Diner*, was published. His hobbies include juggling, games of all sorts, and astral projecting. Also, he likes to sing along with the radio when he's in the car by himself. Find out more about the author at www.aleemartinez.com.

introducing

If you enjoyed
DIVINE MISFORTUNE,
look out for

CHASING THE MOON

by A. Lee Martinez

"Third Rule is don't pet the dog," said Mr. West.

A sad-eyed puppy sat in front of one of the three doors in the hallway. It was white with brown and black spots and big floppy ears, and it whined as they walked past.

"Does it bite?" Diana asked.

"No."

"Whose is it?"

"It belongs to Number Two," said West, "but he lost control of it about a year ago. Now he's lucky if it lets him out on the weekends to pick up groceries."

He wheeled and stared at her with tightly narrowed eyes. So much so she wasn't sure they were even open.

"Mark my words, Number Five. Bad things happen to those who don't follow the rules."

His long mustache twitched, and he scratched his shaggy head then turned back, walked the six steps to Apartment Number Five. He fumbled with an over-loaded key ring. As far as Diana could tell, there were only seven apartments in this small building, but he must've had at least three dozen keys on that ring.

"This'll be yours," he said.

She wasn't so sure. The rent on this place was remarkably cheap, but if a creepy landlord came with the package, she'd have to think it over.

She didn't have to think it over long.

The small apartment was fully furnished. It came with a brand new sofa, a television, an old-fashioned jukebox like she'd always wanted. The jukebox even had all her favorite songs.

"Does this work?" she asked.

West shrugged and mumbled.

The kitchenette was bare except for some silverware in a drawer, but she didn't cook anyway. There were a few Mr. Fizz sodas in the fridge, though.

"I didn't know they still made this brand," she said. "They're my favorite."

"Help yourself."

"Really? Are you sure it's okay? What about the former tenant?"

"He's gone."

"But won't he be coming back for his stuff?"

"I doubt it."

She hesitated but decided that one soda wouldn't hurt anything. It tasted just as good as she remembered. Better.

He showed her the bedroom. Superman posters decorated the walls along with art prints and a huge black and white photo of the Arc de Triomphe and another of the Eiffel Tower. It was bizarre. She knew she had eclectic tastes, but she never expected anyone else to share them.

"There's no way anyone would leave this stuff behind," she said.

"It's not his stuff," he said. "It's yours. If you want it."

The rent on this place was half what she'd expected, and the décor meant she could just grab her three suitcases from the car and be unpacked within the hour. It was too good to be true.

"What's the catch?" she asked.

He smiled. "Ah, there's a smart girl."

She stiffened. Her first thought was that this guy was a fiend who lured innocent young women into a life of orgies and pornography, but it would take more than a jukebox and a case of soda to get Diana to strip on a webcam. Maybe if a good cable package came with the deal....

"Rule Number Two," he said. "Never open this closet."

He pointed to a door.

"Why?" she asked.

"A good question. People who ask too many questions don't usually last. Number Seven asked a lot of questions. Used to."

He fumbled with the key ring and managed, after some rattling and grumbling, to pull the key to the apartment and offer it to her.

"It's all yours if you want it."

She didn't reach for the key just yet. A sixth sense warned her that she was striking a Faustian bargain. Odd, since she wasn't sure what a Faustian bargain was. But it was something not to be taken lightly. She knew that.

"If you don't want it," he said, "somebody else will."

"What's the First Rule?" she asked. "You told me Third and Second Rule, but not the First."

He paused, chewed his lip.

"The First Rule is to turn the lights off when you leave a room. Just because I pay the utilities doesn't mean I'm made of money."

Diana would've sold her soul for paid utilities, so she snatched the key. West was surprised enough to open his eyes to a softer squint.

"Where's the lease?" she asked.

"There's no lease. You stay as long as you're able, Number Five. Leave whenever you're willing."

She followed him out the door. Her three suitcases were already sitting in the hallway.

"Hmm," he said. "Apartment must like you. That's a good sign."

He waddled away without saying another word. The moment he was out of sight, even the jangle of his keys disappeared. Silence filled the hallway. No, that wasn't quite right. Music came from somewhere. So light it almost couldn't be heard. Like a chorus rehearsing. She couldn't figure out where it was coming from, though.

The puppy in front of Apartment Two glanced forlornly in her direction and whimpered.

She glanced around her shiny new apartment. So what if the landlord was a bit of a nut? This place was made for her, and with the run of bad luck she'd had in the last few weeks, this was a good omen. Things were turning around.

She fed the jukebox a nickel. The mechanical arm grabbed the gleaming vinyl disk and set it on the turntable. Frankie Avalon sang about the virtues of beach life, and she smiled.

Diana wasted no time getting unpacked. She needed to claim this apartment. She'd been living out of suitcases too long, bumming off of friends like a vagabond. She shoved her clothes into the dresser so eagerly that she didn't fold most of them. But once she closed the drawer, she felt as if she'd made her mark. She lounged around for an hour, sitting on the sofa, drinking soda, watching TV, just relaxing. Chubby Checker, Aretha Franklin, and The Big Bopper kept her company. And when she was tired, she fell asleep on the nice comfortable bed and dreamt the strangest dreams.

She was herself, but she wasn't herself. She flew across other worlds; strange realms without form or substance, lost cities and ghosts of forgotten civilizations, passed beneath her. Time rendered everyone and everything into dust. From the tiniest speck to the greatest of the ancients. In the center of it all, the slumbering god lay still, wrapped in the dream that foolish mortals and inhuman deities alike called Reality.

The god opened one of his countless eyes. An eye bigger than the sun. And although she was just a mote, the yellow and black orb focused on her. The weight of a vast, incomprehensible universe threatened to crush Diana. She tried screaming. Her throat filled with bile and her brain melted as every cell in her body convulsed in absolute horror before exploding.

She awoke covered in sweat. Her heart pounded. A chill in the air turned her breath frosty. Just for a moment, she thought the walls were moving, and something else was swimming under the covers.

She turned on the lights. Everything snapped back to normal. Her terror vanished as quickly as it had come. The air warmed. She marveled at how alien and real the dream had been, although it was all fading now, transforming into shadowy memory the way dreams did.

Diana got up, grabbed a glass of water, and headed back to bed.

"Bad dream?" someone asked.

She jumped and whirled around. Self-defense courses sprang to mind, and she was ready to shout and gouge and do what needed to be done.

Nobody was there.

"Settle down, girl," she told herself. "You're imagining things."

"No, you're not," said the voice.

She jumped again, but this time had the presence of mind to listen for the source.

It was coming from the closet.

"Hello?" she asked quietly. "Is there someone in there?"

There was no reply.

"Hello?"

No answer.

She went to the bathroom, splashed some cold water on her face, and dried herself with a towel. She was sticky with sweat, and a shower sounded appealing. But she'd seen enough slasher movies to know what happened next.

Part of her said it was time to leave. Don't pack anything. Don't change out of your pajamas. Just walk out of the apartment and never look back. But that was stupid. She wasn't about to be spooked out of her new home by a crazy dream.

Another part of her suggested that this was still just a dream. She'd wake up in another moment and laugh at herself. But it was all so clear, so lucid. She'd never dreamt anything as weird as the flying segment at the beginning. Nor something as ordinary as walking around her apartment, looking for a phantom voice.

"Bad feng shui," she remarked to herself as if that explained everything.

"Oh, I agree," said the closet. "The couch really should be a few more feet to the right. And the coffee table counteracts the openness of the room."

The voice wasn't threatening. Diana was determined to stay calm, but she wasn't going to stick around or investigate. Most stupid victims in movies tended to die because they weren't smart enough to go away from the sound of the chainsaw. She didn't like running around in her underwear since that seemed a cliché, too, but stopping to get dressed in the name of vanity also got you killed in these situations.

The door was gone. Only a wall. There weren't any windows, no other ways out.

She was trapped.

"Don't panic," said the closet. "Let's just keep our wits, and we'll work everything out."

Diana said, "This isn't funny."

"You don't think I find it funny, do you?" replied the closet. "I don't like this arrangement any more than you do."

She tried the phone.

"Don't open the closet," said West's familiar voice on the other end of the line.

She hung up, dialed 911.

"Don't open the closet," repeated West.

"Damn it. You can't do this. It's illegal. People will know I'm missing."

"You can leave any time you want, Number Five."

"How?"

"Open the closet."

"But you just said I'm not supposed to open the closet."

"Stay as long as you're able, Number Five," said West. "Leave whenever you're willing."

The line went dead.

"Looks like we're stuck with each other," said the closet.

Diana pounded on the walls and shouted for a few minutes. Nobody heard her. Or maybe somebody did. More prisoners ensnared in West's bizarre game. She used a tall, standing lamp as a battering ram against the wall with negligible results. She stripped the paint and chipped away some of the wood. If this was her only option, it was going to be a lot of work. Even if West didn't have anything weird planned, even if he was just going to leave her locked in here with a guy trapped in a closet, she'd starve to death before doing any real damage.

Just the realization made her prematurely hungry. She'd have to settle for a soda, though she would've killed for a turkey sandwich. She found one waiting for

her in the fridge. The Mr. Fizz five-pack had regener-
ated its sixth can as well.

Someone was in here with her. Someone other than
the guy in the closet.

Lamp in hand, she searched the apartment. She
came up empty.

"Where is it?" she asked.

"Where's what?" replied the closet.

"The secret door."

He chuckled. "There's only one way out, and you're
talking to it."

"I'm not stupid. Somebody had to put that sandwich
in the refrigerator."

"You did. By wishing for it."

"How gullible do you think I am?"

"What kind of sandwich is it?" asked the closet.

"What difference does that make?"

"What kind?"

She slumped against the wall and glared at the closet.
"Turkey."

"And what kind of sandwich were you just thinking
about?"

Diana dismissed the observation as irrelevant at
first. But she hadn't verbalized her sandwich desires.
Assuming that there was a secret door somewhere and
that someone had sneaked into the small apartment and
slipped in a sandwich before escaping, all without her
noticing, they'd still have had to be telepathic to know

what she wanted and have some sort of superspeed sandwich-making ability.

The rational explanation had a lot of holes in it.

She returned to the fridge. The sandwich was still there. An inspection revealed that it was exactly how she liked it. With just a touch of mayo and mustard, a single leaf of lettuce and three tomato slices. She stuck it back in the fridge, closed the door, and stared at the appliance for ten seconds.

"Orange juice," she said, opening the door.

The sandwich was gone. In its place, there was a tall glass of juice.

She closed the door.

"Deep fried Twinkie," she whispered, throwing open the door.

And there it was.

Diana had spent too much of her life in a logical world to be convinced just yet. Only after she had pulled the refrigerator away from the wall, checked for false walls and trapdoors, and came up with nothing, did she see no other choice. The guy in the closet was strange but didn't require a supernatural explanation. A magic fridge wasn't so easy to dismiss.

"Damn." She circled the fridge twice before admitting defeat. "I'll take that sandwich now."

She ate the sandwich in the kitchen, not even sitting down, and tried to make sense of this, but it didn't click.

The phone rang.

She stared at it but didn't pick it up.

It kept ringing.

"Are you going to answer that?" asked the closet.

She put the receiver to her ear.

"West?"

"About time," West said. "I may be ageless, Number Five, but I don't have all day." He paused. "So did you open the closet yet?"

"No."

"Good. Don't."

"Will you shut up about the stupid closet already?"

"Suit yourself."

He hung up.

"Ah damn it." Diana stared at the receiver, then the closet.

"Frustrating, isn't it?" said the closet. "Imagine how I feel. I was spawned at the dawn of time and now I find myself bound to a small clump of transient flesh."

"Bound by what?"

"Whatever decides these things. Primal forces that make even me piss myself. Or would if I pissed. It's a complicated universe. Sorry if I can't just summarize it in a pithy metaphor."

The phone rang again. She took a moment to steady herself. Losing her temper wasn't getting her anywhere.

"Hello."

"Hello," said West. "Ready to talk now?"

She sucked in a deep breath and replied in an even voice. "Yes."

"Good. Here's how it works. Inside that closet is an

ancient entity known as Vom the Hungering. He's actually a pretty decent sort, as ancient spawns go. But if you let him out of that closet, he will eat you."

She lowered the phone. "You're a cannibal?"

Vom chuckled. "Cannibals eat their own kind. I am a singular entity. There is only one Vom the Hungering, and that is me. And you are?"

She ignored the question. "You're going to eat me?"

"Yeah, probably. Don't suppose it helps anything if I apologize in advance."

She put the phone to her ear. "Pay attention, Number Five. You are now Vom's warden. You will not age or grow sick and you cannot die by conventional means."

"Okay, this is sounding more and more like bullshit," she said.

"Don't interrupt. I have other responsibilities. If I don't bring Number Three an avocado in five minutes California will fall into the ocean."

"Yeah. Sure. Makes sense." She admitted defeat and just listened.

"One day, Number Five, you will release Vom. Maybe not today. Maybe not tomorrow. Maybe not a hundred years from now. But one day, when the crawl of eternity becomes too much for you, you will open that door. He will then devour you, go back into his prison, and wait for the next warden. That is just how this works. There's no point in complaining to me about it either. I don't have any control over any of it."

"But—"

"I'm not even obligated to give you this information, but you seem like a nice young woman. So best of luck."

He hung up, and she knew he wouldn't be calling back this time.

She checked the apartment again. Ran her fingers along every wall, probed every corner, moved every bit of furniture. If there was a way out, she didn't find it, but just to be certain, she checked one more time.

If West was to be believed (although she wasn't quite ready for that) she was a prisoner and her only way out was death. And if she was immortal, then there was only one form of death available: to be devoured by a monster living in her closet.

She found a butter knife in the cabinet and ran it across her palm. It wasn't easy getting the blade to draw blood, but she managed. The shallow cut closed immediately. A scar wasn't even left behind.

It was as far as she was willing to go right now. Maybe in a hundred years, she'd be so bored that sawing her arms off with a dull butter knife would sound amusing.

Stay as long as she could. Leave whenever she was willing. She got it now.

She went back to bed. The clock radio on the nightstand counted the minutes. She turned the bright red numbers toward the wall and tried not to think about it. If she really was immortal, then she had all the time in the universe. It seemed pointless to obsess over every second. Diana turned the clock toward her and frowned. Twenty-two minutes had passed.

Twenty-two minutes.

She put the pillow over her face and reflected on infinity, breaking it up into twenty-two minute chunks. Twenty-two endless bits, one right after the other after the other.

The endless crawl of eternity indeed.

She got up and turned on the television. Nothing was on. Or maybe she just wasn't in the mood.

"Can't sleep either, huh?" asked the closet monster. "I hate that. Of course, I only sleep seven minutes every other century. And believe me, that's annoying. I have a lot of time to kill and a nap now and then might help."

She turned up the volume.

"We're the only company we're going to have for a long, long while," Vom said. "We can at least try and be civil."

She stared at the TV, not really watching it, just thinking about the passage of time, listening to the tick-tick-tick of the clock on the wall. Where did that clock even come from anyway? It hadn't been there before. She was certain of that. She'd been over every inch of this place.

Diana muted the television.

"This isn't fair," she said. "All I wanted was an apartment."

"You seem like a decent lady," said Vom. "I'm really sorry that I have to eat you."

She walked over to the closet. "You keep saying that, but if you were really sorry, you wouldn't. Then I could open this closet, and we could both get out of here."

"Sounds like a good deal to me."

"So you agree then?"

"Sure. No eating. I promise."

She reached for the knob but stopped short of touching it.

"How do I know I can trust you?"

"You don't. And I'll admit I'm not trustworthy. I did promise not to eat all the others. And I really meant it when I said it. But it just sort of happens. Not always, though. There was this Spanish guy who I didn't eat. Good guy, too. Lot of fun. I miss him."

"What made him different?"

"He had the stuff."

"The stuff?"

"You know what I'm talking about. The stuff. The goods. The mojo."

"What does that even mean?"

"It means what it means," said Vom. "When someone has the stuff, you just know it."

"That's not very helpful at all."

"There are mysteries beyond even my ken. Listen. I've done this plenty of times. I know how this game goes. Some people open the closet right away. Others hold out for a while. One guy made it a whole century. But you are going to open this door one day. So why don't we just cut the suspense and jump to the inevitable conclusion?"

Diana wanted to argue, but if what West and Vom had told her was true, then it really was unavoidable. The question wasn't *if* she would open the closet. The question was *when*.